This Christian biogra[...] poignancy of the class[...] [...] with Father, and poems which are reminiscent of Helen Rice Steiner's finest works. To read Pearlie is to experience a rich and inspiring ride back into Oklahoma history and encounter a Christian wife, mother, and writer who saw beauty everywhere and transformed her everyday world into a place of inspiration.

—Hope Harder,
PhD in English literature, author of a series
of books including Silent Voices

Pearlie takes the reader to a time when life was certainly harder but before modern conveniences had robbed it of its soul. You may have heard stories like this from your grandparents but probably not with the depth of detail and feeling found here.

—Ryan Jones, author of Datashark and Specters

I greatly enjoyed this vivid picture of life in Northeastern Oklahoma in the early part of the twentieth century. Her poems are delightful and clearly reflect her joyful appreciation of life, her sense of humor, and her delight in the beauties of nature. The descriptions of the beauty of the countryside in Pearlie remind me of the novel Heart of Glass, by the acclaimed author Diane Noble.

—Rosemary Watson,
former missionary to Laos and author of As the
Rock Flower Blooms and All One Family

You will fall in love with this country girl who loved God, her husband, her children, and her country. I feel as if I personally attended Pearlie's funeral and had a lovely time. This story about Pearlie has shown me that I want to hear laughter at my funeral someday. What a comfort to know when we get to heaven we will see our loved ones. I felt like Pearlie was sitting across the room from me as she read her poems to me personally.

—Yolanda Sampson
Librarian and book reviewer

To Lauren:
I pray you are both
entertained and blessed
by this story.

Russ Jones

www.rfjones.tatepublishing.net
russandjerry@sbcglobal.net
918-622-6036
3712 S. Canton
Tulsa, OK 74135

Pearlie

A Relatively True Story

R.F. Jones

TATE PUBLISHING & *Enterprises*

Published by Tate Publishing & Enterprises, LLC
127 E. Trade Center Terrace | Mustang, Oklahoma 73064 USA
1.888.361.9473 | www.tatepublishing.com

Tate Publishing is committed to excellence in the publishing industry. The company reflects the philosophy established by the founders, based on Psalm 68:11,
"The Lord gave the word and great was the company of those who published it."

Published in the United States of America

ISBN: 978-1-61566-627-0
1. Fiction, Biographical
2. Fiction, Historical
09.12.11

The true parts of this novel are
by Ida Pearl Logan Jones and the
relatively true part by R.F. Jones

Table of Contents

Pearlie

Prologue:

My First Day in Heaven

My Russ and I really enjoyed my funeral. He had moved to New Jerusalem when he died in 1979, after we had been married fifty-four years. I moved there in 1993 when I was eighty-seven. We've been in love with each other since we were children. We felt blessed to be together again and with our first baby.

I arrived in New Jerusalem on a Sunday morning. After several months of being bedfast, I was taken to the hospital because my going-home time was obviously getting nearer. My vital signs were being monitored, and Son had come to the hospital that Sunday morning to sit and talk to me.

The last two days I was alive physically, my speech was very slurred. The last few hours, I couldn't speak at all because my mind was busy with other things. My mind was seeing actual visions of heaven and the city the Bible calls New Jerusalem. I was torn between taking in these colorful scenes and struggling against the chains of physical unconsciousness.

My faithful doctor, Dr. Alexander, had come into the room, and I wanted to tell him and Son what I was seeing with my spiritual eyes. Son stood at the foot of my bed touching my feet. As I got nearer that great city, I saw God on his throne. I summoned all my failing physical strength, and with a surprisingly strong voice, I called out to Son, "The white throne."

I lay back again, exhausted, as Son sat alone beside the bed, holding my left hand and adjusting my wedding band on my swollen finger. He said, "Mother, I called Mary to come see you. She'll be here in a few minutes. I also talked to Betty in Houston to let her know how you're doing."

I thought, *Boy, if you only knew what I've been doing and see-ing while you went to phone them.*

Dr. Alexander returned and said, "Russell, the monitor shows Mrs. Jones's pulse has been getting slower and weaker and has now stopped."

I tried to say to Son, "I could have told him that."

"That may be true, Doctor, but I'm watching a vein on her left thumb, and it's still showing a pulse."

I always liked to get the last word.

Then my pulse stopped, and in the twinkling of an eye, I was standing on a golden street, beside a river with fruit trees on each side. There was my Russ with that sideways grin on his face.

"See. I told you if I got here first we would wait for you."

My Russ was holding baby Francis, who was reaching for fruit hanging from a tree. I laughed with an unimaginable joy that baby Francis seemed to recognize. Twisting around in my Russ's arms, Francis gave me a heavenly baby smile and reached out for me.

We hadn't paid much attention to my funeral until we heard laughter coming from the church where our family and friends were gathered. As we sat beside the river eating fruit, I told my Russ, "I hear Mary and LaMoine and Betty and Buck and Jerry Ann laughing. What does that mean?"

"Ah, you're just hearing the people who are attending your funeral. Ralph Baldwin's going to preach the sermon. But right now Son's reading some of your poems to the congregation."

"Well, I don't see anything wrong with laughter at my funeral. That's really how I hoped it would be. Let's listen to see which poems Son picked out."

After Son read my poems, the first thing the preacher, Ralph Baldwin, said was, "Isn't that just like Pearlie. She preached her own sermon."

After the funeral was over, taking turns carrying baby Fran-cis, my Russ and I took a long walk down the river of life.

"You know, Russ, this river is looking more and more like Old Limbo Creek that ran near the old home place."

My Russ, with that mischievous sideways grin and a twinkle in his eye, held baby Francis out at arm's length and said, "Pearlie, girl, do we have a surprise for you!"

My Funeral

"Our mother's name is Ida Pearl Logan Jones. Her friends and family call her Pearlie. She was born in the Oklahoma Indian Territory in 1906, about one year before Oklahoma became a state. Our father was born in 1905.

"As a child, she lived in a very small Oklahoma town named Lenna. It's still a very small farming community a few miles west of Lake Eufaula in the east-central part of Oklahoma. Our father, Russell Francis Jones, also lived there as a child. A little more than a year after they were married, in December 1925, they moved to Preston, another small town in central Oklahoma. Our father's parents, Horace and Essie Jones, had moved to Preston to open an auto repair shop and gas station business. Our father worked there as a mechanic and drove a school bus for a few years. My two sisters and I were born in Preston. When I was in the eighth grade and Betty was in the tenth, we moved seven miles south to Okmulgee to be closer to the gas station my father operated, to provide me and Betty with better opportunities, and most of all, to live in a house that had indoor plumbing. Mary had already graduated from high school and was married to LaMoine Neal.

"On September 16, 1993, at the blessed age of eighty-seven, our mother moved to heaven to be with our daddy and to see firsthand the things she had written so many poems about. They are the most godly people I have ever known. I've never seen them really angry with each other, with one of us children, with neighbors, or any of my father's gas station customers.

"Our father worked twelve hours, six days a week. He always closed his auto service station on Sundays. Each Saturday night, I watched him prepare a Bible lesson to present the next morning to young people in our Okmulgee church. Over the years, he wore out several Bibles. Betty has one of them. The edges of the pages are like lace, and most of the New Testament pages are pulled loose from the binding. Tucked between the pages is a poem in our mother's handwriting."

> Though the cover is worn
> And the pages are torn
> And though places show traces of tears,
> Yet more precious than gold,
> Is this Book worn and old,
> That can shatter and scatter my fears.
> To this Book I will cling,
> Of its worth I will sing,
> And love it through all of my years.

"Betty keeps our mother's Bible beside our dad's. Inside Mother's Bible is a quote that says, *If all the neglected Bibles in this country were dusted off at the same time, we would suffer the worst dust storm ever experienced in Oklahoma.*

"All of my mother's family except her older brother Troy and his family moved from Lenna to California in 1935 during the Dust Bowl years. Pearlie's childhood days on her family's farm were adventurous and romantic, spent doing things children do that have nothing to do with financial or social status.

"Our daddy was one year older than Pearlie and one year younger than Troy. He and Troy were good friends, and even though they tried to keep Pearlie from playing with them, she could climb trees as well as they could.

"When our mother died, my sisters and I agreed we should invite Ralph Baldwin, a beloved former minister of the Okmulgee church, to preach the funeral sermon. After I read some of Pearlie's poems to give a flavor to the central theme of her life, communicating with others through carefully thought-out poems, Ralph will give his eulogy.

"My sisters and I would like to have some family time with you and together pay tribute to our mother and allow her to encourage us through her poems. Some of the poems will be serious, and some will be humorous. We hope you will feel comfortable to laugh if it strikes your fancy. Many of you in her church family are either subjects of her poems or recipients of them.

"During the last few days of our mother's life, it was clear she knew she was near death. Most of the time her words were slurred, and we really couldn't understand her, but one Saturday she spoke very clearly to one of the nurses in the hospital and said, 'When you see my name in the paper, it will be Ida Pearl Jones.' It's possible God gave her a glimpse of heaven. She wasn't afraid to face judgment, and one of her poems was titled, 'I Dreamed.'"

I dreamed I stood in judgment. It really wasn't hard.

I met my Savior face to face and received my just reward.

I dreamed he took the Book of Life. I didn't feel a dread.

I did feel very humbled, as he opened the book and read.

He looked at me so kindly. I knew I'd won the race.

I'm glad I made him my choice or
didn't make him second place.

It's only those who do his will and walk within his way,

Who enter through the pearly gates,
when comes the judgment day.

"Our mother also wrote about being ready for heaven."

Ready and waiting I want to be,

When Jesus the Christ calls for me.

He'll open heaven's door, and I'll sweep in,

Forgiven and free from every sin.

Waiting and ready and truly yearning,

My lamp trimmed and brightly burning.

A robe of righteousness I will wear,

Pure and white when I get there.

I want my heart filled with his love,

So I can meet him up above.

Ready and waiting I want to be,

And live with him eternally.

"She wrote about her own decision to trust Christ and called it 'My Greatest Step.' It was her preparation for this last earthly step she has taken."

The greatest step I ever took was my first step with God.

I promised to obey his word and in his footsteps trod.

Each Christian will take this step. We
know not when he'll call.

I only hope my lamp is bright for the greatest step of all.

"She also wrote about the necessity to be born again in order to take this great step and called it 'God's Holy Word.'"

Don't live life's frustrations. There's no comfort in despair.

Be ready when Christ comes again to meet him in the air.

The Holy Bible is so true. It will breathe quick relief.

To disobey God's Holy Word will only bring you grief.

Have you been born again? Have you done his will?
He died for one and all on the brow of Calvary's Hill.

"She believed that God raised Jesus from the grave. She tells us that all we hope for is dependent on Christ's resurrection from being dead. It's called 'My Lord Arose.'"

They crucified my Lord. They gambled for his clothes.
He died upon Calvary's tree, and yet my Lord arose.
He died between two thieves upon the cross of shame.
Oh! How I love my Jesus. I want to wear his name.
I've been taught, and I believe, as every Christian knows,
That upon day number three our blessed Lord arose.
I do not dwell in darkness, nor dwell in deep despair.
For I know, and I believe, I'll meet him in the air.

"Mother thought a lot about meeting Christ personally. She wrote about 'When Christ Calls Me.'"

When I think about heaven, I'm filled with delight.
I don't care when Christ calls me. Let it be day or night.
It matters not where I wander, if I be on land or sea.
Peace and happiness will follow when Christ calls for me.

"She loved her church family and expressed it in poems. If you left town, you might get a poem written about you. This poem is written about Sister Dolly Anderson. Dolly only moved fifteen miles away to Henryetta, but it's still worth a poem from Sister Jones."

Ralph said he lost his Dolly. This made him feel so sad.

This was the only Dolly that Ralph had ever had.

Those who know our Dolly will miss her sweetest smiles.

Our loss is Henryetta's gain. Oh! That's just fifteen miles.

"If there was a loss in a family, she would more than likely write a poem. In our mother's things, we found many poems to friends and family members on their birthdays.

"Our mother is a very good cook. I speak of her in the present tense because she is surely alive today and forever. In one little poem she said, 'When I go to heaven, I wouldn't mind being a cook, as long as my name is in God's Book.' She cooked for visiting preachers, and she made food for her family. When my sisters and our families came home for a visit, we had great feasts. Our daddy was her best customer. She might write a poem right in the middle of dinner by saying, 'Goodness gracious, Christmas is here and with it a great big dinner. The way my Russ loves to eat, I'm afraid he won't grow thinner.'

"She used her cooking to her own advantage sometimes. She would make food for neighbors who moved into her neighborhood. While they were moving in, she might make sandwiches and iced tea for them. In one instance, a city policeman named Captain Morrow and his family moved in across the street. She took care of their child and fed them lunch, including a cake and pie. Among Mother's things, we found a newspaper clipping that had Captain Morrow's picture and this note attached to it. 'After they moved in, a friend and I were shopping downtown. It was pouring down rain, so we decided to jaywalk across the street. As we walked across the street, a police car drove by with its red light on. The driver honked his horn. I waved to him. It was Captain Robert Morrow. I told my Russ about it, and he said, "The police are going to arrest you someday." I replied confidently, "Not Robert. I took him cake and pie and took care of his baby."'

"Mother wrote many poems about her grandchildren. Johnny Neal has been one of her most colorful characters. This event occurred when he was four years old."

Johnny boy felt fancy-free.

So he climbed up in the apple tree.

There he wiggled with all his might.

Johnny boy got fastened tight.

So Johnny screamed real good and loud,

Not so fancy-free and proud.

Neighbors could see this thing so wild,

When they heard the cry of Johnny child.

Johnny wasn't fancy-free,

For he was caught by the apple tree.

Then through his tears he smiled at me,

Grateful I had set him free.

Jumped to the ground with a bang,

So happy he didn't have to hang.

"Our mother wrote many poems about our daddy, very tender ones from their first anniversary to their last. Or she would poke fun at him as a way to lecture him. One example of a lecture was 'Hubby Had Better Waste My Time.'"

I had worked and cleaned house all day.

I hadn't stopped one minute to play.

After spending all day alone,

I hummed a tune as Hubby came home.

He walked in and fell into his chair.

I wanted to talk so I went in there.

But he said, "Mother if you don't mind,
I would rather not waste your time."

After I had spent the day alone,
He wouldn't talk when he came home.
He's so spoiled by my devotion.
I'm not mad, but I've got a notion.

No more catering, for I have my pride.
I would like to tan his hide.
Starting today, I'll quit trying to please,
Unless Hubby begs on bended knees.

For I am his and he is mine,
So Hubby had better waste my time.

"Mother confidently expected to see Daddy in heaven. She wrote a prayer called 'My Russell.'"

He is my special angel. Dear Lord, I love him so.
When I said goodbye to him, I was sad to let him go.
But now he is in heaven, in your home bright and fair.
Someday I'm going to see him, when I see you up there.

"The Scriptures say we're supposed to encourage each other with words like these since we have a special hope that people without Christ don't have. I hope our mother has encouraged you today."

When I finished my part of the funeral celebration, Ralph had some really nice things to say about Mother before he preached a sermon. He said, "Pearl's done such a good job of preaching her own funeral I think that anything I have to say will be, at best, superfluous. I do want to express my great joy to the family in this celebration of her being with the Lord and her loved ones who've gone on before. I was so glad when I learned some of Pearl's poems would be recited. It saved me from going through my boxes to gather some of the many poems she has sent to me.

"During the twenty-three years I've known Pearl, I don't believe she was what we would consider in real good health. In fact, she had several surgeries before my wife, Mary, and I and our three sons moved to Okmulgee in 1970. However, that did not keep her from doing what she felt she needed to do as a servant to Jesus Christ, as a homemaker, as a wife, and as a mother. My mind goes back to 1979 when she had first lost Russell, yet she showed great strength to continue as an encourager.

"The one legacy that I want to leave with each of you three children is that if Pearl had been blessed with a good education of a college degree or greater, she would have been a professor in a fine arts college because of her flare for poetry and her love of the arts. Each of you children, in your own way, has some of that good stuff. Each of you has that creative gift, and it comes from your mother. And you have a deep sensitivity that comes from both your parents.

"In 1980, when I resigned as preacher of this church, Pearl said to me, 'This is one time my Russ won't have to cry when a preacher leaves because he's already gone to be with the Lord.' Both of your parents left you a legacy of tenderness. It doesn't mean they didn't have strong personalities. Today, the Lord will be much pleased that we draw attention to the life of Ida Pearl Logan Jones, since she calls attention to God himself."

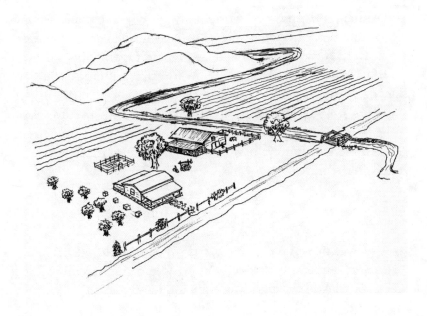

The Common Threads
of My Story

After the funeral service, my physical body was carried to the cemetery and placed beside my beloved Russ. The grave marker showed his date of birth and death on one side, and the other side showed my name, Ida Pearl Jones, and my birth date. In a few days, a man I don't know came and chiseled in the date of my death, and people started talking about me in the past tense. Oh! If more people could only see me now and know how alive I am. My physical body is at rest until that day of resurrection when God's children are given their glorious, resurrected bodies.

When in the physical world, I always hoped I would see my Russ and our baby again when I arrived in the garden paradise of heaven. Now, as the three of us walked together by the river of life, I know it's true. Now I know for sure that God's children live daily in the present tense of God's presence. The reality of my life's story flows past in the river of life beside the stories of other ordinary people who have been as blessed as I have been. I'll tell my story in the past tense, only because that's what my publisher requires.

✝

I was a plain country girl. I loved my Russ. I loved our children and our family. I loved America and my native state of Oklahoma. Most of all, I loved my God and his Christ. I loved nature because its voice is the song of our Creator.

I wasn't what most people would call educated. I only went to school through the sixth grade, and my Russ only completed the eighth grade. We went to a small country school in a wide spot in the road called Lenna. Sometimes I used bad grammar. I learned you don't have to be educated and sophisticated to see the beauty of nature and this magnificent country called America, whose first inhabitants were called Native Americans.

Nature was a part of me. That's why my mind was never very far away from my old home place, the farm where Mama and Papa raised me and my brothers and sisters. It was where I tagged along with my Russ and my brother Troy when they tried to climb very tall trees to get away from me.

From the first time I could remember, I always wanted to be a writer. It started when I was three. I was stood on a table to recite poems at the beginning of town meetings or town parties.

I learned a new, sophisticated word. I could have called my story *Pearlie's Soliloquy* because I tried to reveal my most transparent thoughts and dreams to a willing audience. It was as if I just talked to myself and put together my memories that were a little painful a few times but abundantly joyous most of the time.

Most dramatic stories, like ones my grandson Ryan wrote, seem to rely on escalating levels of conflict. My story was one of escalating levels of happiness and fulfillment. There were times of hardship, but those times were greatly diluted in my memory by the love and laughter of my family and the beauty of creation's creatures and colors.

These sights and sounds were the colorful healing oils that painted over and mastered circumstances that were out of my control. At times, I felt overwhelmed by the vast impersonality of circumstances and conflict. Then, with the passage of time, my smile was given back to me by the person and personality of nature's power to make me feel alive and in control again.

When I was young, before my Russ and I were married, the natural settings of the old home place provided the healing balm for my few disappointments. After we were married and had to move away from the farm, my memories of those glorious young days at the old home place became the common thread that ignited my imagination when I began to talk to myself through poetry. I learned encouraging words to see God's good humor in my spoiled longings when I had to accept that I couldn't have my way in all the scenes of my life's story on earth.

Since my story couldn't deliver great dramatic conflict, I had to rely heavily on its characters. Ryan, in his novels, believed that it was vital to a good plot that the readers cared about and believed in the characters on which the story was built. But this is also a problem because my characters are all nice, decent people. I felt like Jetta Carlton, who wrote *The Moonflower Vine*. I echo her sentiments. Why couldn't I write a book about ordinary, decent people who love each other, who love God and his creation, and who love America and my Oklahoma Indian Territory?

Why couldn't I write a book about how much and why I loved my Russ?

I wrote more than 1,600 poems. Most were handwritten on

lined, three-ring-binder notebook paper. Many of them were written on scraps of paper or on the backs of envelopes. Or one might have been written on paper made from a white paper sack, which, after being cut open, had a clean, white surface quite suitable for a thought that cried out to be recorded.

One of my last poems was penciled following my eighty-fifth birthday, after I had undergone radiation treatment for lung cancer. I wrote many about the old home place in Lenna, and almost one hundred were love poems to my Russ. A small number of my poems were written as songs. No songs were published, and only three of my poems were published in national magazines, one being an *Ideals Magazine* Easter publication. Most of my published poems about God were published in the Okmulgee church bulletin.

Son said I was the original antique copying machine. If I wrote a poem about someone, they would receive a handwritten pencil copy just like the original. If I thought one of my poems was particularly good, I would handwrite as many copies as required for my selected audience.

The Carefree Life at the Old Home Place

1906 through 1920

The joyous life that my Russ and I, our children, and our grand-children were blessed with was built on a heritage of God-loving parents and grandparents who practiced what they preached to their descendants. In almost every dinnertime prayer, we gave the Lord thanks for the godly lives these wonderful people lived.

My Russ's parents, Horace and Essie Jones, came to Oklahoma from Arkansas, where my Russ was born September 9, 1905. Mr. Jones's mother was a full blood Kiowa Indian.

My father, Bill Logan, came to Oklahoma from Missouri.

I was more fortunate than a lot of people. I was a farmer's daughter. Growing things from soil was my greatest joy. Papa never achieved great fame and fortune, nor did he care to. He was blessed with happiness and contentment. Not only was he a farmer, he was a carpenter, blacksmith, hunter, fur trader, well digger, logger, stonemason, and casket maker.

He made caskets for friend and foe alike. He made our baby's casket. For this emergency, he removed lumber from our barn loft floor.

After going hunting, he would have to clean and age the furs. We children and Mama could hardly stand it when he brought furs into the house to get them ready so he could take them to the post office to be shipped to a fur company.

My mother, Mary Hargus, was a neighbor of the Logan family in Missouri. There was a lot of American Indian blood in Mama. She was Cherokee with real black hair when she was young. She had dark eyes that snapped when she got angry, and that was often.

My twin brothers, Troy and Roy, were born in 1904. My family moved to Lenna when I was a tiny baby. I was born in Ada, Oklahoma, on March 9, 1906. I wasn't old enough to remember when we moved to the sandy knoll in Lenna.

My life was simple and far from luxurious in possessions. We were often in need but never hungry. I wasn't accustomed then to having things like we had in the last half of our lives. So many threads of gold are woven in and out of my life. I know God walked with me all my eighty-seven years on his dear earth.

I was born on a farm, free as the wind and weather.

Nothing marred my day 'cause God and I walked together.

Even before my birth, my parents prepared for a home of strong ideals and love for me. They filled my life by teaching me right from wrong. For this, I was always grateful. All of their teachings were woven into my conscience in such a way that they were unbroken when trials came along. In my youth, while wandering through the maze of growing up, my parents' example shone as a morning star and as a dependable and constant guide.

In 1907, Oklahoma changed from being Indian Territory to become the forty-sixth state. My family didn't know that we were an important part of history by being very small players in the Oklahoma farming industry. I had no idea then how much I would learn to love my native Oklahoma and our beautiful America.

In 1908, when I was two years old, my papa built the house where I grew up. I remember when we moved into it. My brother Roy, Troy's twin, died from being badly burned in an accident while we were there on the sandy knoll. While Papa was building the house, Roy and I would pick up the little blocks of wood and put them in a pile. We played with them when we moved from the shed we were living in while the house was being built. As the pile of discarded pieces of lumber grew, Papa would burn it. After being burned, it left soft white ashes that we ran through after they cooled because they felt so soft to our bare feet.

After one of these burnings, Roy ran through the ashes too soon, not realizing that beneath the fluffy ashes, the red hot coals were at their most dangerous temperature. Roy died before we moved into the house, so I divided the blocks with Troy. Both of us missed Roy very much.

We didn't understand about death because we were so young. My mother had twelve children. Only seven lived: Troy, Pearlie (me), Blanche, Whitey, Bertha, Mae, and Thelbert. We were a very close and happy family. I was closest with Troy because he didn't move to California in 1935 with the rest of the family because of the damage to the family's farm from the Dust Bowl years.

✝

At our little country school of about eighty students from the first through eighth grades, they set aside time for performances before each town meeting as we waited for everyone to arrive. There was always a nice crowd, and anyone could get up a dialogue and perform. As early as three years old, I would always cry if they didn't let me say a little poem. Mama would always say, "You can't if they don't ask you." But somehow, I always got to perform. They stood me on a desk because, at three, I was so little. How I loved it when the audience clapped their hands. Mama taught me to say "The Little Short Eskimo."

Away up north where very little grows,

But fish, seals, and Eskimos,

A little short Eskimo I know,

Was very fond of ice and snow.

So when they want a hearty meal

They dine upon a big fat seal.

When I was a grown woman, these performances were a subject of one of my poems. Here's part of it.

When I was a little girl, I was as spoiled as I could be.

Mama taught me poems, just right for a child of three.

At every schoolhouse program, I'd cry to have a part.

If Mama said I couldn't, it would break my heart.

I struggled as a child for a little laugh or two.

Some were those I composed. Some my mama knew.

Reciting words of poetry, that was my cup of tea.

Standing on a teacher's desk at just the age of three.

In 1910, the Jones family arrived in Lenna with seven children—two boys and five girls. Three more were born to them in Lenna. Mr. Jones was thirty-seven years old, and Mrs. Jones was thirty-two. Ola was fourteen; Jessie was twelve; Purl was ten; the twins, Walsie and Elsie, were seven; Russell Francis was five; and Gladys was three. They bought a big farm near Lenna. The house had a porch that went all the way around, affording the small children a good place to play out of the wind if it was cold or to enjoy the breeze if the weather was warm. Besides being a farmer, Mr. Jones also became the local blacksmith.

This same year, my sister Audra Blanche Logan was born. We called her Blanche.

For me, town life was never able to compete with my best memory of country living. I thought if a person was lazy, it would be a miserable life to live on a farm. My twenty-five years of farm life were so happy because I loved nature so much. I always felt like I walked and talked with God in the country. I didn't even mind the birds as they eavesdropped on my conversations with God because I loved the birds too.

I spent much of my time canoeing in the creek near our house and hiking in the woods. I was very proud to grow up as a country girl. Unlike children who grew up in town, there was always something to do. I would sit on our front porch at night in the moonlight, or I might just sit under the cottonwood trees in our country yard and wait for stars to come out at night.

The nights were intense and quiet. The insects gave their own sound effects. The beauty of the soaring moon and the shadows of the trees gave a melancholy serenity to a perfect night. I could hear Papa's hound dogs barking in the distance. If Papa was sitting with me, he would teach me the different way they barked when they treed some animal, such as a coon.

Papa was a skilled stonemason. Oklahoma sandstone had for many years been an excellent building material. Papa used it to build a horse trough, the wall around a deep well he dug, and the walls for a tater (potato) house.

At my old home place, it was almost impossible to describe the endless and special beauty God gave me to enjoy when the evening sun bathed the green valley.

A red sun was poised above the mountaintop west of our farm. Then there were the colors of amber, red, and gold as the sun passed from sight. The western skies were awesome to behold. Even as a young child, it was developed in my memory as a permanent mental photograph.

I asked Papa, "Why is the sun moving so fast?"

He said, "God never allows it to stop because it must hurry around the world to give a colorful sunrise tomorrow."

I told Papa, "I'm going to stay awake tonight so I won't miss the sunrise."

He promised, "I'll wake you early in the morning when I get up to plow the garden."

Sure enough, the next morning, there was a faint circle of pink touching the edges of the clouds. Then the sun made its long-awaited appearance above the horizon. As the sun ascended, its light lit up the sky, touching each cloud with a splash of gold. I lay on my back in the yard for a long time, struck with awe as the fluffy clouds broke up and drifted away. I was never the same after that glorious sunset and sunrise. I couldn't wait for God's and Papa's next nature lesson.

We were still clearing timberland to make more farmland when I was five years old. I was only big enough to gather the smallest limbs and throw them in a pile, but I liked to feel a part of it.

We'd clear the land and pile up the green limbs to dry, and later we would burn them in the spring. It always popped and sparkled as the smoke drifted away to make big, dark clouds. The flickering fire would cast uncertain and strange shadows after sundown as it blazed high in the air. As it died down, Papa would pile more limbs on the fire, and those mysterious shadows would come to life again, forcing me to imagine ghostly creatures. It made a fantastic show as darkness fell with a wonderful, lingering afterglow in the west against the golden red of a clear sky. Then, through the wet ashes from the next summer's rains, we would be captivated by goldenrod blossoms pushing up through the ashes and nodding along the roadway.

Mr. Jones taught children and teenagers how to sing at church. Because he thought I was special, he talked to me often about building my life on Bible scriptures.

I didn't know then, but I learned the great importance of Proverbs 22:6, which says if parents train children in the way they should go, then when they are old they will not depart from it. I learned early in life that I couldn't be a faithful servant of God without studying his Word.

In our small country school, we had more than one grade in each room. In 1912, when I started school, I cried to sit with Troy, but they wouldn't let me, even though I begged Papa. Papa was so tenderhearted that he left the spanking to Mama. I guess that's why I always thought he was so good and Mama was so mean. Believe me, Mama didn't spare the rod or spoil the child.

My Russ and I knew each other almost all our lives. As soon as the Jones family moved to Lenna, he would come to our house to play with Troy. Of course, they had to play with me too. I followed them around and proved I could do anything they could do. Oh, they quarreled at me, but they didn't get rid of me. They were two selfish little boys.

They would say, "Pearlie's a tagalong," and pull my ponytail.

I returned, "You're just jealous because I'm strong."

Sometimes they climbed real high in a tree and laughed big and loud. "Ha, Ha. You can't catch us now."

I would climb even higher.

They yelled, "You should stay in the house and act more like a lady!"

To which I yelled back, "Oh yeah? And let you call me a 'fraidy cat?"

Troy had to get the last word. "I bet you could get down this tree faster than we can if you knew your bloomers were showin'."

Well, they didn't know then that just a few years later, I would put Troy's little friend Russ in a whirl. I did grow to be a young lady, and after a little flirting on my part, my Russ had fallen for me and was very happy to have me tagging along with him.

✝

We learned early in life how to work hard, even as small children. Mama taught me how to cook when I was quite small. Papa and Mama were both early risers. Often, Papa and Old Slim, the mule, were up before daybreak. They would plow the garden or fields while it was still cool and pleasant. That's also when, at a very young age, I worked in my flower garden.

Only today was of much importance to Papa. He lived for the moment and the pleasure he got from each day's labors. He often quoted from his own observations, "Take care of your today properly, and you will have no regrets about your yesterdays." "Treat today as it deserves, and you won't need to worry about your tomorrows."

I think I was like my daddy in many ways. It always made him feel bad to see a tree die. Papa's orchard was his pride and joy. The death of a fruit tree or grape arbor hurt him visibly. He seemed to feel personally responsible. They were like friends. He felt he must have failed them or they wouldn't have died. They were more than vines or trees to him. He knew God had made them and given them life also.

He did a good job on both trees and children. He would

say, "You can prune a young tree and shape it properly, and its fruit will be a blessing. A child is like a tree or vine. Let it have its own way, without some restrictions and training, and it will seldom amount to much."

If that's true, I should have been a pretty good girl. Sometimes Mama would prune a switch from a peach tree to shape me in the way she wanted me to grow. We kids knew not to be asked twice to do something we were told to do by either Mama or Papa.

My parents tried to instill the knowledge of right and wrong in our minds before we got too independent to accept advice. Since most of my married life outside the house revolved around vegetable and flower gardening, I put Papa's philosophy about children into my own words. "Children's minds and hearts are like seeds planted in fertile soil. Plant only good seeds in your family garden, and don't let any weeds grow."

We ate supper together as a family. No matter how late Papa worked in the fields, Mama always kept the food warm and insisted we wait on him before we ate. We didn't have electricity in our Lenna farmhouse. If Papa came in after dark, Mama would clean the glass lamp chimney and fill the lamp with kerosene so it would brighten the simple house we called our home.

I loved it when Mama called,
"Children, come in right now.
Papa's home from the field and he's tired from the plow."
We rushed to the table, so happy and filled with glee.
Papa's home from the field, as hungry as he can be.

Once I went with Papa to Eufaula to ship some furs and sell some produce. I noticed children playing in their yards and wondered what it would be like to be a city kid.

With part of the produce money, Papa bought us a little red wagon. When we got home, I pulled the wagon to the top of a hill and rode down the hill over and over. I felt sorry for the children in Eufaula since they couldn't have country fun because they lived in a crowded city.

I asked Papa how many people lived in Eufaula. He said, "The population is about a thousand." I'd never heard that big word *population* before. I just wanted to know how many people lived there.

At my country farm, I felt free because to me, it seemed I had the whole world as a playground. Between the clay hill and Old Limbo Creek, I could slip away for hours to meditate and dream. I loved to walk barefoot on the dusty ribbon roads, winding and unwinding mile after mile. Sometimes on hot summer days, the deep dust was boiling hot to our bare feet. Just to think about it always gave me an honest-to-goodness smile.

Often I loved to dream, when I was a barefoot child.

They said I was unbearable and nearly drove them wild.

Each day of my existence found me in more trouble.

I overdid each thing I did; to them it all seemed double.

Once I caught a garden snake and carried it up the path.

Oh my! It upset Mama so. I surely felt her wrath.

Once I took our rowing boat a ways down Limbo stream.

I stayed lodged in drifted logs until they heard my scream.

If anything did go wrong, my mother would declare,

"I can't prove a single thing, but I'll bet Pearlie was there."

One time Troy and I were playing and wandered off our farm to a house where loggers had once lived. First, we picked up broken dishes for our playhouse. Then, as we went into the house and were meddling around, we discovered a man in a bed. He lifted himself upon one elbow and said, "What're you kids doing in my house?" I was scared pink—not of him, but that he would go and tell Mama what we had done. We didn't go there anymore.

Mama had an old violin which she played by ear. When I was a little child and time for Mama to rest,

She reached for her violin and pressed it to her chest.
So many times, I recall, she'd sit on the porch at night,
Softly playing for everyone, with only the moon for light.
Her playing often stirred my mind, as I went off to sleep,
But some tunes played on her violin
made me want to weep.

In 1914, when I was eight years old, my brother Hiram Eugene Logan was born. We called him Whitey because his hair was light colored. He was entertainment for us older children.

One of our winter entertainments was to skate on the edge of a pond or at the edge of the creek. We didn't have ice skates. I truly believed we had colder and harder winters back then than when I died in 1993 at the age of eighty-seven. We always had so much fun skating on ice. Papa wouldn't let us skate when he knew about it because he said it wore out our shoes.

This year, another regular entertainment entered into our lives. A circus started coming to Lenna each year. From then on, Papa took us kids every year. We sure did enjoy it. As we walked home with him on these cool, winter nights, I sometimes walked in the back so I could see what we looked like and sounded like as we chattered to this tall, kind man who helped us sum up all we had seen.

Mama was also full of fun and did her part to entertain us. One day, she got one of the young bull calves out of the barn lot so my Russ and Troy could ride him. She had as much fun as they did. I was beginning to get the idea that this was too undignified for me, so I didn't join in because I had decided I wanted to be a grown-up lady, except when I got a chance to go hunting with Papa.

I tagged along with my daddy as if I were a boy. I went hunting with him more than Troy did. I enjoyed the nature of nighttime as much as the hunting and having Papa all to myself.

One September, when we started out after dusk, the moon was an orange color. It was near the horizon, rising just behind the trees. After we had walked for an hour, the moon had risen higher and turned yellow. I could look up and see clouds passing over the moon and the stars shimmering like crystal. From a distant ridge, I could hear a coyote yipping mournfully, and the dogs in the woods would answer. The crying coyotes kept me pretty close to Papa's side.

I might as well have been a thousand miles away from a town in this old, untamed, and unspoiled land I loved so much. Even in my old age, the black bottomland I called my old home place still called me back.

Papa trapped and sold his furs. We hunted far and wide.

We had much fun together, when I was by Papa's side.

I held a lantern in one hand, a possum sack in the other.

When I heard the coyotes howl, I longed for my mother.

The lantern gleamed in the darkness. We followed the barking hounds as they zigzagged through the woods. In a short time, they would tree a coon or a possum.

I asked Papa, "Why do the coyotes sound so sad?"

Papa answered, "Maybe they're singing a happy song. It just sounds like mourning to us because we listen with human ears and minds."

Sometimes we would hunt almost all night. I hunted with Papa until I grew up and got married and had to move away from the old home place. When I was little, I would ask questions just to stay awake. I didn't want to admit to him that I couldn't keep up with him. That's when Papa knew it was time to put me on his shoulders so I could rest my little legs. If I hushed talking in my elevated position, I could smell the sweet fragrance of the mint and evening primrose. Also, when I hushed talking, I would go to sleep. Papa would hold one leg, bow his head to make a pillow, and head for home.

Another night we went hunting when the weather was cold, clear, and brittle. The snow crunched underfoot, and the stars were so brilliant I imagined they could cast a shadow like the sun.

We bought our cow feed in brown fabric sacks. We called them tow sacks. We always took one or two with us in case we caught a possum. Papa would say, "Carry it away from your legs or they will try to bite you."

You might think the woods at night would be really quiet and peaceful. But they weren't. The owls hooted; dogs bayed; insects chirped; and dry, crisp leaves rustled underfoot where no snow accumulated. I wasn't afraid of the dark as long as I was with Papa. I knew I had good protection.

Near our home was a metal bridge over Old Limbo Creek. From our house, we could hear the horses' hooves clippitty-clop as they crossed the loose, wooden floor of the bridge. When a horse-pulled wagon crossed over it, I enjoyed hearing the loud sound of the wagon wheels as their echo was amplified by being echoed from the hill in the background.

If it was hot summertime, we knew a neighbor would soon pass by our house and stop for a cold drink of water from our well and for an exchange of news or gossip. The gossip was passed in both directions past our house and across the bridge. Mama kept a gourd dipper hanging on a hook near our well for people who came by when we were in the barn or out in the field.

The bridge stood many years, through my childhood days.

We had fun and little fear, in our old-fashioned ways.

All my years, I clearly hear wagon wheels rumbling slow,

To bring reality to my mind of my home place long ago.

The steel frame was black, and the
floor was made of wood.

Now I wish I could stand where once the old bridge stood.

I'm gone from my old home. The road goes past the hill.

The creek is dry, but I can hear the horses' footsteps still.

Old Limbo Creek was fed by some springs that released cold water. These springs kept the creek near our house unseasonably cold for our swimming. Papa warned us against going swimming without his permission.

The creek had a magnetic pull on me, just like I wanted to go barefoot on the dusty roads before it was warm enough. I was drawn by my own impatience to risk Papa's discipline if he caught me. More than once, I took a short dip without Papa's permission and always breathed a sigh of relief when I got away with it.

In warm weather, we kept our milk in the spring closest to our house that fed cold water into the creek. Mama would send me there again and again to store it after the milking was done or to bring some to the kitchen when she needed it to cook or feed us.

You haven't experienced all of nature until you've been through an Oklahoma thunderstorm or experienced a river-bottom flood. One particular day in the late part of May, when I was eight years old, I took a long, leisurely walk down Old Limbo Creek where it meandered lazily. I stopped to rest under a sleepy weeping willow tree on a bank of the creek and lay down behind the curtain of branches.

After an hour or so of listening to the babble of the stream, I opened the curtains of my dream room to see silent, puffy clouds drift through a blue sky. The clouds were moving from southwest toward the northeast, a relatively sure sign that the storm was making up its mind. I measured the speed of the clouds as they raced past some stately oak trees. The darkening clouds had a lacey edge around them, created by the bright sun behind them. Even though the clouds were moving rapidly, a breathless hush served as an additional warning.

A gust of wind blew through the trees as if testing them and their limbs to see which trees could win the fight. A spatter of rain fell against my face and then subsided. Then everything became perfectly still. I'd heard about the calm before the storm and took this as a final warning to head for the house. As I ran, I looked up and was captivated by a bulging, billowing mass of clouds that seemed to climb higher and higher into the heavens. They formed a thunderhead that looked like there had been a great explosion followed by bright lightning that was immediately followed by a blast of thunder that snapped me to attention as if God was saying, "Run, Pearlie. How many warnings do I need to give you? You know my rains sometimes overflow the creek."

Big drops of rain and penny-sized hail began to fall from dark, rushing clouds that were so low they seemed scarcely higher than the treetops. With all this came the sound of roaring wind. There was no chance I could escape the driving rain. I could only hope to avoid the worst of it. The wind drove through the brush and stunted trees until it appeared they would be sheared off at ground level or be uprooted. I saw the birds trying to escape by flying in among the clouds to avoid the blowing debris.

As suddenly as the storm came, it was gone, leaving dark and hanging clouds that shadowed the hills and hollows into gray and black as the day turned into evening. The storm acted like it was in a hurry to move from farm to farm to teach its warning signs to other children for their own protection.

I was lucky that time. And even though I carefully memorized the warning signs, there were other times when I wandered too far away from home and had to take cover in a neighbor's house. There were even times I put myself in danger because I didn't want to miss out on anything God was doing.

As I weathered many more storms, I concluded that the thunder of God's voice precedes the first flash of lightning. Otherwise, how would the winds get the signal to gather the vapors and rub them together with such intensity that the friction could generate the needed electric shock?

I've seen God in nature and in the heavens be as gentle as a blue sky kind of day or in the rebellious disarray of an Oklahoma thunderstorm.

Rain is hard on the flowers, but they have to have it. So do the fields need rains to usher in harvest time at the end of summer. Even when I was young, I knew to have gratitude to God for the extremes of nature. I always felt close to God in the nature that surrounded me. If I looked into space, I could see him walking in the clouds with outstretched arms in the lightning and falling rain. I saw his smile in the blossoms of flowers and when he waved his hands in concert with the limbs of trees. Best of all, I felt him beside me when I prayed.

I often walked the dusty roads at the end of a happy day.

I loved the days in redbud time in the early month of May.

I loved the dogwoods on a hill, lifting blooms into the air.

I could feel his holy presence as I talked to him in prayer.

I really loved the little creek that rambled by our home.

I could play there all day long and never feel alone.

I was born on a little farm, free as the wind and weather.

Nothing there to mar my day, for
God and I walked together.

✝

In 1915, Mrs. Jones gave birth to my Russ's youngest brother, Roscoe.

By this time, I was ten years old, and I had to begin the transition from being a child who played much more than I worked to being a child who worked as much as I played. I enjoyed both. In fact, most of the time, I couldn't tell the difference. Season by season, my parents expanded the simple farm chores a child could do to the more responsible ones I had to learn to do without being asked.

To stretch my day, and because it was so hot in the middle of summer, I slept outside in the yard as soon as weather and Mama would let me. I slept there until cold temperatures ran me into the house in October. I had no fear because Papa's two hunting dogs kept watch day and night. By this age, I had become a flower girl. By sleeping outside, at the first glimmer of daybreak, I would get up early in the morning, sometimes before my folks.

Have you ever slept out under the stars,

When the night was warm and still,

And the last faint rays of the setting sun

Were fading over the hill?

Do you know the joy of a quiet place

Far from the city's din,

Where nature heals your troubled heart

And gives you peace within?

In the quiet of the dusk,

Do you hear a night bird call?

Do you hear a murmuring stream,

Or the sound of a waterfall?

So if you're tired and weary of life,

And if you're burdened down with cares,

You'll find while sleeping under the stars,

God really answers prayers.

For heaven can come so close to you,

With no roof to shut it out,

And when you see God in the stars,

There's no more room for doubt.

I was crazy about flowers. I had my flower plot near the place Mama had her garden area. Mama taught me how to control the weeds in my garden and in my life. She taught me to expect and be thankful for the rain that would damage the flowers just like the storms that come to our lives. It must have been from Mama that I learned the proverb, "Rain is hard on the flowers, but they have to have it."

I would work with my flowers as if they were my children. Flowers, with their gemlike colors, were constantly changing each hour and unfolding new charms. That's why I had to walk through my garden several times each day. I thought flowers were the sweetest things God made. I wondered why he didn't put souls in them. My flowers were one of my main entertainments.

The creek near our house was both a source of heartache and entertainment, peace and danger. On the creek we had many good times. We learned to swim. We had a rowboat, and even the least of us knew how to use the oars. We had a few fights about who would get to row next.

When I got out alone in the boat, I felt really deep in nature. I would lie on the bottom of the boat at night and watch the silent stars, listen to the whispering wind, the soft ripple of running water, and the patter of a gentle rain. These sights and sounds gave me a great sense of calm. Nature's peace flowed into my life as sunshine flows into the trees.

However, one time, several of us were swimming, and I got caught in a whirlpool. If our neighbor across the creek hadn't been there, I would have drowned. When we had a heavy rain, the creek became swift and dangerous. It turned into a raging river and overflowed its banks.

My mind goes back to the old home place,
There on the steep hillside.
Memories flow back of my childhood days.
When I had to leave I cried.

I can see the creek where we learned to swim.
There we learned the crawdad stroke.
From an old grape vine we'd swing across the creek,
Or dive from the limb of a stately oak.

And the boat we paddled up and down,
Up and down that crooked stream.
All alone, on the bottom I would lie,
And dream from dream to dream.

I will never forget the old home place,
There on the sandy loam.
Before our baby died, I had to leave.
Someday, I must go back home.

A major heartache the creek brought with it in some of the rainy seasons was when it overflowed its banks. It could wash away our crops and leave us with nothing for that year.

I'd seen my parents with heavy hearts. Papa would console Mama with, "Mary Logan, aren't you proud we have the garden on the hill near the house. We can always live out of the garden from spring until winter." And we did.

That was the year I learned to make my famous soup. I was quite a soup maker when I was a girl. I would go to the garden and get what I needed or what was available. Everyone said they liked my soup, and that made me happy. It was a good meal when served with cornbread.

Another close call I had on the creek was when I was standing up in the rowboat, and a sudden thunderstorm blew in. The boat went out from under me, and I had to wade to the shore that was away from our house. The river was rising so fast even the bridge floor was covered. I didn't dare go back across that day. I had to spend the night with the Allen family. My family had no way of knowing whether I was alive or dead. The next day, the river had gone down enough that Mr. Allen felt he should get me home. We crossed the bridge in a horse-pulled wagon. The team of horses had to almost swim the river, and the wagon bed almost floated off its frame. I began to wonder how I could love that old creek so much.

I started making faint trails for my walks in the woods to soak up all nature had to offer. These trails became much more distinct from year to year. I didn't know at the age of ten that I was designing the path my Russ and I would walk hand in hand after I turned fifteen.

My nature trail meandered to places I selected to watch the wildflowers and trees as the seasons changed. At other places, I observed many animals and birds darting about. As I walked, rabbits would scurry out of the path, looking for cover.

At one particular spot on Old Limbo Creek, I would often watch a kingfisher bird swoosh down through the air to catch a fish firmly in its beak. Its long beak also allowed it to spear a fish. Then it would fly back up to its perch on a limb above the creek. The bird would kill its catch by repeatedly smacking it against a limb, flip it in the air, and swallow it headfirst. The kingfisher birds always fascinated me because they could dip into the water and come up with a fish so fast. They have their own sound and color like other birds. They have a blue body with a white necklace, and the tops of their wings are blue, but underneath they are white.

My path made its way to the rocky ledges on the hill where the going was a little more rugged. As I climbed, the wind moaned through the pine trees. As it blew across the cave openings, it made a sound like you make when you blow across the top of a pop bottle. From there, I could look down on the farm fields in their seasons as a reward for the climb. What a happy feeling! A gentle spring rain would remind me that a miracle would recur when, in the sun-warmed earth, millions of seeds were waiting for their rebirth.

On its way back down, I designed the path to go by a spring where I could get a cold drink. There was a big log there where I would sit in the balm of solitude and watch the clouds flying by and sometimes the wild geese. As I watched, I heard a crow caw from the trees on the slope, and a doe ran by toward the stream, followed by her twin fawns.

I carved my name, *Ida Pearl Logan,* on a tree there. I thought, *Someday I'll come here when I'm old and see if my tree's still standing and if my name is still there.*

Just six years later, my Russ and I would sit on this log to start a three-year courtship. After we got married, we walked the trail again and added my new last name to my tree. I knew I would never want to leave my beautiful life in the country where, on the circle of my woodland trail, I was surrounded by God's nature. It was so beautiful.

✝

In 1917, at our farm, World War I was a greater distance from Europe than almost any other place in America. We had no electricity, no radio, and no newspaper. Even though farms were critical for the war effort, quite a few of our farm men joined up. I was eleven years old when the U.S. declared war. At that age, I had other things on my mind since, at the end of the sixth grade, I had to stop going to school to work on our farm. I had less time to dream, and therefore, I didn't feel very patriotic. The war was just too far away.

Now, at twelve years old, I had to learn to plow in the fields, gather corn, cut tree sprouts from the fields, and saw wood. I worked almost as hard as a man. I didn't realize that in just three more years there would be almost no time for play or dreaming or walking my nature trail.

I must admit I found a way to enjoy plowing. It turned into a delight to walk barefoot in a newly plowed field as the wind played through my hair. I followed behind the mule, wrestling the plow into the upright position. The mule knew where to walk better than I did to make the row straight. Papa had taught him well, and the mule must have known I wasn't very strong.

Newly plowed earth has a special fragrance all its own. I became addicted to it. That's why, after I had to leave the farm, I still worked in a vegetable garden to feed my own children well. In my older years, I crawled around in my flower beds, turning the dirt over so I could get a daily whiff of newly turned soil.

But not all was work and no play. We had plenty of fun things to do on the weekends when we were growing up. On Saturday night, there would be singing performances, and on Sunday morning and Sunday night, we went to church. My Russ's daddy led the singing. He worked hard to improve the singing, using it to give the young people something to do and places to go. We would go to singing conventions in nearby towns.

We also had big fish fries in those days. Large crowds would gather at the Deep Fork River for those occasions. The men would stomp around in the water to make it muddy, and the fish would come to the surface of the water to get air. That way they could be easily caught. Later, this was against the law. I didn't like to eat fish, but I did like to wade in the soft, blue stream before the men muddied it.

My faith in God grew stronger as I grew older. Daily, I saw the miracles of things growing in nature. I saw these miracles in the woods, the cornfield, and Mama's garden. But I gave the prize to Papa's two orchards. They were Papa's pride. We kids spent many hours in the orchards. Mama made apple cider from the apples we picked for her.

It was a big chore for Papa to protect the trunks of his fruit trees. He wrapped them in fabric from cow feed sacks to protect the bark from the rabbits. Another thing Papa did to protect the trees in the orchard was to go rabbit hunting. It wasn't unusual for him to return with as many as eight rabbits at a time. As he skinned the rabbits and cut them up to be cooked, Mama would make biscuits, gravy, and whipped potatoes. My, how we kids did eat! We even held our plates up to our faces so we could lick them clean.

Mama had seen how young people often didn't respect older people. So when I was twelve, she told me, "Don't turn away from older people, Pearlie. Don't regard them as have-beens. To ignore them would be a terrible mistake. Stay close to them. Regard them as precious gems. Love them. Learn from them. Take what they have to offer. Like God, they have given life to the younger generation. They can teach you how to use it, appreciate it, and understand it if you will let them." I did what

Mama told me. I had no idea then how much I would have to rely on our older neighbors three years later.

At fourteen years old, even though I no longer went to school, I stayed active in the youth group that Mr. Jones led at church. All his life, he was interested in young people. He took a special interest in me. Perhaps it was because I had to drop out of school before the other young people. My Russ had just graduated from the eighth grade. Perhaps Mr. Jones thought my hard work on the farm and my love for God made me more serious about life than the other young people.

On most Saturday nights, he would ask me to lead the singing. I didn't dare turn him down or I would get into trouble with Papa. The country people really turned out for the Saturday night assemblies. It was nice, and we had lots of fun. We really had some good singers in those days, and Lenna was rated very highly when we sang as a group at singing conventions.

Mr. Jones talked to me about Jesus. It wasn't a subject that Mama or Papa knew a lot about at this time of my growing up. Mr. Jones knew the Bible really well and pointed me in the right direction. I treated him as a second father on these kinds of matters. He told me, "Pearlie, you will clearly know when God is speaking to you because you have a heart for it. He speaks to you in nature. Someday, he will speak to your heart. I know your family isn't well off financially, but when you find Jesus, you'll realize you're the richest girl in the world."

The glow of youth upon me, I searched for things untold.

And when I found my Jesus, I found my heart of gold.

I can't undo my yesterdays. Those days are forever gone.

Why wait for my tomorrows, for they may never come.

I had walked in darkness, putting off what had to be,

I searched for God's answers, while Jesus looked for me.

With the glow of youth upon me,
I found the thing untold.
Since my Jesus found me, I've found my heart of gold.

I guess my parents loved us as well as any parents could. They really made us toe the line. They only told us to do something once. We quickly learned the hard way that they meant what they said. My parents didn't tell us they loved us. I guess we had sense enough to know they did by the way they took care of us and made us mind. They saw we had plenty of food and as much of the material things as they could afford in those days.

Nevertheless, I wish they had shown more love in words and hugs. I decided, from these thoughts, that I should show more love and look for expressions of love from the other person's point of view. I decided that if I had children, I would use words and poems to express my love, not only with my mouth but in writing as well. I really longed for this outward show of affection and understanding from my mother and father.

I realized love was the most powerful force known to mankind when I realized the love God showed for me by hanging his son on a cross for my salvation. God spoke to my heart and told me, "Pearlie, think of the many times your parents have kept working to provide for you kids when they were dog tired. It's their kind of love that motivates them to action when their bodies are crying out for rest." I didn't realize that in just another year, God would require me to show that kind of love to my parents.

✝

The barn loft was my sanctuary when I was a little girl. I sat there while I played with my paper dolls. As time passed and my interests changed, my use of Papa's barn loft also changed. It became my lookout station. My Russ frequently rode his horse by our place or stopped to visit Troy. The way he looked at me told me it was really me he came to see. The way I looked at him told Mama how I felt about him. Because of my history of risk-taking and her observation that I used the barn loft to spy on my Russ, Mama would just as soon he didn't come around.

It seemed to me Zula McCraken and Thelma McDanel always happened to be in the road just in case my Russ came by or stopped by our house. I could understand their interest. My Russ, with his wavy black hair, combed straight back, was oh so handsome. I had heard his grandmother was a Kiowa. So at fourteen, the barn loft became my sacred high ground where I went to watch my Russ to see if he would stop to talk with Zula or Thelma. After all that time and effort, I never caught him at it.

We were just children when we first met.

We needed no reminder, and yet,

We grew and grew as children do,

And fell in love as if we knew.

At first they called it puppy love.

We said it was from God above.

They said romance would fade away.

They learned that ours was here to stay.

For years, he was my handsome man.

"Puppy love?" They just didn't understand.

Mama knew I spied on him, and she told my Russ about it after we were married. He never let me forget it.

I had another high ground I liked to go to as often as I could. It was the mountain ledge that was part of my nature trail. I could go there and think of God and the way he had blessed me with his nature. I suppose that's why I never felt lonely. I always felt that the trees in the forest were my friends. I would climb to the top of this ledge and look down on the valley below to see if there were any remote places I had missed.

I wasn't a stranger to any part of the woods or their inhabitants. The birds were my special friends. It would thrill me to see a bird building a nest. From my vantage point on the mountain ledge, I could watch the many large birds that swept the sky with their wings spread wide. I longed to fly with them. These were the kinds of images I wanted to store in my memory, to be dusted off when I needed to remember God's glory in nature through the young eyes of girlhood.

Only flower lovers can understand that gardeners talk to their flowers. My private flower garden continued to thrive. I ordered a rosebush from a catalog as a gift for Mama. There were many of them, and all had different names, such as Peace, Abraham Lincoln, and Tropicana. Mama had noticed me looking through the catalog, and we had talked about the names of the roses.

After I received the small bush and set it out in the corner of my flower garden, next to Mama's vegetable garden, I told her, "I bought it for you, Mama. It's the connection between our gardens and a way to tell you I love you."

She smiled and asked. "What's its name?"

"It's named Mama's Rose," I answered.

As I went toward the house, I looked over my shoulder and noticed she had gotten down on her knees, facing the rosebush, and was talking to it. When my family moved to California, I dug it up and took it to my marriage home in Preston. I promised to talk to it like she did.

My mother knew how to stay as young as springtime. When I was fourteen, she was thirty-seven and expecting my sister Bertha. She could sing and whistle like a bird. By now, she played a violin, a French harp (harmonica), and a pump organ by ear.

I loved to hear Mama play her violin. She lent it to a crippled boy, and it was never returned. This worried Mama then and was always a great disappointment to me each time I thought about it during my life. To soothe my longing to hear her play again, I imagined the boy took it to heaven with him when he died at a young age.

Mama's friend came by. Her son couldn't walk or run.

So Mama loaned her old violin to give him a world of fun.

She didn't guess the loss as she shared it with this boy,

Knowing well, within her heart, that
it would bring him joy.

About its loss I often worried and was never able to learn,

Why, after the little boy died, Mama's violin didn't return.

God knew how she loved it; so much she shared this part.

So we lost Mama's violin, and it nearly broke my heart.

If I could only hold it again, even if it had not one string.

Just to hold Mama's old violin, what joy it would bring.

Hard Times at the Old Home Place

1921 through 1924

In 1921, when I was fifteen, my sister Bertha Lavern Logan was born. We were always very close. At first, because of the age difference, we were more like mother and daughter than sisters. This was accentuated because of Mama's illness soon after Bertha was born. Bertha even looked very much like I did as a young girl and as a grown woman.

During Mama's illness, Bertha was just a baby, and we bonded more closely than any of my sisters. Bertha thought I was her mother for the longest time.

It was about this same time when my Russ really started paying close attention to me, although he had quit riding his horse by our place as often. I concluded he had eyes for Zula or Thelma. Then, one day, the church youth group cleaned around the graves in the Lenna cemetery. When we finished, I left to walk home, and I was almost there when he overtook me on his horse. We walked along with the horse following us. We talked a while out in front of the house before I went in.

I remember real well on a certain day,

We met to work and not to play.

The work was finished. I left alone.

You overtook me, with thoughts of your own.

I'd say silly things, and you would agree.

You were taken with me; I could plainly see.

I remember those walks from church to my home.

How I flirted with you when we were alone!

Then as quiet as the stars slip away from the dawn,

I knew you'd be mine from that day on.

The next Sunday, as I was leaving the church house, he said, "Wait a minute until I get my horse." He didn't ask if he could walk me home. He just did, and we were never apart since. After almost fifty-four years of marriage, he went to be with the Lord, about fourteen years before I did.

When my Russ rode away that day, I thought he was downright beautiful sitting astraddle his dapple gray horse. He wore shiny black boots that came just below his knees. He removed his white, broad-brimmed hat; gallantly waved to me; and called out, "See you at church tonight, Pearlie."

I smiled all the way into the house. Mama had watched the whole drama and gave me a knowing smile when our eyes met. She knew that day that my life was set upon a whole new course.

I fell in love with Russ when he was just a boy.

He was then, and still is, my greatest pride and joy.

He would ride his dapple gray,

As each day he passed my way.

He would smile and tip his hat,

Oh! My goodness! I did like that.

Every day I watched for him.

How I loved him was a sin.

Mama also watched him every day.

She wished that boy would go away.

But to him it didn't matter.

It wasn't Mama he was a'ter.

I didn't want a husband who smoked and drank or wouldn't say where he was going when he went away from the house. I was blessed because my prayers and wishes were answered. My Russ made all the difference in my life. He provided for me and our children as well as he could. When times were hard and money was short, we always got by somehow. He was always the best man in the world to me. But our thoughts about marriage would be delayed by a typhoid fever epidemic. This seriously cut into the time my Russ and I could spend together.

At fifteen, I was fairly well prepared to take over all the housework when Mama and Papa and Troy had the typhoid fever. Adding to the workload, Bertha was only seven months old when this occurred. The worst of it lasted about five weeks, but they were so weak afterward it took another two months for them to regain the strength required to harvest the crops that had been planted before they had begun to show symptoms of the disease.

Typhoid fever occurs more frequently in the country because of unsanitary conditions related to drinking water, outside toilets, and the flies that are always abundant around a farm. I probably didn't get the disease because I was always very careful about washing my hands and keeping flies off my food. And I stopped drinking from a stream no matter how clear it looked. This was before antibiotics. Fortunately, the older ladies in the community were able to tell me how to nurse the family back to health. I was highly motivated because I had been to the funerals of people who died from the fever.

The treatment was simple: cleanliness. I boiled the water they drank but cooled it before they drank it. I washed their food with boiled water and bathed them with cool, clean water to control their temperatures. I buried or burned their body waste so the flies couldn't carry the germs around our house or the neighborhood. I killed more flies than I could count. I didn't have a thermometer, but later I learned that their body temperatures during the second week may have gone as high as 103 to 105 degrees. I know this must be true since all of them spent a few days when they were delirious.

We had one particular neighbor who was a blessing to all of us and especially to me. Her name was Eddie Beebe. She was a widow with six children and never let the fear of this serious disease keep her from helping us when our family was so sick. None of her family took it, and I was so thankful. I wrote a letter to her for all the things she did for me and my family. I don't believe I could have made it without her. I never forgot her or stopped thanking God for her.

It was hard for me to believe that while I was doing all this hard work, my weight increased to more than 148 pounds. I suppose I did too much eating on the run at the cook stove. I hadn't even had time to look in the mirror. After the worst was over, I went to the store to restock Mama's pantry and Papa's cow feed in the barn. While in the feed store, I stepped upon the scales. I saw how much weight I had gained. I took care of that problem because now that I had more free time, I wanted to look trim for my Russ.

The Deersaw family lived down the road from us. They were very important neighbors. They knew about many Indian remedies for any illnesses that were common to people like us, who lived far from towns where doctors and medicines were readily available. I learned later in my life that vaccines for diphtheria were newly available when I was twelve years old.

For diphtheria, the Deersaw family showed us how to build a tiny teepee around a victim who was struggling to get air through his throat passage. They taught us to burn beeswax inside the enclosure. The fumes would open the passage and bring relief.

In an emergency, when our daughter Mary was a child, I had to use this old method to help her breathe until the doctor could get to our house and treat her with a vaccine.

Everyone recovered. I didn't know it then, but two years later, Papa and Troy would have accidents that kept them out of the fields again. Again, I transferred from being a homemaker to being a full-time farmer, and my hopes about marriage were again delayed.

After Mama had fully recovered, she wanted to reward me for the nights and days I couldn't go to Saturday night singings or even meet my Russ in front of the house to talk. He would have come, but I wouldn't let him because the fever was transferred by direct contact with the person who was a carrier. Besides, I didn't think I could get that close to him without wanting him to touch me.

Mama had been a bride at my age. She knew what was going on in my mind, and she knew she owed it to me to give us a little time to be alone with each other. With an appreciative look she said, "Pearlie, I want to do something special for you.

Why don't we invite Russell over to eat and spend the afternoon Sunday after the two of you go to church?"

All I could say as I jumped to my feet and hugged Mama was, "Sounds pretty special to me, Mama!"

Mama was a very good cook, and I got a preview of how much my Russ enjoyed good food. During the meal, Papa would tease me by threatening to tell some secrets about me. Mama noticed how my Russ didn't quite know how to take it and tried to make Papa hush.

To save myself from further embarrassment, I got up from the table and said, "I'm going for a walk. Does anyone want to join me?"

Papa jumped up real fast with a grin on his face, and Mama grabbed his shoulder and pulled him back down into his seat.

Mama said, "Russell, I think she wants you to go with her."

My Russ is the only other person I ever took on a personal tour of my nature trail. To make conversation, he said, "I heard from a schoolteacher that during your last year of school you could memorize poems quicker than anyone he ever met. He also said you showed him some of the poems you had written."

"Would you like it if I would make up a poem just for you?" I challenged.

"You mean just make it up out of your head as we walk along your trail?" he questioned, with his hands extended out from his sides, as if to punctuate his surprise with body language.

So, like a classroom poem teacher, I instructed with a deep man's voice, "Come with me, young man, and I'll show you how your eyes and ears and feelings can write the poem for you. Listen and tell me what you hear."

"Well, it's so quiet I don't hear much of anything. I see clouds in the sky. I feel the wind and see the tree leaves moving."

"Very good, young man," I complimented him. "I believe you have the makings of a very good poet who may even get your poems published in a magazine someday. Here's how it's done."

There's quietness on my country trail.

"Isn't that what you heard, or didn't hear?"

A very good start, you know.

"Next, we need to set up a word that rhymes with *know*."

I love the whisper of the wind

"Now we must do something with the clouds."

When clouds are hanging low.

"That wasn't difficult, was it? Okay now, young man! It's your turn to start the next line. How did we get to the trail?"

"We came down the road from the house," the budding poet replied without much imagination.

"Was the road straight?" encouraged the teacher.

"It was a winding road," the student replied, as if he had invented a new adjective.

I thought to myself, *This beautiful boy, who went to school two years more than I did, is going to require a lot of instruction, and I'm prepared to give him private lessons.*

"Okay. Make up a sentence about the road and the trail, describing them with an adjective," I instructed.

There upon the winding road,

"Is that with a comma or a period? A comma? Okay."

And on the narrow trails.

"Now. Just blurt out what you hear."

I can hear that old bobwhite.

"Perfect. What do you see?"

I see some birds we call quails.

"See. It rhymes. This is fun, isn't it?"
By now, we were holding hands and laughing and acting silly. I hoped nobody was watching. To get us back on track, or back on the trail, I might say, I put back on my teacher voice. "I'll do the next three lines, and your exam is to see if you can complete the last line. Here goes. Pay attention, young man."

Here we stroll the forest deep,
And pick any flower that we choose.
Where country folks come to play

"Here's your chance to shine. Don't mess up."

By pitching old horseshoes.

This he added with the squeaky voice of a child.
"That was really a sorry line, young man. But since you're not too bright, we'll have to use it." I giggled as I watched the first of the sideways grins I grew to love on this poor boy's face. "Come on. I have a special place I want to show you on my nature trail."
Taking his hand again, I led him to the big log beside the cool spring, where we stopped to get a drink. We sat down, still holding hands. He saw my name carved on the tree.
"Ida Pearl Logan. Why did you carve your name on the tree?" he asked.
"Because this trail belongs to me, and I love to live out in the country, and I never plan to leave it." This brash demand

seemed to startle him, and he had nothing to say for a while, as if he were thinking very deep thoughts.

Then, to bring the gaiety back and to suggest that we go back to the house, he encouraged me by saying, "Before we go back to the house, give me three more lines about how much you love living on a country farm."

So I took the challenge as if what I said in these three lines and what he said in one might be a prophecy about a choice I would someday have to make. I chose my words carefully because now he was giving *me* a test.

Each day I love it more and more.

I must always tell my Russ the truth.

It holds a sweet, peaceful charm.

How could I ever love him more than my home place?

Although I'm falling deep in love,

He answered me with a question.

Mostly you love your country farm?

Oh God! I think he understands.

We went back to the house with me knowing I might have made one brash commitment I might not be allowed to keep but had made another commitment I knew I couldn't help but keep. I also knew God had given me someone who would understand me and make it as easy for me as he could.

As we walked up on the porch, twilight was falling, and crickets were beginning to chirp. Mama and Papa were sitting on the porch waiting for us, and Mr. Charmer said to Mama,

"Mrs. Logan, do you suppose I could have some more of that good dessert?" The way she smiled!

As we ate dessert, Mama suggested we play a game to describe the sounds we were hearing from the woods. All of us made the sound of an owl, but we had to debate about whether it was *Hoo hoo* or *Who who* or *Oo oo*. We even had to argue over whether the frogs around the pond were saying, *Knee deep, knee deep*, or *Ribbit, ribbit, ribbit*. When we each did the wolf howl, our hound dogs started barking, and my Russ bent over in his chair with the silliest laughing I had ever heard.

Fortunately for me, a horse-drawn buggy clip-clopped, bounced, and rattled across the wooden-floored bridge near our house. Behind the buggy, we saw the headlights of a car that stirred up the sandy dust from the road, passing the buggy quickly. It honked, *Uh-oooooo-guh*, to the buggy driver, asking him to make way.

My Russ said to Papa, "That's a 1920 Model-T Ford. I've been reading books about how to repair cars. I've found an old junk car that I can remove the engine, transmission, and rear end so I can learn how to take them apart and put them back together. I can use these as samples to show potential customers that I know how to fix their cars. My daddy said I could use a part of his blacksmith shop to work on customers' cars. He's even made me some wrenches to get started."

Papa was very impressed.

Then I could tell Papa had some joke up his sleeve. He said, "Mary, you're the best whistler around these parts. Whistle what the whippoorwill and bobwhite sound like."

Mama blew the sounds from her puckered-up mouth.

"See how easy it is," Papa said. "Anyone can whistle."

I saw what Papa was up to. He wanted to get an idea how far our courting had gone. He turned to my Russ and said, "Now Russ, it's your turn. All you have to do is pucker up your lips like this and blow." As he puckered his lips to make them look like a kiss, he jammed his elbow in the poor boy's ribs and then hee-hawed like a mule.

My Russ caught on to the joke and laughed along with Papa like it was really funny. Mama and I gave both of them a steely-eyed look, but it was too late. My Russ saw the look on my face and decided it was time for him to go home. Mama and Papa went into the house to give us a few minutes of privacy.

I loved Papa so much I couldn't get mad at the way he teased me. I couldn't be mad at my Russ just because he was trying to impress my daddy. So as I walked with him to the road, I took his hand to let him know I didn't really mind the joke. When we got to the road, my Russ looked deep into my eyes and said, "I love you, Miss Poet."

It took me a few seconds to recover as he gave me that sideways grin. I answered, "I love you too, Mr. Poet."

As he walked down the dark road to go home, he looked back several times and waved until he disappeared in the darkness. Under my breath, I said to myself, "Someday, when I'm Mrs. Poet, we will make some little rhymes together." I was glad it was dark because I felt my face redden from embarrassment.

Mama had done something special for me. I mentally looked around our not so prosperous farm as I sat for a while longer on the porch. A whippoorwill called from the hills. A whispering wind gently stirred the trees. We never did know we were poor because our hearts were happy, and I thought, *Why wouldn't I want to stay here forever? And why do I sense that I will be forced to leave?*

In 1922, my sister Ina Mae Logan was born. We called her Mae. My Russ's baby sister was also born this same year. She was named Lena Loyale Jones. My Russ carried her around when she was tiny and pampered her more and more as she learned to walk. One time, he rode to our house, supposedly to show his new dapple-gray horse to me. He brought Loyale for me to see also. I wasn't sure which one he was most proud to show off.

I liked to watch the way he treated his baby sister. It gave me an idea how he would be with our children when we got married. We weren't formally engaged, but I had no doubt how we felt about each other. He handed Loyale down to me. She was a pretty brown baby with black hair. I thought to myself, *If I ever have a little brown-skinned girl, I'm going to name her Loyale.*"

Bertha was barely three years old. She really loved my Russ. She came running and calling, "Wuss. Wuss."

Mama came out on the porch carrying Mae and said, "Pearlie, bring the baby in the house, and I'll let her play with Mae while you show Russ the new calf."

My Russ lifted Bertha up on his shoulders, and we held hands as we walked to the barn. It was a beautiful day because spring was bursting out all over the valley, and my heart was about to burst for this unexpected visit. Redbud and dogwood were a riot of glorious color on the mountainside. I felt my cup running over with happiness and contentment. We were surrounded by the love of nature and our love for each other. The sun added its radiant glow to this picture as we stood there inspired by the little calf trying to frolic on wobbly legs.

My Russ took Bertha off his shoulders and held her in his left arm and gathered me close with his right arm. With his arm around me, I felt so safe and fulfilled. Bertha was kissing him on the cheek. I could read his face that he had something on his mind. His voiced cracked just a little as he asked, "Pearlie, will you marry me?"

The hills were never prettier, the sky no deeper blue,

The sun never so golden, that day I stood by you.

Your voice wasn't as steady as a man's voice should be,

When you said, "My Pearlie, will you marry me?"

I kissed you again and again, my cheek against your brow,

And said, "my Russ, my darling, I'll marry you, and how!"

When we got back to the house, Bertha blurted out to Mama, "Mama, Wuss kiss Pulie on the mouf."

Because of this unexpected revelation, he decided he urgently needed to take Loyale back home. I carried her until he got on the horse. I kissed her and said, "You're a wonderfully beautiful girl, Lena Loyale from Lenna."

As I lifted her up to him, I informed him, "If we ever have a little brown, black-haired girl, I'm going to name her Loyale, so try to get used to the idea."

As he turned the horse's head with the reins, he replied with a mixed tone of disbelief and pleasure, "You'd better watch it, Miss Prissy, or you'll give me other ideas."

I laughed at him and said, "Tell your mother I'm going to write a poem for Loyale's baby book."

I reached seventeen that year. We began to talk more about marriage, not knowing that by this same time next year another event in my family would delay serious marriage-date setting by a year or two. It was fortunate because it gave us time to grow up a little more, as if any young lovers are ever really prepared to take on the responsibilities of marriage and family. The delay also gave my Russ more time to polish his skills as a car mechanic and save some money toward a house. This common sense didn't make it any easier for me to wait.

I was a silly little girl looking for romance.

And when I found my Russ, I knew this was my chance.

"Marriage is not for me," my Russ once had said.

But I had a lot of patience and a very level head.

I flirted and I waited and made him chocolate pie.

I was awfully sneaky and wasn't one bit shy.

So we courted and we courted, five years and maybe more.

When I got him in my house of love,
I closed and locked the door.

Not only did I keep my mind on my Russ and our future; also, I thought about the house we would live in near my old home place. I will admit I didn't know enough to think it completely through, but I surely did want our house to be on a farm not far from my old home place and my nature trail, where I had learned more than I learned from reading books.

Only the Lord knows what every day and year holds for his children. That is surely why this particular day of this year he let me stroll with him over my winding trail.

I sat on a rock in a shady nook and dreamed. *When I grow up and have children, this is the kind of life I want them to live. I want them to have a home in some of these green valleys where, as a child, I played so pleasantly under the lacy trees.*

On that sunny day, shadows danced on the green grass under the trees as the wind bent every bough, like long arms reaching out to the sky. That same wind would blow upon the prairie fields of grass, making them look like waves upon the sea. Often, when the fog would drift in from the river bottom, we couldn't see very far, and the nights would be ghostly in their silence.

I wanted my children to enjoy the country life where there is plenty of wildlife to study, such as rabbits who live in their cages made of thickets and surrounded by good forest land. No one was afraid of danger in this animal freedom where coyotes can howl above the singing of the wind. I wanted my children to see with their own eyes the prairie grass turn from gray to green. I wanted them to see the bluebonnets massed for miles and miles beside the North Canadian River, where I played often as a child.

That day finally came when my Russ gave an engagement ring to me. Actually, it was a real wedding band. I asked, "Why a wedding band for an engagement ring?"

He replied, "I'm not trying to be cheap. This is the ring we'll use when we get married. I just don't want you to have any doubt in your mind about my intentions." So in return, and not to be cheap, I wrote my Russ a poem.

I warned my heart, "Now don't fly away,

This is just the beginning. Our love is here to stay."

Why shouldn't we call this *love?* No other name will do.

That's why my heart stood still. I am so in love with you.

In 1924, Troy got married to his first wife, Ivy. This was also the year Mama put the wrong medicine in Papa's infected eyes, and Troy injured his hand in a gristmill. Papa's eyes were damaged for several months, and Troy could only do one-handed chores. These accidents occurred just a short time after my eighteenth birthday and right before planting season.

Thoughts of marriage had to be put from my mind because I had to concentrate on preparing the land and planting the corn and cotton fields. This was one spring the landscape became as dark as the soil that had to be exposed, turned, harrowed, and furrowed.

Even though Ivy helped, Mama did both housework and fieldwork. Ivy, with her frail body, worked as hard as she could. Blanche was fourteen, and Whitey was ten, so they already knew how to do most of the barn and garden chores after school each day. The neighbors came to our rescue even though they had the same work to do on their farms.

Some nights, my Russ would gallop his horse and work in

the moonlight. He said he did it because it was the only way he could see me during those weeks. Seeing him kept me going.

Each night, I'd go to bed and couldn't straighten out for half an hour. My back muscles were so tight I would just lie there in a tired trance. Papa knew what the hard work was doing to me. He sympathized with me by prophetically telling me, "Pearlie, as much as you love the farm, you're not made for this kind of hard work." I took what he said only as his way of being so sorry he and Troy couldn't carry their full load.

Even though this was a painful experience, behind our backs, the orchards were in full bloom in competition with the redbuds, dogwoods, and daffodils. Summer was showing promise that it would work its magic on the many seeds we planted. And before our eyes, the prairie grass had grown thick and green before the hay mower. The cotton stalks began to show off their soft, white fruit, and the corn we planted marched off in straight rows taller than a man.

Finally, that day came when I went down to the spring and sat on the log on my nature trail and said out loud in a satisfied voice, "I'm going to take a cool siesta now and call it a day."

My Russ and I had to rebuild our close relationship because the long days were consumed by work, and the short nights only gave time for rest. In addition, my Russ was inclined to be jealous of other young men who came to help. Over the years, he got over it when he saw he couldn't change me. So I sat him down on the log seat of my nature trail and gave him a lecture.

Let me say as we sit and listen to my teardrops fall,

If you don't trust me now, you never will at all.

I'm too proud to give my heart to someone full of doubt.

You have little faith in me, nor trust me when I'm out.

I will not toss my life away on a future I can't see.

I've said what's on my heart. What will your answer be?

We never ever had to have that frank conversation again, and I was just as friendly as ever. However, I must admit I wasn't being totally fair with my Russ because I had a tinge of jealousy too. I just didn't let it show on my face and in my voice like he did. Besides, my Russ was too sweet to chew me out about it. Even though I was wearing our engagement ring, that didn't keep other young women from making it clear that they would take my Russ from me if they could. One of them was a very good friend of mine. I got my comeuppance one Saturday at a community get-together. My friend got my Russ off to one side, and I could tell they were having a serious talk. This time my Russ could see the worried jealousy in my face.

I feared he'd fall in love with someone else but me.

I told myself, *This isn't true. This just cannot be.*

She told me things he said or nice things he would do.

So I would wonder to myself, *Does he love her or you?*

Then he walked away from her and stood by my side.

With his grin, he said to me, "I want *you* for my bride."

As he walked home with me, there was a yellow moon near the eastern horizon, and the stars seemed to fall at my feet as if God himself were speaking reassurance to me.

My Russ held my hand and squeezed with all his might.

I looked in his eyes and said, "I believe the stars are right."

The yellow moon rose higher. The stars kept teasing me.

I didn't mind. We were in love, as all could plainly see.

It was a wonderful feeling to be young lovers whispering sweet nothings to each other and building dreams on a star.

I sometimes felt like a thief the way I would steal glances at my Russ when he wasn't looking; take time from him when he was busy with other things; selfishly steal him from his friends when he wanted to play baseball with them; and most of all, when I stole the poor boy's heart away.

> "My life's a path of sunshine," whispering shadows say.
> Yes, I'm the lucky one, for I stole your heart away.
> I want you for myself. You mean the world to me.
> I looked into your heart; only happiness did I see.
> It wasn't really necessary for me to write a book,
> For I remember every word and just the way you look.
> My life's completely happy. I need you every day.
> I'm so glad you understood when I stole your heart away.

Between planting time and harvest, we had time to take walks on my nature trail. It was a relaxed time after the exhausting days we had gone through because of the accidents Papa and Troy experienced. They were on the mend, and the distribution of the farm's workload would be back to normal come harvest time. As my Russ and I sat on the log by the spring on my nature trail, we had another go at composing a poem together, with me doing most of the work. My hard experiences and our delayed dreams were drawing both of us closer to God.

> As we sit on our fallen limb,
> I hear love in nature's hymn.
> It takes love to challenge all.
> That is why we hear his call.
> We turned our faces toward the sky.
> Saw stars at night, heard winds that sigh.
> We drew a breath of scented air.
> We know now God answers prayer.

Our hearts are so full of cheer.

We really have no room for fear.

And there's no need for us to cry,

Since love did not pass us by.

We both said the next verse to each other.

It takes you to make my day,

With lots of love along the way.

A whisper from your tender voice.

I whisper back, "You are my choice."

We kissed and hugged with the tender intimacy that only other young lovers can imagine or older ones remember. My Russ said, in a way that hinted that these carefree days of our youth were nearing their end, "Let's climb the mountain path of your nature trail and look over the ledge again."

The trees were so thick we could only see patches of sky. The trees seemed to hug each other high above as we held each other, trying to outdo them. It seemed the only sound I could hear was the leaves beneath our feet and our hearts beating as one as we stood breast to chest.

It was a hot day. The forest was very quiet. As we began to ascend the mountain path, we could see the dancing heat waves shimmering; their watery veil floated across the fields. As we climbed higher, we saw places where water lay in basins of solid rock that had been hollowed by centuries of God's sculpting hand. On top, we could see the trembling water in the North Canadian River and the little waterfalls in Old Limbo Creek.

The sun was beginning to set, and we could see the shadows gathering to make their contribution to the nighttime. We made our way back down the mountain, but we didn't need to hurry because we had learned my trail by heart. We felt the coolness as the sun faded out of sight. The stars began to come out, and by the time we reached the bottom, the stars held their stillness like the far-off conifers that made a silhouette on the horizon. As we walked, with my arm around his waist and his arm around my shoulder, we came to the creek again. There was almost silence, only the gentle lapping of water; a faint stir of wind; and overhead, bright stars hung in the darkness above us.

Presently, the birds ceased their singing, and the silence was all the more noticeable. We contributed to the silence because we sat for a long time without saying any audible words. We felt so isolated from the rest of the world. We both admitted we had a lonely feeling that this precious day would never happen again. We knew it would be replaced by others just as dear, but we knew that we must bid goodbye to this one so it could make room for every single day that God would allow us to be together.

We stayed there until that quiet night broke into a melancholy but memorable dawn. Mama and Papa didn't say a word because they too sensed that we weren't far from another time of testing.

The Tough Start of a Happy Marriage

1925 through 1926

Nineteen twenty-five was a bittersweet year. On December 5, I would get married to my Russ but would be forced to leave my precious country home. Mr. Jones had sold his farm and would move to a town about thirty miles north of Lenna, where he had bought a business. There, he and my Russ would operate two school buses to transport children to and from school. Between the morning and afternoon bus runs, Mr. Jones would work as a blacksmith, and my Russ would work as an auto mechanic and run the gas station.

Everyone knew I loved farm life and country living, including Papa and my Russ. Papa also knew that my Russ wasn't cut out to be a farmer. Papa had seen how skilled he was at repairing cars and knew he would never be successful unless he lived in a town or on a highway between two larger towns.

My Russ asked Papa's advice, and they talked about my needs. They knew I would be awfully sad when I was told I would have to leave the farm. They talked about how Preston was a small town not much larger than Lenna but located on the highway between Tulsa and Okmulgee. Papa said it would be the best compromise he could imagine, knowing I would need a home that had some semblance of country living.

After they had gone over all the details, Papa said, "Russell, I believe it would be best if I talk to Pearlie first. There's something I've needed to say to her for a long time. Your job and your dad's business opportunity give me a way to tell her what's best for her, even though she won't like it."

So Papa was the one to bring me the news. "Pearlie, do you remember how tired you were when Troy and I had our accidents and you had to work so hard? Remember how dog-tired you were every night of those weeks? Remember how it took you several months to recover physically from that hard daily ordeal? Do you remember how you teased Russell and told him he would never make a farmer because he couldn't plow straight rows?"

My first thought was that something very horrible had happened to my Russ. "What are you getting at, Papa?"

He picked up again on the questions he had just asked me and insisted I give him an answer to each one. Then he confessed. "Seeing what the planting season had done to you was harder on me than the fear of losing my eyesight. I've been living in greater fear of losing you if you're forced to live the life of a farmer's wife. Pearlie, you and I know how uncertain farming is, and you work too hard to be a farmer's wife. When you marry Russell, he must have a job that keeps you from working so hard."

I trusted Papa, but I didn't like the things he was forcing me to accept. "What's the rest of the story, Papa?" I was wondering, *How many deaths must my dream die?* Then I thought of Troy's wife, Ivy. After only one year as a farmer's wife, she had aged incredibly. Even I could see that farm work would kill her before her time.

Papa continued. "Pearlie, the rest of the story is an answer to my prayer. Just listen to the whole thing very carefully, because you must tell Russell what you've decided."

So Papa told me every thing he and my Russ had discussed. He told me how my Russ would be a farmer before he would lose me. Papa told me how he had advised Russ that farm life would ruin my health. Papa said he told him he wouldn't want him for a son-in-law if he did that to his precious girl. Papa really did a selling job.

I cried. I was no angel. I was really angry at Papa and Russ. Papa held me through my long, angry, trembling sobs.

"I know you love me, Papa."

"Not as much as Russell loves you. He'll listen to you. You must listen to him too. I don't think Mr. Jones's business will be successful without Russell. Russell's life won't be as successful without you. You know, as I know about your Mama, your lives won't be complete without each other. The two of you must decide this crossroads of your lives together. You think and pray. Then you can talk."

That was the first time I ever heard Papa say he was a praying man. Papa said we would have to make this difficult decision together. That wasn't really true. I was the one who was expected to bury my dreams. *God, why did you give these dreams to me if they weren't going to come true? I thought you said it was the man who was to leave his father and mother, not the woman!* How I argued with God!

After I had emptied myself and began to listen, God spoke to my heart. *You say you trust your papa. Why don't you trust me? If you don't trust me, who you know loves you, how will you trust your husband, who also loves you? You won't have to give up your old home place. You'll carry it in your mind and enjoy writing poems about it. You'll long for it just like you'll long to be present with me. Trust me with your dreams. Who gave them to you? Enjoy the life I have for you. Enjoy the husband and children I'm giving you. Let me have your old home place and keep it for you in a place where "moth and rust don't corrupt."*

I must admit that this thought from God helped. But I was very stubborn about my dreams and didn't give up easily. Like a silly child, I decided to take a wait-and-see attitude. I met my Russ at a town funeral later that afternoon. We didn't say one word to each other. My Russ was afraid to, and I didn't want to. He took my hand and held it the whole time.

What's wrong with me? I get a thrill when he touches me!

The words in the preacher's sermon helped me make up "our" mind. After everyone left the graveside, I stubbornly stood there with tears running down my cheeks as I half-rebelliously buried my dreams with Grandmother Deersaw, thinking, *Here we are in the heart of what was once Oklahoma Indian Territory that is in its eighteenth year of being Oklahoma State. How many dreams has this full-blood Indian matron buried along the trails as they were forced to move from their dear home places and hunting grounds?* In the deep, youthful sadness of my own forced move, I thought I knew how the Indians had felt.

My Russ saw my tears and after a while said, as if reading my mind and understanding my pain, "You're not just weeping for Mrs. Deersaw, are you?"

With the last ounce of my angry hurt and with fire in my eyes, I pleaded, "No, I'm not!" He didn't respond, and I didn't say any more that day. But I didn't let loose of his hand or stop him from holding me in his arms. We really didn't have to use any words to understand that I had decided to trust him through the hurt, no matter how long it took.

As he walked me home, I said, "I really didn't think you'd make much of a farmer anyway."

I had a surprisingly good night's sleep. The next day, my Russ came to the house. In one hand, he was leading a tan Jersey cow and in the other a small, gift-wrapped box.

"Now what are you up to?"

"I've bought our first milk cow for our place in Preston. I've got to go there for several weeks, without you, to help Dad start his new business and get a house located for us. Do you want to keep the cow here, or do you want me to take it with me?"

I asked, "What makes you think I'm going with you? I guess you think your old milk cow will be a good substitute for you." My curiosity got the best of me. "What do you have in that little ol' package? Is it a gift to keep Mama from dusting your bottom with her broom?"

Oh my! He started giving me that sideways grin again as he handed the package to me and led the Jersey off to the cow lot. It was a gold coin mounted to a gold chain. As he came back to the front porch, where I had gone to open the gift, he called out, "Now you have two gold pieces: your ring and your necklace."

I ran to him, smiling and laughing, and gave my biggest kiss. I took his hand, and, running, I pulled him to our log by the spring on my nature trail so we could have some privacy.

Papa could see we had accepted his advice and called out, "Thanks for the cow, Russell."

I scolded him about spending so much money for my necklace. He said, "It's an investment."

I countered, "No. It's an insurance policy."

As we negotiated, I roughed out a poem about our future that, over thirty years later, I would try to get published as a love song or ballad.

I have two gifts that I treasure dear.

I'll wear them always; you need not fear.

One gift is this little band of gold.

I'll wear it forever to hold.

These two gifts didn't come from the sea,

But from a gold mine from you just for me.

One was a piece of gold on a chain.

I'll wear it as I wear your name.

Remember we said many years ago,

If we were in need this gold would be sold.

But the good Lord has blessed us in every way.

I'm still wearing my two gifts today.

I'm still wearing my two gifts today.

I would like to say everything was rosy after I received my necklace from my Russ. It wasn't. The only thing I could truly claim was that I grew up some and accepted, to some small degree, that there would be other unpleasant truths in my happy life. No matter how I tried, I knew deep down I would never completely get over leaving the security of the good home of my father and mother and our old home place.

Just as deep down, I knew I had been given the security of a nice, loving man, the one I played with as a child and went to school with. Until these few months that my Russ must go to prepare a new home place for us, we had never been more than a mile or two apart. After we were married, we were never apart again except the few times I went alone to California after most of my family moved there.

I used the remainder of that year to talk to myself about coming to peace with the adjustment I knew I must find the courage to accept. I used the time to soak up as many memories of the old home place as I could. I built a wall of poems around my Russ to protect our love for the future when we would need to depend primarily on each other.

I got as close as I could to the marvelous land God had so blessed me with to enjoy. I had fun visiting the country folk as they worked in their fields or were on their way to work. Knowing I was leaving home, they would listen kindly as I said things like, "You don't know how lucky you are to live in a place like this, where you can stretch out your arms without hitting someone in the face."

One old practical friend, attempting to help me face reality, responded, "Oh, I doubt if it will be all that crowded in Preston. I heard it wasn't much bigger or busier than Lenna except for the number of cars passing through on the highway and a few trains on the railroad that parallels the highway."

I walked to the North Canadian River to leave my footprints in the sand, imagining they would really be there when I returned someday. Part of the security I was afraid I would lose was the peace and contentment found in the traditional values of like-minded people who had a strong sense of each individual's worth. Then I would think, *All of this won't be lost. I can teach my children how to be free and independent. I can teach my children that they will have to bear hardships.* I didn't know then how much I had yet to learn in order to survive the tough times. I also didn't know how much the joyful experiences at my country home would help me through my few future hardships.

Then, in the depth of my meditations, God wisely gave me an illuminating insight about the future, and I spoke to the fields as a gentle breeze blew past me, causing the wildflowers to dip their little heads and say, "Yes. Yes."

So I joined them and also said out loud, "Yes. I can help my children have joyful experiences in any home God provides for us to live." As I waded through Old Limbo Creek on my way home, I thought about the children God would surely give us and about the times I had broken Papa's rule and gone to the creek by myself to swim.

Papa would say to us kids, "I don't want you to swim in the creek without letting me know when you're going. There are so many springs draining into the creek that often it's too cold."

I remembered breathing a big sigh of relief the few times I

disobeyed and went swimming without telling him. Then I had to admit, *I don't want my children to be nearly as independent as I am.*

I didn't know what kind of fear my Russ experienced during our months away from each other. I only knew I had my own fears. To encourage my Russ, I sent poems with the letters I wrote to him. For all I knew, this could have been the greatest adventure he had ever known. He had already so spoiled me that I was too intent on my own preferences to graciously enjoy the adventure with him. I tried to join our two separate experiences by calling him my wild rose.

In the garden of wild roses, the evergreens grow so tall.

You can hear bluebirds singing down by the garden wall.

I'll meet you there, my Russ. We can plan a future day.

Don't keep me waiting 'til the wild roses fade away.

In our secret garden, as the moon shines high above,

With all the stars twinkling, I'll tell you of my love.

The wild roses in our garden are blooming just for you.

And with the bluebird, I'm singing, "I still love you true."

In our garden of wild roses, I have something to propose.

If you'll be my husband, I'll call you my wild rose.

The more weeks we were apart, the more hopelessly mushy my letters and poems got. When I sent this one to my Russ, I told him I would sing it to him. When he came back to Lenna the next weekend, he reminded me to sing it to him. He loved it, but he still thought I was a little nuts.

Walk with me by this stream that flows cool and calm.

And hold me next to you, my dear, tightly in your arms.

Caress me close, my Russ, and whisper you'll be true.

Tell me I'm a pretty one, how I hold you with my charms.

When far from the quiet stream that flows cool and calm,

Year by year, with all your strength, hold me in your arms.

I sealed away the last few months of the year before we were married by keeping a record of the memories of that last year so I could maturely compare them with my memories and thoughts in future years. I wanted to see how the memories of the old home place, in the mind of a young woman, would compare with the memories of a young wife and mother, the memories of a mature woman with grown children, and the memories of an elderly grandmother and great-grandmother.

My roots had grown so deeply at the old home place. I had a sense that the memories at each future age, with their different surroundings, would year by year have a more comforting reality than the one I was seeing as a young wife who felt uprooted from her very soul.

Fall was coming on, and a soft wind was blowing. I was restless. Maybe it was because of the wind or the way the sun shone like lace behind bright, fluffy, white clouds. The wind moved a shadow across the cliff at the upper part of my nature trail. I thought, *I'm sure this will be the last time I'll feel this way again. If I see it when I'm older, it will probably look much smaller. I'm certain it will never be this pretty, but I'm certain I'll never forget the beauty of it all.*

Along the winding river, there were oaks, pecans, dogwoods, willows, and redbuds. There was driftwood along the riverbanks. Leaves rustled under my feet. I smelled the brewing coffee of some fishermen.

At night, the stars seemed dark and mysterious. A faint light gleamed from the moon. The Milky Way was subdued. There in the dark, I could hear the hum of insects and the occasional cry of a bird. A nighthawk wheeled in the sky above. The night would have been very still, except for the crickets' chirping. I could smell the earth. I could smell the pine trees carried by the coolness of the soft wind whispering among them.

If I'd had a choice, I would have chosen the birds to be my friends from all of God's creatures that live on earth. I could watch them for hours. Even the little sparrows were interesting. When a mother sparrow fed her babies, they crowded around with their mouths open. If one baby bird had too much food in its mouth, the mother bird took some out of its mouth and fed it to one that didn't have any food. That seemed really smart to me.

I watched a woodpecker on a sweet gum tree going *rat-tat-tat*. I didn't tell Papa because he had killed one the previous year, and I didn't like it. The woodpeckers could fill a tree full of holes, but I doubted if they'd ever killed one. They were just doing what God told them to do as they freely took sap and worms from the tree. I always felt like birds were serenading me as I walked along.

One day, I walked along the edge of a clover field. A mockingbird followed along from tree to tree. Then a meadowlark sprang up from near my feet and perched himself on a fencepost. The two of them poured out a melody well suited for a church hymn. It was as if they were singing sweet, gossipy songs about what the three of us were seeing in the woods and fields. The mockingbird would imitate other birds with a more mellow and liquid tone.

Even more wonderful was the journey of the bobolinks with their song that rang out long before spring was in the air. Some of these birds were just plain home folks who stayed around all year long. Others must have thought they were from the sophisticated upper crust of the bird kingdom because they had both summer and winter homes, separated by many long miles.

Mama was a wonderful cook. I would have given anything to be able to cook food like she could. Before I left home, I soaked up as many of her cooking skills and secrets as I could. During this year, I also gathered some seeds from my private flower garden so I could transport that part of the old home place with me. I acted as if God couldn't use the wind and the birds to carry his seeds to my new garden when the time was right. I didn't believe he was offended because I wanted to help him make my own selections. I always thought flowers, like the birds, were the sweetest things God made that didn't have souls in them.

I had one more special place I had to record in my memory before I moved away from home. The week before we were married, I spent a large part of one day in the high barn loft thinking of the things connected with it. The barn had been my sanctuary when I was a little girl. I passed away many hours in the loft playing with my paper dolls. I had saved some of my best ones, hoping my little girls could touch something I had enjoyed at their age. I played with the paper dolls again and prayed for the gift of some daughters God would allow us to share with him.

Also, the barn loft was sacred ground because it was the

high ground I had used to spy on my Russ. I reminded myself that my Russ would never have known about that covert activity if Mama hadn't blabbed it to him after he asked me to marry him.

By now, my Russ had bought a used car, and he drove it to Lenna to move me to Preston. He arrived early the cold Saturday morning of December 5, 1925. After picking me up (I had never been kissed in a car before), we picked up his older sisters, Ola and Gladys. Ola was already wed to Rob Smith, who owned the grocery store and post office in Lenna.

We drove hurriedly to the Eufaula city hall, where we met Mr. Chapman, the justice of the peace. He came in on his day off. Before eleven o'clock, we were married. Ola and Gladys and Mr. Chapman signed the marriage license for us. We had to leave the marriage certificate with Mr. Chapman because it had to be recorded, and city hall was officially closed on Saturdays.

The marriage certificate actually showed that both of us lived in Lenna. Not knowing we would be in Preston, the court clerk finally mailed it to Lenna on December 14. Fortunately for us, Rob Smith knew where to forward it, and we received it in Preston on December 17. We received it after being married twelve days. We had a big, hugging laugh about what good service we had gotten from a two-cent postage stamp we didn't have to pay for. We called it our most special wedding gift. I saved it so it would be in the legal papers our children would find after my funeral.

This is a day to remember.

It's the fifth day of December.

We were pronounced man and wife,

So happy, so young, so full of life.

A gold band upon my finger,

We said, "I do," and didn't linger.

This day in 1925,

Life is beautiful, and we're alive.

The snow is deep. The weather is cold.

We are so young but very bold.

Our earthly possessions are but a few.

But you love me, and I love you.

And with the help of our dear Lord,

We'll try to live in one accord.

Many times, I'll be mad at you.

And in return, you'll be mad too.

But we will learn that this is life.

And we will learn as man and wife.

Many years later, I added another happy verse.

If someone brushed this hour away,

I'd do the same again today.

If I live to grow very old,

I'll want your love instead of gold.

We dropped Ola and Gladys off at Ola's house and went home to eat the noon meal with Mama and Papa.

My Russ asked Mama, "Do you think Pearlie will be able to cook food that tastes this good?"

Her quick reply was, "Well, if she can't, you can just send her back."

My Russ couldn't think fast enough to make a response to this. Papa and I had a big laugh at his expense.

After we had eaten, my Russ told me, "Let's take a quick walk down your nature trail."

I was so surprised I didn't know what to say. Was he doing it because he really understood how much it hurt for me to leave this place? Did he just want to get away and have some private time with me before we drove to Preston?

"You want to go for a nature walk in this weather?" I asked.

"I have something important I need to do there."

"Must we walk the whole trail or just go to one particular place?"

"Just one particular place," he answered. "Come on. I'll show you."

We bundled up with our warmest clothes. We held onto each other, slipping and sliding on slick places and laughing like two children instead of a grown-up, married couple. He took me to the place by the spring, and we sat down on the big log. With his arm around me, he gave me that sideways grin and looked straight ahead and asked, "Pearlie, what's your full legal name?"

"What a dumb question from a dumb young man who doesn't have enough sense to stay in out of the cold. My name is Ida Pearl Logan, as you well know."

He got up and walked straight to the tree where I had carved my name. He took his pocketknife out of his pocket and started carving. And then I saw what he was up to. He took on the deep tone of a professor like I had when I tried to teach him how to write poetry on one of our walks.

"Now, young lady, your first lesson as a new bride is to correctly state your full legal name so I can give you full credit for this course."

So I gladly joined the game with a meek child's voice and answered, "Oh, Mister Professor, as of today, my full legal name is Ida Pearl Logan Jones. But if it's all right with you, while we're in class, I'd like for you to just call me Pearlie Jones. That's the favorite thing I'd like to be called."

I ran to him and gave him the most icy-cold, wet kiss I hoped he'd ever have. We held each other, only restrained by our heavy coats. But we were no longer legally restrained from the freedom of intimate touch.

I said to my Russ, "This is my nature trail at its finest. This is the best marriage ceremony any bride could ever imagine. Thank you, my dearest."

When we got back to the house, I said, "Let's go to the kitchen to remove our coats because it's the warmest room in the house."

My Russ readily agreed by joyfully cutting his eyes toward the table. "That's a good idea. Besides, that's where the chocolate pie is begging for attention."

Lesson number two for this new bride: my Russ liked chocolate pies, and I had that recipe down pat.

Mama and Papa could tell from our faces that we were anxious to get on our way. Papa said, "The road may get worse if you kids hang around too long. Don't you think you'd better get started home?"

Papa looked at me by emphasizing the word *home* as his way of reminding me and himself of the reality of this change.

My Russ agreed with a phrase I would hear many times over the next fifty-four years: "Yes, I believe we'd better check it to you."

The car was already loaded with my remaining things. The old Franklin was very cold, so of course, we had to sit very close to each other during the thirty-mile drive. We rehearsed the day with each other as a way to secure it into our memories. Then we talked about children we would have and how strange it might feel for someone to call us "Mother" and "Daddy," to have a little soul call out, "Come, Mother, and see what I can do."

It was dark when we arrived. The lights of the car revealed that the house was painted a brown color. Mr. Jones had the house toasty warm from the flames of a small natural gas stove. The house had electric lights that revealed food on the table that Mrs. Jones had prepared for us. The house had only two rooms, but I felt I had fallen into the lap of luxury because our house in Lenna had wood-fired stoves and kerosene lamps for lights.

Home, I silently said in my mind. *Our home, and our first house.* Then I scolded myself. *This is not the time to be thinking about a poem.*

The afternoon after our arrival from Lenna was Sunday. My Russ took me for a walk around town to show it to me and to show me off to the townspeople. The highway was a busy national highway that ran from the north through Kansas and Tulsa to Okmulgee and then on down through Texas—Highway 75.

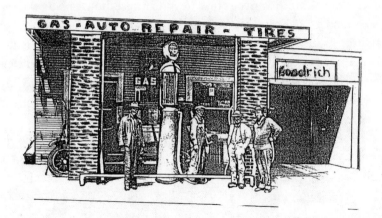

First, he showed me the gasoline filling station with a large garage attached to it where my Russ worked on cars. Mr. Jones worked as a blacksmith. The gas pumps were the old-fashioned kind with a hand lever to pump ten gallons into a glass cylinder that used gravity to flow gasoline into a car's gas tank.

Two school buses were parked in the garage at night because Mr. Jones had the school bus contract. Each of them drove a bus twice each day to pick up and deliver first- through twelfth-grade children of farm families in the surrounding area. The big garage was across the highway from our little two-room brown house. The Jones family house was just a little farther from the highway.

The town itself was about the size of twelve large city blocks, divided in half by the highway. The population was under five hundred. The railroad, which carried both freight and passenger traffic, ran parallel with the highway, less than three hundred feet behind the gas station and garage. The passenger trains dropped off and picked up the mailbags each day except Sunday. There was also a bus passenger service that stopped near our little house.

This was during the days of segregation. The small Negro school was across the tracks, where a mixture of both white and Negro families lived. Just beyond these houses was a large lake next to a Boy Scout camp, which the town could use for swimming, fishing, and bullfrog hunting for frog legs. Not many Indian families lived in Preston, but several Indian children came to school on the school buses because Okmulgee was only seven miles away, where the Creek Nation counsel house was located.

The grocery store and post office, run by Mr. and Mrs. Forrest Kaylor, were on the same side of the highway as the Jones filling station and garage. On the opposite side of the highway were two churches, another filling station, and a drugstore owned by Dr. Oliphant, who lived across the street from the Jones family in the only two-story house in the town. The highway was paved with concrete, but all the other streets in town were dirt roads.

The main industry for the town was the big school located on a very large city block, next to the block where the Jones family house stood. The school had three buildings and playgrounds large enough for a baseball field and outside basketball courts. The school building was a two-story, redbrick building on one corner of the lot. It had a partial basement. On the opposite corner was a redbrick building with a basketball court, places to sit on each side, and a large stage with curtains at one end.

The school had both boys' and girls' basketball teams that competed with surrounding schools of similar size. Next to this building were boys' and girls' showers, locker rooms, and restrooms. Each building had running water supplied by the school's water well and pump. Unfortunately, the town didn't have a water system, so each home had its own water well and outhouse.

Our tour was almost finished when my Russ said, "I still have one more place I want to show you." It was obvious he was doing a selling job on me by making comparisons between Lenna and Preston. I had to admit that there were some advantages. And it was surrounded by farms and farm people. But our little house wasn't out in the country on one of these farms.

His main selling point was the school and how our children could get twice as good an education as we had received and how they might even go to college and be teachers or professional people. The school had a superintendent who was also the basketball and softball coach. Also, it had a principal who was also a high school teacher and four ladies who were elementary teachers.

My Russ acted like no sacrifice on our part could be too great for this one reason alone. "Okay. You've convinced me," I told him, though I still had a nagging prejudice about living too close to other people and not close enough to nature. He saw it in my face that I wasn't totally sold.

The superintendent's house was directly across the street from the school. Across another street, beside his house, was a small house with a garage, a chicken house, a large garden, and a small cow pasture with a cow barn. Near the house were some large oak trees. All together, it was about the size of one-half of a city block. Behind it were some woods that gave it the flavor of being out in the country.

"I've got my eye on this place," he said. "I've met the couple who own it. They think they may want to sell it in two or three years. I think it might be a good compromise for you to be on the edge of town and still have our children across the street from the school and for me to be in walking distance to work." He was doing everything he could think of to give me hope so I'd be more confident that this new life could be a happy one.

I thought, *It takes barns and farms and covered bridges and nature that's so sweet. And it takes country living to make my life complete.*

So we moved to Preston, where my Russ worked with his father for a little fewer than ten years. A lot of water flowed under the bridge since that first day in Preston. Eventually, I learned that whenever I wanted to go back to that little farm where I grew up all I had to do was turn back the pages of my memory to hear the gentle murmur of Old Limbo Creek and the birds singing in the shady nooks.

We were married in December, and before my next birthday in March, I was expecting our first child. Also that year, Troy and Ivy had their first child, a girl they named Dolly.

Mr. Jones and I were still very close because of our association from the youth group back in Lenna. I owed so much to him. As soon as he learned I was expecting a child, he encouraged me to decide in advance to take my children to church so the Lord could help us bring them up right. He told me, "Without the knowledge of God, your spiritual lives will be a failure."

He told me to memorize Proverbs 22:6: "Train up a child in the way he should go: and when he is old, he will not depart from it" (KJV). That night, my Russ and I prayed to our Father that we would be good spiritual examples to all the children and grandchildren he would give us.

My parents were certainly good examples to me. I saw them in happiness and heartache. They had twelve children. Five of them didn't live. I saw the sorrow of my parents when it happened or when they talked about it. I knew enough to imagine this could happen to us also, even knowing Mrs. Jones had ten children and none of them had died.

I told Mr. Jones about my worries. To start the conversation,

I said to him in a grown-up and confident voice, "Since I'm going to be a mother and a wife—oops, it looks like I got that backward. I should have said a wife and a mother."

My face flushed, and Mr. Jones put his arms around me and laughed with me and then asked, "Why don't you tell me how you think you should handle this worry?"

I was silent a while as I thought about my answer, and, in a not so grown-up voice, I told him my thoughts. "I think because I have Christ in my life, I have a source of comfort and courage many people don't have. I'm also aware that there is sorrow along the ragged paths of life and that into each life some rain must fall."

He patted me on my shoulder. "Just hold onto that, Pearlie, from year to year and on into heaven, and you will be comforted."

I didn't entirely take my own advice. All I wanted to do was sleep. I was so lonesome for my family. I was grieving for my old home place. I was depressed, and my body was going through the strange activities of pregnancy it hadn't experienced before.

Living so close to our little house, Mrs. Jones was well aware of my inactivity and my inexperience. More than once, she came to warn me that lack of exercise could affect my baby's health. Being just as inexperienced as I was, my Russ didn't know about the dangers of childbearing and did all he knew to do during those months. Mrs. Jones reminded me that she'd had ten successful pregnancies and knew what she was talking about.

In October, our baby boy was born dead. He never breathed a single breath or gave a single cry. Somehow, this jolted me into action, even though in the back of my mind I was arguing with myself whether it was my fault. My Russ never accused me. It seemed in a moment we had grown up and started making the necessary burial arrangements. We got word to Papa to make a casket.

Even though I wasn't physically ready, I lay in the backseat of the car holding this little nameless child while my Russ drove us to Lenna. I was adamant that our baby be buried there.

We talked very little on the way. My Russ searched for something comforting to say. I knew my Russ wanted a little boy very badly. We talked about that, and I tried my best to comfort him.

When we were about halfway to Lenna, my Russ looked over his shoulder and with a breaking voice said, "Pearlie, we do know our baby's soul is in heaven."

We were both weeping, so I answered back, "Thank you." I had enough faith to put none of the blame on God, so I whispered, "Thank you, Lord."

My Russ answered back, "Yes."

When we arrived at the old home place, Mama and Papa and my sisters and brothers were waiting on the porch with the tiny casket in front of them. The trees around the house were blazing in fall colors. Bertha ran to her Russ for him to pick her up and carry her. I handed our baby's body to Mama, knowing she knew how I felt.

I noticed that the wood of the casket looked old and weathered. "Where did you get the lumber for the casket, Papa?"

"I took it from the floor of the barn loft where you played paper dolls and spied on Russell."

I couldn't believe we laughed and cried and hugged each other all around.

Troy had harnessed the two mules to Papa's wagon. Ivy was standing in the background, holding their new baby named Dolly. I read her face with its dear, imploring look, sensing that she was offering to let me hold Dolly. I held out my arms and gathered Dolly to my breast and face. I wept some more while Ivy gathered Dolly between us. No words had to be spoken.

Mama laid our baby in the casket, and Papa closed it with nails he had drawn from the wood from which he made it. Mama and Papa asked to carry it to the wagon. I rode in the wagon beside my Russ as he snapped the reins to get the mules to move down the road. As we moved along toward the cemetery on the other side of town, our friends walked along behind the wagon, looking up into our faces to make eye contact with us as they came out to the road. We laid our little son to rest. A little poem came to me as we stood by the grave when the casket was being covered.

A rosebud from heaven,

To earth he was sent.

We hoped he was given.

But he was only lent.

Later, we laid a headstone over the tiny grave with a tiny lamb cast on the top and with the engraved words, *Infant son of RF and IP Jones, Born and Died Oct. 27, 1926. Gone but not forgotten.*

We stayed at the old home place a few days for me to complete my recovery. The day we left, I walked back to the big log by the spring on my nature trail and talked to God. I had to understand, to some degree, why this had happened to us. I prayed about my level of responsibility or forgiveness. I talked to my God about my reliance on his Word.

In this quiet place of mine, I felt my heart mending, but I didn't feel at peace. So I asked for peace and forgiveness for any way that I had failed our baby or my Russ. And he gave me peace.

My Russ gave me time to be alone, and then he came to join me. He said, "You're composing poems, aren't you?"

"And you're getting to know me way too well," I replied with a confident smile on my face.

I could tell I also needed to encourage him just as the Lord had encouraged me. "Remember the first time you walked with me on my nature trail and I gave you a lesson about how to write poems by what you were seeing, hearing, and feeling? I think it's time for another lesson."

I recited the little poem that had come to my mind in the cemetery. "Help me write a poem about our little rosebud, and see if that will make you feel better. What are you thinking now?"

"I don't understand why God took our baby," he said.

I answered, "That sounds like a good starting place."

Lord we don't understand just now

"Do you think we will understand someday? Say it!"

But someday we will know.

"Good! You finish the first phrase."

Why you took our firstborn child.

"What's the best answer you can imagine?"

We think *you* loved him so.

"You're a very good poet. Now it's my turn."

He was our little rosebud,
Tiny, pink, and wonderfully sweet.
I think I know the reason.
You need him to make heaven complete.

"I'll do the next line. See if you can finish it."

Someday we will meet again,

"When?"

When our time has passed away.

"Now look at the first line."

We will understand it all,

"See how easy it is? When? Look at the preceding line."

On that precious, golden day.

"Makes you feel better, doesn't it? Poetry does that!"

I saw my Russ relaxing. Then he abruptly sat up straight. He looked directly at my name carved on the tree in front of us.

"Our son needs a name. He'll never even have a birth certificate."

With a sudden inspiration, I cried out, "Let's give him your middle name: Francis."

"Why do you suggest that name?"

"Because it connects him with you, and I want to save Russell for your next boy. Yes, sir. Your next son will be called Russell. And one of our girls will be named Mary Lavern after Mama and Bertha, and if we have a little brown girl, we'll name her Loyale, like I told you when you brought your baby sister to meet me. Now, that's settled. Let's go home."

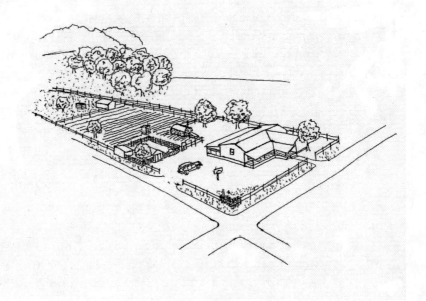

Starting a Family and a New Home Place

1927 through 1932

Before my birthday in March 1927, I was expecting again. I decided to take Mrs. Jones's advice and get plenty of exercise this time. I asked her, "May I work in your garden for my exercise and plant a little extra for my Russ and me? I want to can some fruits and vegetables for the next winter when I'll be busy with our new baby." She also gave me a place in her yard to grow flowers.

The newly plowed and harrowed dirt smelled refreshing as I planted the various seeds at the proper time, just as *The Farmer's Almanac* recommended. I made several trips to Mr. Kaylor's store to buy seeds and always stopped by the garage to see my Russ.

My Russ could see me working in the garden when he came out of the garage to put gas in cars. He and his customers waved to me. We were bad in love and looking forward to our new baby. Mr. Jones used these excuses to wave encouragement to me also.

As the weather got hotter, I would go to the garden to hoe the weeds and gather the fresh vegetables for summertime meals. One day, Mrs. Jones came out on her back porch and called to me with a very stern voice, "Pearlie, you're working too hard. You won't have a healthy baby if you work too hard. Go home and rest a little, and I'll tell Russell to finish the garden work this evening." I couldn't help but smile about this reversal of her advice, but I minded her. After all, she'd had ten healthy births.

Mrs. Jones turned fifty that year. Her hair was still black. She bragged, "I celebrated this birthday by registering Republican."

I suppose that set our family's politics for the remainder of our lives.

As fall came and the fruits of the garden had been gathered and the canning completed, I exercised each day by walking the half mile around the school. I was beginning to show. I timed my walk while the children were on the school grounds playing. The three youngest Jones children—Loyale, Grace, and Roscoe—waved to me when they saw me and sometimes came to the iron pipe fence to visit, even though they spent considerable time with us in our little brown house. My Russ would let them ride the school bus he drove sometimes. After all, they lived a whole block from the school.

The house my Russ said he wanted to own was the midpoint of my walk. So I used this corner of the street to stop and rest.

One day, the lady who lived there called to me, "Aren't you Russell's wife? Come on in and rest a bit." The two-room house had bigger rooms than our little house, and it looked more sturdy.

"Russell told us to talk to him as soon as we're ready to sell. I thought you might like to see the house. He told us your father was a carpenter and could build on some extra rooms as you need them. It looks like you're going to need some extra room soon. Make yourself at home any time if you want to walk around the garden and the cow pasture. Russell said you are quite a gardener. You can go walking in the woods next to the pasture. The owner won't mind. His name is Bert Hodges. He works at the *Okmulgee Daily Times* newspaper. He went to school with Mrs. Jones when she lived in Yellville, Arkansas. I suspect they might have been in love once. You go walking in the woods any time. Russell said you are a country girl and need to spend a lot of time around nature. You'll like this place. It's almost like living in the country. If you go walking in the woods, let me know when you go and come back. I sure don't want anything to happen to you in your condition. This place needs a young couple and children—close to the woods, chores to make them feel productive, and close to a good school."

She did most of the talking. It also sounded like my Russ had done considerable talking. I wondered whether they were in cahoots to do a selling job on me. I excused myself. "I believe I'll take you up on that walk in the woods."

I enjoyed my walk in the woods. It looked more suited for a boy to hunt in than for a girl's nature trail. I knew what good hunting grounds looked like. I saw plenty of squirrels and rabbits and big rocks to climb around on when you used your imagination in play. I called, "Thanks," to the housewife as I went by to let her know I was leaving. Now I knew where to come to stay caught up on town gossip.

As the weather got colder, I spent most of my time in the house, reading my Bible and thinking deep thoughts. Little by little, I was solving the mystery of both life and heaven, connecting creation's nature with God's supernatural grace. I'd always known, in this life, grace must come before greatness. When we lose the peace in our spirit, our work for our God will be considerably lessened. Prayer begins where human capacity ends. Pain and heartaches are part of this life. But what a difference Christ makes!

In a world torn with strife, on edge with tensions, and divided by misunderstanding, it can be refreshing to one's soul to see the quiet leaven of the true gospel at work. Again and again, I expressed my gratitude to God for having been privileged to find the truth while I was young and tender in years. My soul had been lit with wisdom from heaven. I prayed I would never forget this.

One morning, I watched the sun rise under brewing storm clouds. I prayed, *I pray for strength this day in all things that I do and say. I pray, dear God, you will help me lead others to our blessed Lord. I humbly ask in Christ's name. Amen.*

Mary Lavern was born four days after our second anniversary, in the midst of rain, sleet, and snow. When they placed her in my arms, I said, "Now hush, tiny gift from heaven. No one will harm you."

She cuddled up and grew very still. She was the softest little thing and as red as a red rose. I looked at her feet and tiny, drawn-up toes. Her hair was as fine as silk but long enough to tie up a little bunch with a ribbon. I moved over to the big mirror and watched myself singing a lullaby as I held her close to my heart. Then over my heart there swept a great thrill. I prayed, "Lord, thank you for this healthy child. I love her, and I love you."

Mary was Mama's name, and Lavern was my sister Bertha's middle name. I was twenty-one years old. We called Mary our anniversary gift to each other. By garden-planting time, we moved to our place across the street from the school, where I wrote a poem for Mary.

Your socks are little, and your shoes are too.

There's a little, long dress that belongs to you.

These little socks will become ragged and worn.

And the heels of the shoes will be tattered and torn.

The little, long dress will grow yellow with age.

And you'll save them as your life's first page.

Mama made the dress. Oh! She was very proud.

When she put it on you, you cried so very loud.

My Russ was a friend with the old colored farmer who plowed, harrowed, planted, and harvested the big school garden between the superintendent's and principal's houses. His wife, Lillian, helped him in this occupation. He also plowed our big garden for the eighteen years we lived at this home place in Preston.

The school garden was used to feed a big, healthy lunch to the children. Some of the children my Russ and Mr. Jones brought on the buses came from poor families. You don't have to be college-educated to know children must be healthy to learn well. The school in Preston was very progressive.

The deep peace and the feeling of country living began to soak into my body and bones as we worked in the garden. My Russ did the very heavy work. There was a peach tree near the house and a green apple tree near the back, beyond the outhouse. The sour green apples were excellent for making apple pies. Every year, our impatient children had to learn again the cruel lesson that green apples pulled directly off the tree to eat caused severe bellyaches.

Because of our garden, like most country people, we were well fed, even during the Great Depression, which started in 1929. And working in the garden together was one way to give our busy minds a rest. All of these allurements of our country garden became the food of love and a place to grow closer to our children.

I didn't know then, but in only ten years, I would see my Russ and our little boy begin an annual ritual. My Russ would tie a small rope to the front of the small garden plow so Sonny could pretend to be a big horse pulling the plow. They plowed between the rows of potatoes to plow up the weeds. From the time Sonny was in diapers until he went away to college, they found a way to work together.

When I was still at the old home place, I had observed that Mama was Papa's constant helper. She did things she didn't have to do and should not have done, which was the most dramatic expression of passionate love. In this way, I was a little like she was. I wanted to get the milking done, the hogs fed, and the chickens taken care of before my Russ came home from work. I just wanted him to sit down for our dinner and not have to hurry. I knew I spoiled my husband just like Mama did Papa, and our husbands spoiled us right back.

Just after we completed the canning and had butchered two hogs in the fall, I learned I was expecting again.

When Mary was a little more than one year old, we started a tradition of taking our children's photo in a butter churn with the Preston Consolidated school building in the background. The top of the churn was just above Mary's waist. We rushed it with Betty Loyale after she was born. We took her picture when she was less than nine months old, and the top of her shoulders were barely above the top of the churn. When Sonny was born we forgot to take his picture until he was eighteen months old, and the top of the churn was even with his belly button. We also used the churn to make sauerkraut.

I had always been afraid of Oklahoma thunderstorms and the tornadoes that developed out of them. My Russ had promised that when we got our own place, he would hire Papa to build a storm cellar that would also serve as a place to salt down pork and store our canned fruits and vegetables in glass jars. The storm cellar was partially underground to keep it cool during the summer. The top was an arched shape made of reinforced concrete. Papa built it in 1928.

Papa also hired a crew of men and drilling equipment to drill a well one hundred feet deep for our water supply. All year round, the water was about seventy degrees temperature and had a mighty good taste, especially in the hot summertime.

Before planting season, Papa came again in 1929 and built on two extra rooms to the house. Now it was L-shaped with a covered porch on the front side.

One day, as Papa was putting shingles on the roof of the new portion, he came down the ladder for lunch. As I was preparing his lunch, Mary slipped out a door and climbed the ladder. When we realized she wasn't playing in the house and that the door was open, I went to the yard to bring her back in but couldn't find her. I called to Papa for help. Then we heard her babbling and discovered her on the roof, straddling the peak of the new roof. From then on, the ladder came down when Papa did.

The following year Papa made the final addition to the house. This addition went the entire length of the backside of the house. Half of it was kitchen and everyday eating space so we could have a more formal dining room and family room. The other half was a screened-in back porch that enclosed the well so water could be drawn without having to go outside.

My Russ and I moved our bed to the screened-in back porch, where I could get back to the old enjoyment of sleeping outside the way I had as a girl back home. We slept there year-round. In the coldest or most windy days, we had a canvas cover that could be rolled up and down as it suited our fancy. I loved it. My Russ tolerated it for my sake. I finally got over this fanatic habit when we moved to Okmulgee about nine years later.

The wind moaned, sighed, and cried loudly in the night.
It blew and banged and shook the hanging electric light.
The wind kept my Russ from sleep.
All he could do was yawn,
Although it did let up a bit, just before the dawn.
Then, as the sun began to spread its rays across the sky,
I said to the red-eyed man beside me,
"I think it passed us by."

I was twenty-three years old in March, and Betty Loyale was born in July. She was born on the screened-in back porch my Russ and I used for our bedroom. It was Saturday, about five thirty in the afternoon.

We gave her Loyale for a middle name, just as I had promised if we ever had a little brown-skinned, black-haired girl. When I first saw her, I held her close to my breast. Her daddy cupped his big hand around her tiny head as I talked to her in baby talk.

> "Hello, my child. I'm glad to say,
>
> What a lovely day to come our way.
>
> You're very sweet, plump, and round—
>
> The sweetest baby in our town.
>
> We are as proud as parents could be.
>
> And how we love you. Can't you see?
>
> Because you are our baby!"

So now we had the proof that we had some Indian blood. Two generations later, Betty would have a granddaughter with the same dark coloring. Mary's hair was an auburn color. When Sonny was born, he was a cotton-top like my brother Whitey.

We made frequent trips to Lenna to see Mama and Papa and my family there. When my brother Troy and his wife, Ivy, had Roy, their baby boy, this was a good excuse to make the trip and show off each other's new babies. They named him Roy after Troy's twin brother. Ivy looked very frail but also very happy.

My Russ seemed to give the baby boy a lot of attention. At first, I thought it might be because he and Troy had been good friends since they were young boys. As I carefully watched him, I thought, *He's longing for a boy of his own. I'll see what I can do about that.*

It began to rain late in the afternoon, and I said, "We'd better start home. You know how easy it is to get stuck in Deep Fork bottom when the roads get muddy."

It rained harder and harder, and before we got to the surfaced highway, we got stuck several times. I put Betty in the backseat with three-year-old Mary. My Russ showed me the way to gently accelerate to spin the wheels slowly while he pushed the car to help it move forward. The mud was up over his ankles.

It got dark. Sometimes he would need to get down on his knees and shovel the mud from beneath the axels so the car could go backward and forward to break out of a deep rut. Finally, we broke loose from the deepest mud. My Russ was soaked and dirty and tired, and I was trying to say soothing things to encourage him. Then from the backseat we heard Mary Lavern's tiny, pitiful voice say, "I wish I was home in bed." This broke the tension, and we had a big laugh at Mary's expense.

For the longest time, when something wasn't going well and we felt like we were stuck in the mud of Deep Fork bottom, one of us would break the tension by crying, "I wish I was home in bed!" So I wrote a poem to record this great saying of Mary's that gave us a chuckle from year to year.

> Every problem has a solution. You can't just sit and say,
> "I will not pay it any attention. I know it will go away."
> Maybe a problem is simple, like getting stuck in the mud.
> Don't wring your hands in deep despair.
> Don't be a muddy-fuddy-dud.

Many years later, the road through Deep Fork bottom was paved, and we could sail right through in rainy weather.

When we got home, I wrote Papa a letter and thanked him for the cellar he had built for us. I told him about the muddy road and Mary's words that had transformed our circumstances into perspective. Then I reminded him about the sudden Oklahoma thunderstorm that had caught us in Deep Fork bottom, where he and Mama and all of us kids went to pick blackberries to can for winter.

Papa had put the wagon cover on the wagon because of the hot sun and because the fast cloud movement was hinting about a possible rain. But we knew when the blackberries were ready, we had to take our chances.

We finished gathering the berries and were making our way to the wagon when a strong wind blasted through. None of us could stand erect. It even blew the small children off their feet. All of the streams were rising fast, and we children were scared to death, none more scared than I was.

It was an awfully loud storm. Even inside the wagon, under the wagon cover, our voices couldn't be heard above the wind. From the sound the mules made, we could tell they were afraid too. The sheets of rain battered the wagon cover, seeping through around places where we couldn't keep the wagon sheet fastened to the sideboards. The thunder was almost a continuous sound, and lightning flared again and again. It was still daytime, but the darkness was like late twilight. The rain continued to roar down, slashing at us as we made our way home. I looked from one to another and sensed that each one felt as if he were all alone with his own private fears and uncertainties, isolated by the storm.

Almost at once, the rain ceased as the storm blew past. But the sky remained dark from a heavily overcast sky. We could hear the thunder in the distance as it grew faint. When we got nearer home, the storm had moved away. Everywhere were the evidences of a storm. Trees were down. Streams were rushing bank-full and overflowing the road.

After the fury of the storm, it was welcoming to be at home to settle down and start canning the blackberries.

✝

Not very many months went by between love poems I wrote to my Russ. Some of the cold, winter days were long and lonely when he was at the garage. He was working long hours repairing broken cars, trucks, farm tractors, and the two school buses he and Mr. Jones drove twice each weekday.

The first time we were apart for a night as a married couple was in 1931 when he had to travel to Oklahoma City to replace a school bus that was no longer worth repairing for the daily use required of it. That night, after I got Mary and Betty to bed, I sat in front of the gas-fired stove and thought through a poem so I could read it to him the night he returned.

Soon after his return, I was expecting. And again, I realized it right after my birthday in March. I told my Russ, "We need to be more careful about my birthday celebrations."

This year was an eventful one. The Great Depression took the nation into an economic valley. And 1931 was the first year of the great seven-year drought with its rainless days in Kansas, Oklahoma, and Texas. The great Dust Bowl did its most damage during 1935 through 1938. My family in Lenna was one of those that would be driven to California by the dust-filled winds of those dry storms.

The drought, added on top of the Great Depression and the coming of mechanized farm equipment, drove more and more farmers from their farms.

Our son was born the fourth day of January, 1932. I did move from the back porch into the house for this event. Even I knew the back porch bedroom was not practical for this big event this time of the year.

We named our son Russell, just as I had promised the day we buried baby Francis. We gave him the middle name Forrest. The grocer, Mr. Kaylor, assumed we had named our son after him, and for several years, he gave Sonny nice Christmas presents until the Kaylors moved to Tulsa. Most of the time, the presents were large, high-quality toy cars or trucks. This and his daddy's love of nice cars must have marked him because he was always a lover of four-wheeled and two-wheeled vehicles.

Some people called our boy Russell Junior or Little Russell. We decided to call him Sonny, and that was the name he was known by until we moved to Okmulgee when he was in the eighth grade, where he was called Russell and then Russ.

As bad as my Russ wanted a son, it seemed only natural to call him Sonny. When Sonny was around twelve or fourteen, the name on the auto service station in Okmulgee was changed from Russell Jones Service Station to Russell Jones and Son and stayed that way until after Son graduated from college. Then my Russ had to accept that our son had to follow his own chosen profession as an engineer in a Tulsa manufacturing plant.

Near the end of 1932, Troy's wife, Ivy, became very ill and died a short time later. About a year later, Troy began to court Olga. She had a boy named Rallo, about the same age as Troy's son, Roy. They were blessed with a long, happy marriage and had seven children within the first ten years.

The Transitioning Years in Preston

1933 through 1945

After Sonny was born and the year before Mary started school, my Russ took us to Lenna and left us for a week. It was during the school year, when Bertha was twelve years old and Mae was ten. Every day, Bertha could hardly go to school. She was afraid we would be gone by the time she got home. I took Mary and Betty to some of my favorite places while Mama looked after Sonny. This was as much for my benefit as for them, knowing they were probably too young to remember. Mary was old enough to play around the yard and orchard by herself.

We brought her little dog along to keep her company. I kept my eye on them, lest they wander too far, as I had been known to do at her age. I checked to see that no ladders were around to tempt her.

Mary would wander off. She could not be denied.

She was picking wildflowers with her doggy by her side.

I would call to Mary. She pretended she didn't hear.

I'd watch as she found new things, her doggy always near.

They were like two kids. They loved each other so.

And when I spanked my Mary, her dog would hunker low.

When I put Mary to bed, her dog would lie close by.

He pretended to be asleep and didn't bat an eye.

A few days after we got back home, I had another experience with Mary and her dog. I jumped to the conclusion that Mary had followed her dog and had gotten lost. I called for her outside and hunted around in the chicken house, the garage, and cow barn. I asked neighbors if they had seen her. Finally, I decided I had better search more thoroughly inside the house. I found her and her doggy asleep under one of the beds.

Betty was a toddler at this time, and this harmless experience alarmed me so much that I started using a small rope to tie Betty to a bedpost for the twenty minutes it took me to milk the cow each morning and evening.

Later, when Sonny was about seven years old, he took over the milking and hog-slopping chores. He loved to work and hardly ever complained, except when I called him to supper when he was busy playing baseball. He and other boys and girls played in the wide dirt street in front of our house.

One day, we couldn't find Sonny after school, when he was in the fourth grade. We called and called and looked in all the likely places he might go after school. We were certain he hadn't come home because we saw no evidence that after school he had eaten his regular peanut butter and jelly sandwich. We even searched around the Boy Scout lake a half mile from the house, fearing he may have drowned. It was getting dark when his daddy came home from work and asked if we had looked in the house. We found Sonny asleep in his bed. We didn't wake him for supper, and he slept straight through until morning.

I asked my Russ how he'd thought of this simple solution. He told us about his parents not finding him one night after church, assuming he had come home with the rest of the family. Mrs. Jones had eight of her ten children at that time. They even came to our Lenna house to see if he had come home with Troy.

When they asked Troy if he had seen Russell, he said, "The last I saw of him, he was asleep in one of the church pews." That's where they found him. My Russ had heard the story so many times a sleeping boy was the first thing he thought about.

In 1934, Roscoe was almost twenty years old, and he and Lillian wanted to get married. The Jones garage could no longer support this many families. Mr. and Mrs. Jones converted part of the garage into a small grocery store. My Russ loaned them money to stock the store after taking a job in Okmulgee with another service station business that operated a tank truck to transport gasoline from the Tulsa and Barnsdall refineries to the Okmulgee area. My Russ drove the tank truck. He also made deliveries to farmers who had replaced their teams of horses and mules with motor-powered tractors.

When my Russ was making deliveries to farmers in the Preston area, he would stop by our house, put some diapers in a sack, and take Sonny with him to make deliveries. When Sonny was almost five years old, his daddy started taking him to Tulsa and Barnsdall to pick up a load of gasoline or oil.

At the Tulsa refinery, they had a rule that Sonny couldn't go inside the refinery. So Sonny would stay with the guard at the gated entrance. The first time this happened, Sonny ran into the house, all excited, and said, "Mother, I helped the guard stand in the guard house and keep the bad guys out of the refinery."

Sometimes Sonny's daddy would use a hoist to remove the tank from the truck and replace it with a flatbed so he could haul back drums of motor oil, boxes of canned oil, and auto-lubricating greases. On those days, Sonny would tell me, "Daddy is really strong. He hooked chains to the tank and hooked it on the pulley. Then he pulled on the pulley chain and lifted the tank off the truck. The flatbed was even heavier, so I had to help Daddy pull on the pulley chain."

Sonny weighed about fifty pounds and was now able to draw the bucket of water from our water well on our back porch. My Russ never missed a chance to take Sonny with him.

Forty years later, when Son was about forty-five years old, his daddy decided to retire and close the gas station. Together, he and Son removed the big, twelve-foot-long Barnsdall sign from the roof of the station, and Son took it home to Tulsa. He restored the colorful, porcelain shiny surface of the sign and placed it as the central decoration in a room of their house where he had a pool table.

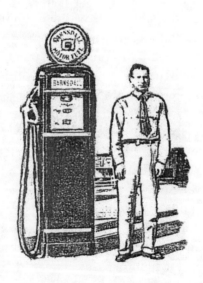

Those were the days when oil companies required their service station employees to wear matching uniforms with colorful patches on their shirts. The patches identified the brand of the products they were selling. My Russ sold Barnsdall products. The patch on the chest of his shirt was round with a *B* inside a square. The company's motto was, "Be square to your motor." Also, they claimed to be the world's first refiner. My Russ was no exception. He wore a cap with a bill on it and a tie around his shirt collar. He was oh so handsome dressed as if he were going to church. I took great pride in sending him off to work in a uniform that was starched and ironed.

When my Russ got his own service station in Okmulgee, he never opened it on Sundays. He had all the business he could handle. Each year, as business got better, he hired high school boys to work for him after school and on Saturdays. Saturday was his busiest day because that was the day the farmers and their families came to town. Most of his customers were very loyal and arranged to fill up on weekdays and Saturday.

Sonny went to work at the station on Saturdays when he was tall enough to stand on car running boards to wash windshields. He got paid a penny per windshield. He put a mark on a piece of paper for each clean windshield. When he got enough marks on the paper, his daddy would take him to the bank and send Sonny to a teller to put money in his savings account.

In the summers, Sonny stayed at the station all day. When he was small, his daddy boss would park the car in the shade on the east side of the station so Sonny could take a well-deserved, two-hour nap after lunch, waking him at three o'clock when station traffic was the heaviest.

Before we moved to Okmulgee, when Sonny was thirteen years old, it wasn't unusual for him to ride his bicycle the seven miles from Preston to the station after school. He would work an hour or two, tie his bicycle on the front bumper of the car, and ride home with his boss.

As he grew older and more experienced, Son had his own ideas about how things could be done better at the station. It wasn't unusual for his boss to remind him that at the house, he was his daddy and the rules were different. It was the only way he could shut Son up.

After harvest time in 1935, all of my family except Troy and me moved to Delano, California. Papa got a job on a very large farm where irrigation ditches were used to water the crops, using water from drilled wells.

When I learned they were leaving, I knew we must go back to the old home place for our final visit there with my family. I had the same kind of lonesome feeling I had when I learned I had to move from there to Preston. I knew I needed to soak up as many things into my memory as my natural and spiritual senses could absorb. I needed to talk with my family about the special things we had done there and dig up some of Mama's flowers that she would leave behind.

One final time, my Russ and I strolled hand in hand along my winding nature trail. We watched the clouds hide the sun and then journey on eastward in their daily rounds. We sat together on the log by the spring where my full legal name was carved on a tree. This was a place for dreams. The log was becoming more rotten, as if to say to us it also wouldn't be there the next time I came to visit the old home place.

I said, "We've shared a lot of dreams sitting on this log."

My Russ brightened, saying, "Yes, and most of them have come true. Why don't we dream some more? Dreams are one of the best things we need to take back home with us from your old home place."

I thought, *He's trying to keep me focused on the dreams that can come true at my present home place.*

We looked at the enormous trees around us, hundreds of years old, and talked about how they could represent our dreams and the dreams of the generations of other young couples who had sat on their own logs before us. As we sat there a little longer, we noticed the wisps of clouds entangle in the branches of the tall trees on the high part of my nature trail.

I had a sensation this was God's way of saying, "Those clouds are your new dreams on their way to meet you at your own new home place."

I stood up, pulled my Russ close to me, held him tightly for a while, and then took his hand and walked into the new dreams with him. The silence was broken only by the silvery chimes of birdsong from every direction.

The last thing we did before returning to Preston was to dig up some of Mama's roses. They had come from the rosebush I bought for Mama from a mail-order catalog fifteen years earlier—Mama's Rose.

Mama's Rose shines with dew. It doesn't look the same.

I think it is a lonely rose, even with my mama's name.

I still call it Mama's Rose. Today, it receives my love.

I'll talk to it like Mama did when it received her love.

It has the sweetest fragrance as it did in days of yore.

I'm thankful to have Mama's Rose, with me forevermore.

As we dug up Mama's Rose, we remembered going to the hills and gathering huckleberries for youth group outings. I loved the berries for their sweet taste, but they had one negative feature. We ate them as we gathered them, and the more of them we ate, the darker our mouths and teeth would turn. Of course, that was part of the fun.

When we got back to church from one of these youth outings, Mr. Jones would get us to look at each other's lips and teeth and express ourselves about our favorite foods that God made sweet and good for us and about favorite verses we knew from God's Word that were sweet and good food for our souls.

As I remembered these times, it came to my mind that Mr. Jones hadn't been looking well lately. I thought it might be from worry about business falling off at the garage or about grocery sales not being as high as they had anticipated. I decided to watch him more closely when we got home to see if the hacking cough and breathing problems he had been having lately would go away. I decided to use our reminder of eating huckleberries as my excuse to talk to him about his persistent cough.

In 1936, Mr. Jones was diagnosed with tuberculosis. That was the reason for his coughing and breathing problems. Because of our close bond that developed when I helped him with the church youth, near the end, he insisted that I come and take care of him. He and I talked the same language when it came to the Bible. He made it clear to me that it would pay very big dividends for many generations if we faithfully took our children to church every Sunday. He died in August.

We hadn't been regular about going to church on Sundays. We got into the habit of driving to Okmulgee to go to the movies on Saturday night, causing us to sleep late on Sunday mornings. After my talk with Mr. Jones before he died, I outlawed Saturday night movies so we could go to church regularly on Sundays.

I found Jesus when I was young.

He made my heart light and full of fun.

As I grew older, I didn't do

The things I knew he wanted me to.

I strayed, didn't meet with the fold;

I lost many treasures more precious than gold.

I was wandering through life on the brink of woe.

Then he found me again because he loves me so.

By now, the subject of baby Francis didn't come up so often. It seemed the girls thought it was appropriate that Sonny at least have it explained to him. It came up in conversation about Mr. Jones's death. Sonny was on the front porch of the Jones house when the hearse came from Okmulgee to take his frail body. The image of the gurney and a sheet covering his grandpa's face had to be explained in some way. And in some way, Sonny made the connection between Mr. Jones being dead and baby Francis being dead. Sonny's only comment was, "I wish I had a big brother. If he was still here now, would he be a baby or older than Mary?"

After Mr. Jones's death, the Jones garage was closed, except for the grocery store and gasoline sales. It was very much like the convenience stores that oil companies began to operate in the 1970s, acting like they had created a new marketing idea. One of Son's favorite photos is a picture of his grandmother Jones standing beside the hand-operated gasoline pumps out in front of her business. Gasoline was nine cents per gallon in 1936.

During this time, Mr. Kaylor closed his big grocery store and moved to Tulsa to work in the Tulsa post office. The Preston post office was moved from Mr. Kaylor's store, and Mrs. Jones became the new postmistress. She also added feed and seed to her inventory and continued to run this business for many more years.

✝

In 1938, we went on a family vacation to California. This was the only time we went there as a family. The other times I went were because Mama and Papa were getting older. We drove our 1933 Chevy sedan. It was summertime and very hot. There was no auto air conditioning at that time.

The greatest memory I have of this visit with my parents was to see them read the Bible together and talk to me about it.

The second-greatest memory was to walk in the ocean for the first time. I had imagined how it would feel and sound and taste and smell and what it would look like. I had even written some poems from my imagination and read them to my Russ. He didn't think too much of them.

While we were wading together on the beach he asked, "What do you think about the poems you wrote about the ocean waves? Remember how you let me help you write poems by telling me to observe things that I was seeing, hearing, tasting, touching, and smelling in nature?"

I tried to take the focus off myself for breaking my own rules. I complimented him for remembering this rule I had taught him. "I'll get those poems out and do them over," I promised. He just gave me a sideways grin, and we continued to walk along. I wasn't about to give him additional satisfaction by asking him to start a poem just then.

The restless sea is wide and deep,

With restless waves that never sleep.

Night and day, wild breakers roar,

Washing shells upon the shore.

And if you walk in the mighty deep,

The tide will soon around you sweep.

I tried to run, couldn't get away,

From the tide chasing me that day.

My Russ beside me laughed with glee,

When the tide rushed in and covered me.

I was as scared as scared could be.

And I'm still afraid of the restless sea.

While standing on the wind-swept sand,

I said, "This is made by my Master's hand."

I looked here and listened there

And ended this day with a little prayer.

On our long drive back home, we went to the Grand Canyon. Everywhere, there was rock. Rocky cliffs and crags. Great mesas rising abruptly. Shelves and plateaus of rock. The colors of the rocks were pink and white with streaks of rust, red, and maroon, all carved by wind and rain into weird shapes and giant forms. There were pinnacles that pointed their ghostly fingers at the sky. There were other beautiful shapes like flames of fire. A river on the canyon floor was doing its ageless work of tearing tiny particles of sand away from stones as it churned and turned the water over and over again and again. At sundown, the cliffs turned red and gold with the setting sun. In those last minutes before sunset, darkness filled the canyons, and then the gigantic walls magically disappeared. It was a beautiful sight to see.

When we got home from our vacation, it was time for our children to start their next year of school. The school superintendent lived across the street from our house. He knew my Russ well since my Russ drove one of the school buses and had recently been added to the school board.

Sonny had an adventurous, creative, and somewhat rebellious streak much like I had when I was his age. I often took small limbs off the peach tree just outside our back door to serve him some "peach tree tea" on his bare legs as my mother did to me when I misbehaved.

Knowing this, when Sonny started to school, I felt I needed to reach an understanding with the superintendent about Sonny's discipline while at school. We reached an agreement that I would discipline acts of poor behavior done at home, and the teachers would be free to execute appropriate punishment at school. We agreed I wouldn't have to know everything about misbehavior at school unless a teacher felt I needed to know.

I summarized our agreement by saying, "Mr. Duke, when you catch him, you spank him, because punishment needs to come as quickly as possible after the crime. As all of us learned, a fair and speedy trial is Sonny's right under the Constitution."

Mr. Duke and I had a good laugh about that, and he said he should ask me to teach government classes to the high school students.

Each classroom had two grades in it. Fortunately for Sonny, Betty was two grades ahead of him, and he was protected from her tattling. A pattern was soon established. If Sonny was in love with the teacher and if she kept him very busy, he had no behavior problems. If the opposite was true, he got spankings.

First and second grade were examples. Sonny fell in love with his first grade teacher, Miss Gillespie. She was a young, beautiful, blonde-haired teacher. She left to get married after the beginning of Sonny's second grade and was replaced by Miss Martin, a stern, older, not very attractive teacher. Sonny decided to test her.

He brought one of his favorite toy cars to school and would play with it in his lap while she taught. Naturally, she took it from him and put it in her desk. After school was out that day and she had gone, little mister Sonny retrieved it from her desk and brought it home. The next day, she intended to give Sonny a lecture and give it back to him at the end of the day. When she didn't find it in her desk, she quizzed Sonny about it.

Watching her, as she pulled the truth out of him, Sonny could see the anger on her face and said, "My, my! Aren't you a red-hot mama?"

He had overheard his daddy say this about someone and had been looking for a chance to use it. Poor, dumb kid. And to think he had gotten a scholarship award from Miss Gillespie at the end of the first grade.

So Miss Martin gave him what he deserved: a spanking. Mary, now in the sixth grade, heard about it and went to smooth things over with Miss Martin.

There were similar kinds of events as Sonny moved from grade to grade. Even with this behavior, he made good grades. I wish I had known to ask the school to give him more homework than he could get done because he really did enjoy learning new things. In Okmulgee, in the eighth grade, he would figure this strategy out for himself.

✝

Our house in Preston was within walking distance of the railroad track. When hobos came to our house, summer or winter, I would have them sit on the tree stump in the front yard while I fixed them something to eat. In the beginning, they would go from door to door. Then I noticed they began to pass all the other houses and come directly to our house. They seemed to know to say, without me asking them, "I'll just go over and sit on this stump to eat if that will be fine with you."

Most of them would ask if I had a job they could do. I always turned down their offers. Because of the children, I wanted them to move on as soon as possible.

I suppose the word had been passed around that the lady at this particular place would feed them. It was almost like a stage play where each of us played our part and stepped offstage at the right time. After a while, I was no longer very afraid of them. It was as if they needed to be polite and appreciative so that the next hobo would be welcomed.

The first beggar I met going door to door wore a black derby, and his coat was torn. When he came to my door, he knocked very loudly. He said, "Good mornin', lady. I want to be fed. My pack's so heavy it feels like lead. The wind is cold, and the snow is deep, and I don't even have a place to sleep."

I might have sent him on his way without feeding him if he hadn't introduced himself with poetry. After feeding him, I asked him why he lived this way, thinking he might have been forced into it by misfortune.

His answer was simple: "Lady, I like it. That's the reason why. I like to tramp the highway and catch a ride on a freight train. It's a good way to see the country and meet interesting people."

I asked him what his mother thought about his way of living.

He said in a low voice and without raising his head, "Lady, you don't know it, but my mama is dead."

One snowy day, I wrote a poem as a prayer for the many hobos I fed.

It was a long time ago on a bitter, cold day.

I fed a poor beggar and watched him hobble away.

I shall never forget how he trudged through deep snow.

With one good leg, the other a peg, I watched him go.

He had a pack on his back, a walking stick in his hand.

Long hair and a beard of white—he was an old man.

He sat down on my porch because the snow was deep.

I couldn't keep from wondering, *Where will he sleep?*

He moaned as he ate. He shivered in the cold.

I couldn't ask him in, although he was so old.

This was a long time ago, when my children were small.

Had my Russ been at home, I wouldn't mind at all.

So I shall remember, when it is snowy and bad

And my mind drifts back, "Was he somebody's dad?"

✝

In 1939, my Russ started teaching Sunday school Bible lessons to teenagers in the Okmulgee church. He was about thirty-three years old. I think Sonny must have been subconsciously marked by his daddy because he would sit at the dining room table late on Saturday nights as my Russ studied and outlined the next morning's lesson after a hard day's work at the station.

Sonny always wanted to be like his daddy by duplicating how he acted around his customers at the station. He never heard his daddy use a curse word. One evening, when Sonny was about fourteen, my Russ came home with a badly bruised thumb. He hit it very hard with a big hammer while working under a car on the grease rack.

I decided to tease my Russ about it and asked Sonny what his daddy said when he hit his finger with the hammer. He proudly proclaimed, "He didn't say a thing. He just sucked air through his mouth and made a sound that sounded like *Eshh*."

The Preston schoolyard had concrete sidewalks that ran between the classroom building, the gym, restroom, and the home economics building. The sandstone home economics building and the concrete sidewalks had been built by the WPA as part of President Roosevelt's stimulus package during the Great Depression. A sandstone rock stairway was built over a fence made of pipe at the bus-loading stop. Sonny often used these sidewalks to ride his little red wagon. He liked speed, and he and the other boys would race to see who could go the fastest. There was one safety hazard. The sidewalks had some ninety-degree turns that were too sharp if a boy didn't have enough sense to slow down.

I tolerated it because it wasn't nearly as dangerous as things I had done in the boat on Old Limbo Creek when I was his age. Sonny just didn't have enough sense to slow down for these turns, or he was purposely going too fast for the thrill of it. Many times, he would wreck and bump his head. At least two times, he landed hard on his head and was cut over an eyebrow. Both times, he was bleeding so badly I had to ask someone to speedily drive me to Okmulgee so I could take him to Dr. Michener to put in several stitches. That boy!

I didn't drive our car. It terrified me. I didn't know why. Lots of my Russ's customers were women who could drive cars. My Russ taught me how to drive and shift gears. My decision to refuse to drive came one day when I had to drive our car home from the Okmulgee service station back to our house in Preston. All three children were with me. Even Sonny, only seven years old, could tell by the way I drove how incompetent and terrified I was. I never drove again after that day unless it was an emergency. I know I was a burden to my Russ, but that's just the way it was. He could either like it or lump it.

After Papa made the last addition to our house, I changed one room into a combination living room and sewing room. I was thirty-four years old, and I felt a need for more artistic, dignified culture in my life. Being at one end of the house, I kept the French door of this room closed much of the time so it would not be exposed to normal household clutter. I also used it as my sewing room. I bought a treadle-operated sewing machine so I could make most of my own and our children's clothing.

I also bought a used upright piano. I hoped the children would take an interest in playing it. When they were all at school, I would take one of my poems and pick out a tune to go with it. I wanted to see my poems and songs published so others could enjoy them and so I could get some recognition.

The only one who made real music come from my piano was a neighbor we called Grandma Fox. She played by ear and wasn't any help to record my tunes on paper. She was an elderly lady who moved into the house across the street, catty-corner from the superintendent's house. We visited often, and she even came to our house to play the piano to entertain our children and sing to them.

Grandma Fox was old and bent and gray. It seemed I liked her best that way. I would tease her and say, "You're my very best old friend."

Her response was, "Yes, I'm old. I'm old enough to go to heaven and sit on the throne beside Jesus."

Being only thirty-four years old and energetic, I hadn't stopped to think much about my own death. But she wanted to talk about it as a glorious event she was looking forward to. She had read the Bible through many times and could tell me many things I had missed. She taught me to expect some Bible verses to say different things to me as I grew older and as I had new experiences with life and with God and his Holy Spirit.

Sonny felt at home at Grandma Fox's house and often went there on his own or played in her yard. One day, she walked across the street to tell me that Sonny was playing on top of her chicken house with two other boys.

Over the past few weeks, I knew Sonny and the boys he played with had found a grapevine on the fence of our cow pasture. He learned the small, dry limbs were partially hollow and that they could use a match to light one end to play like they were smoking a cigar or cigarette. He made no secret of it because he brought some of the sticks home to share with his sisters. I didn't make a big deal out of their youthful, adventurous need to experiment. I had done such things as a child also.

The smoking experiment went to another level when a new family moved in next door to Grandma Fox. Rather than growing vegetables in their garden, the father of the family grew tobacco and hung it up in their barn to dry. One of the children of the family showed the drying tobacco to Sonny. Sonny suggested they make themselves some cigars. This is why Sonny and his friends were on top of Grandma Fox's chicken house.

They thought they were well hidden for their experiment. I watched as they rolled the tobacco leaves into a cigar-sized roll.

I saw small puffs of smoke. I got a bucket of water ready in case this experiment went out of control. I was pretty sure of what was going to happen and that the tobacco could teach Sonny much more than my scolding or a spanking.

It didn't take long for Sonny to crawl off the chicken house and make his way home. I was sitting in the living room when he came in. He looked at me pitifully and plopped down spread-eagle on the floor, as sick as I expected. The pale look on his face was a mixture of, *I need your help,* and, *I know when I get well you're going to beat me.*

All I had to say was, "You've been smoking, haven't you?"

This is one of those times when a boy asks himself, *How does she know?"*

I decided, like the teachers during the school year, that I needed to keep Sonny occupied during the summer. It occurred to me one of the reasons Papa took me hunting with him often was to tire me out so I wouldn't get into so much adventurous trouble. So I started going on walks with Sonny in the woods behind the house and the big rocky hill across the highway from our cow pasture.

I showed him how to see the squirrels more easily and how to discover places rabbits might live. When he got a little older, his daddy taught him to kill squirrels with a .22-caliber rifle. If we saw a snake, I taught him how to identify poisonous ones. I would pick up non-poisonous snakes and let them crawl around on my arms to remove his fear of just any snake.

We only killed rabbits in the winter, for health reasons. After a good snow, when Sonny was old enough, his daddy took him out and taught him how to kill rabbits with a 12-gauge shotgun. By the time Sonny was eleven years old, we were allowing him to go hunting by himself.

My Russ had three sayings that were repeated over and over and were as predictable as daylight and dark. On school days, he would wake the children with a happy voice to start every day.

"Early to bed and early to rise makes a man healthy, wealthy, and wise."

The children surely didn't like this but learned to tolerate it. After all, is there any pleasant way to wake up a child? I often expected each of them to say, "I'm not a man!"

At six o'clock every morning, when it was time for him to go to work, he would say, "Time to go." For all of the fifty-four years he worked, he left the house at six in the morning and returned again after six in the evening, six days each week, almost never missing a day of work. He felt it was perfectly natural to sacrifice for his family and his customers. Men like my Russ are what made God's America great and what makes Christ pleased.

At night, when it was time to go to bed he would say, "I believe I'll check it to you." When the children were young they would already be in bed, and this would be the signal for me to join him, which I was always very willing to do. As the children grew up and would return home for a visit, he would use it as a signal to excuse himself so they could keep visiting with me or with each other.

I made a sack lunch for my Russ each day. In Preston, we had no phone, so I couldn't call him during the day. The school had a phone, and there were only two or three homes in town with a phone. At seven miles away, those calls were long distance. So, after we moved to Okmulgee, I sent frequent messages or reminders with his lunch. One day, I sent a poem to thank him for providing for us. More than twenty years later, I put the poem in another lunch by only changing, "We'll be waiting here, and you won't be alone" to, "I'll be waiting here, and we'll be all alone." If that sounds like a come-on, it was.

The time has come for you to go.

Now take good care, for I love you so.

There's a nip of winter blowing in the air.

Wrap up real warm, for you know I care.

Please be careful to not take cold,

For if you do I'll have to scold.

Do your work well, and hurry home.

We'll be waiting here, and you won't be alone.

The time has come for you to go.

Now take good care, for we love you so.

†

During one summer, Sonny spent a week at Troy's farm, between Lenna and Henryetta, playing with Roy and Rallo. It wasn't a very prosperous farm. There was no electricity. Troy still used a team of horses to till the soil. Their water well wasn't very productive, and often water had to be carried from a spring across the field from the house.

There was no refrigeration, so for more than half the year, the children had to drink warm milk directly from the morning and evening milking of the cow. It was such a contrast to the cold milk Sonny was accustomed to that he told his aunt Olga he didn't like milk.

The time with Roy and Rallo was a big adventure for Sonny, except for the warm milk. The boys slept out under the stars on the bed of the horse-drawn wagon and roamed around in the woods, stopping often at the spring to get a cool drink of water.

After Sonny returned home and told me all his adventures, I asked him if he would like to live on a farm like that.

His answer was, "Oh no! I like my milk cold and my bed soft. I liked it that I didn't have to take a bath while I was there."

When the children were young in Preston, we had a weekly required back porch bathing routine. It started with placing the metal bathtub next to the deep well on the back porch. Next, one of the children would draw water from the well and pour it into the tub. It would take a minimum of six buckets full of water to get six inches of water in the tub. This chore alone would keep them from using too much water from the well.

Mary, being the oldest, would get to bathe first; Sonny, being the youngest, would be last. Mary and Betty would use soap, of course, which turned the water varying shades of gray. When he was little, Sonny couldn't care less what the color of the water was, since he didn't want to take a bath anyway.

As he got a little older and preferred to use soap, he began to complain, not only from having to always be last but because of the dirty water. However, he would rather complain than draw enough water to dilute the color or have a shallow bath of clean water. Besides, every gallon of water weighed seven pounds and had to be emptied from the tub, bucket by bucket, until the tub and its contents were light enough for two kids, one on each end of the tub, to carry it into the backyard to dump it.

When Son grew up and repeated this story, the water got grayer and grayer every time he told it. He insisted he could vividly see it in his mind's eye.

As autumn came in 1940, we were coming up on our fifteenth anniversary. The brown oak leaves were beginning to drift silently to the ground. There was a chill each dawn and sunset. I was delighted to see the vivid scarlet berries hanging against the dark green leaves. The chrysanthemum blossoms lifted their brilliant heads. Sonny was milking the cow as my Russ and I walked by the barn door. The persimmon tree in the cow lot behind the barn was bright with its golden fruit. Some had fallen to the ground. We watched the full moon growing smaller and smaller as it arched higher and higher into the heavens. The night wind had sprung up, and across the sky, a procession of fluffy white clouds whirled with the speed of great snowy birds. We held each other and spoke of love. As we walked past the barn door, my Russ took one side of the handle of the full milk bucket and helped Sonny carry it to the house.

The leaves began to fall.

We heard the robins call.

Hurry up, all you lovers.

This surely must be fall.

You held me very tight

Under the moon tonight.

We wished on the stars above

Because we're still in love.

I was learning to ease my yearning for the old home place by taking walks in the woods while the children were in school. I never felt lonely because I loved nature too much. In the spring, I picked wildflowers like a child gathering them for a class assignment. I looked for nests—never to bother them, just to find them and count the eggs or the baby birds. They were so tiny with no feathers and only down on their heads and wings. In the winter, I would track rabbits in the snow just to watch them at their daily chores.

When I really felt adventurous, I trekked into the woods on the hills to look for tucked-away places as private as my inmost thoughts. The breeze rustled leaves of the trees in sooth-ing whispers. Before I knew it, I would be dreaming about my childhood as nature's peace flowed through me. The wind blow-ing through my hair gave me new energy while cares dropped away like falling autumn leaves. Even though I was thirty-five years old, I began to feel like a country girl again. I suddenly realized I was the happiest person in the whole world.

In 1942, Sonny was in the fourth grade on the lowest floor level of the classrooms in the school building. Betty was in the sixth grade on the next floor of classrooms, over the kitchen and lunchrooms in the basement. Mary, in high school now, attended classes on the top floor of the building. Mr. Duke, the superintendent, had his office on the top floor. When he had to discipline someone, usually boys, and often Sonny with a group of other boys, he left the office door wide open so each spanking could be advertised by the gossip that would spread quickly from room to room.

On one particular day, Mary passed by Mr. Duke's office. With his paddle in his hand, he was lecturing a group of fourth-grade boys. Sonny was among them. Mary halted out of sight to hear Mr. Duke say, "Now, it was bad enough for Miss Estes to have to make you boys stay in from recess, but it was even worse for you to do what you were doing when I walked by the room and caught you. Sonny, you and Porter Lee are going to get extra swats because the other boys probably wouldn't have gotten into more trouble if you hadn't been such sorry leaders."

Mary didn't hear what they had done. I waited for Mr. Duke to tell me. He never contacted me, so I kept my agreement with him and let him handle the discipline at school, even though I was very curious. I concluded that Sonny and Porter must have some leadership talents that needed to be channeled in more positive directions. I kept my eyes open.

When Sonny was ten years old, he and some of his friends built a clubhouse in the corner of our front yard. The corner fence was covered with a honeysuckle vine that made two of the walls of the clubhouse. They gathered leaf-covered limbs from bushes and trees to make the arbor roof and the other two walls.

They must have plotted many adventures there. There was a rival group of boys led by a ruffian named Jimmy Green, who came one night and dismantled the clubhouse. Jimmy had even been threatening Sonny at school, saying, "I'm going to beat you up after school," though he never did try it.

The next morning, it was Betty who discovered the damage and was ready to retaliate. Sonny wasn't a coward. He just didn't like to fight or even get angry at others. Betty had no such qualms. She caught Jimmy Green and his friends together at school and gave them a scorching threat. "If you guys ever do such a thing again, I will give you a good beating you will never ever forget." Just to get her point across, she gave Jimmy a good shove that almost toppled him.

After he knew what Betty had done, Sonny said to me, "I wish I had a big brother to do my fighting."

Mr. Duke must have gotten wind of this fourth-grade rivalry because he bought some heavily padded boxing gloves and took these young boys out beside the gym at school and let them have at it under his supervision. Sonny's friend Porter Lee was stocky. From working on his family farm, he already had muscular arms. He was the best boxer of the group and seemed to enjoy taking on Jimmy Green. This strategy of Mr. Duke's seemed to work because they soon lost interest in boxing and concentrated on softball and basketball games.

It wasn't long after this that Sonny began to bring Jimmy Green home with him after school to eat peanut butter and jelly sandwiches. If Betty walked through the kitchen, Jimmy would watch her out of the corner of his eyes because she still had her bluff in on him. Sonny loved jelly sandwiches, so Jimmy started calling him Jelly Jones at school.

✝

Since we didn't live on a farm where our children could learn to work hard, my Russ and I decided that they should go to work to earn money as soon as possible. This also had its practical side because our income wasn't big enough for Mary and Betty to have all the nice clothes they wanted.

One summer, I decided that during cotton-picking season it would be a good experience for our children to get a feel for that part of farm life.

A farmer we knew named Mr. Rainbow picked us up early each morning in an empty flatbed truck with tall sideboards. I sat in front with Mr. Rainbow. Riding back home was more comfortable for the cotton-picking crew because the truck bed would be full of cotton, almost to the top of the sideboards.

I made each of the children a canvas cotton-picking sack. The sacks were properly sized for each child's age. They had a broad canvas band on the open end to go around their shoulders as they dragged the sack behind them down the cotton row.

I found I hadn't lost my knack for this work because I could pick over 220 pounds of cotton each day. Mary could pick about 150 pounds. Betty never got over 120 pounds per day because she would have to leave her sack and go over several rows to give one of the young boys a whack for teasing her. Sonny was very competitive and wanted to do better but seldom could pick as much as 80 pounds each day.

Sonny had grown beyond washing windshields at the station. Now he was filling customers' cars with gasoline, checking their oil and water, airing up tires, sweeping dirt from a car's floorboards, fixing flat tires, washing cars, changing oil, lubricating suspensions, and hosing down the whole driveway every Saturday morning. He was being paid the same as high school boys who worked there regularly.

He saw no merit whatsoever for the educational or cultural

values of picking cotton when compared to the more professional activities of working with his daddy at the station.

Sonny's first major purchase was to buy a fancy bicycle that
his uncle Roscoe no longer used. It had a battery-powered head-
light, a battery-operated horn, a chain guard, a carrier behind
the seat with spring-loaded metal arms to secure a load, and lots
of reflectors. Of course, his primary goal was to buy his first car
when he was sixteen.

✝

For the girls, most businesses wouldn't hire them until they were
sixteen. However, Mary's daddy thought fifteen was a good age
for her to start, particularly since she was dating LaMoine Neal,
who was two grades older than she was. Her daddy suggested
that she get a job on Saturdays in Okmulgee. She could ride to
and from work with him.

Mary's first job was at Cowden's Laundry. Daddy could see
how hard the work was, so he suggested she ask for a job at the
large Kress variety store.

She said, "But Daddy, they won't hire me until I'm sixteen."

His answer was—and Mary knew he meant for her to at
least go and ask—"Just go and check. You can always ask them
to contact you when you're sixteen. I think they'll want to hire
you."

Mary returned to the station all smiles to ride home the
day she interviewed at Kress, very excited that she had gotten
a job. She worked there until after she was married and until
LaMoine returned from the Philippines in 1945 at the end of
World War II.

Betty would also work at Cowden Laundry. Then she worked
at Okmulgee Laundry, Kress, and as a telephone operator for
Bell Telephone in Okmulgee. She worked for Bell in Tulsa after
she and Buck were married.

Betty was fourteen when she went to work at Cowden Laundry in the summer of 1943. The weather was hot, and so was the job. Sonny had taken the service station receipts to the bank for his daddy. After making the deposit, he walked past the big door of the laundry, where he could watch Betty folding bed sheets used by the hotels in town. Sonny acted like he was responsible for Betty. He told me how hard the work was that Betty was doing.

After we moved to Okmulgee in 1945, he even felt like it was his job to pass judgment on the boys she dated. This didn't go over very well with Betty.

Mary heard our conversation. Having done the same job at the laundry, she agreed that it was a killer. So Betty changed to Okmulgee Laundry ironing shirts before going to work at Kress. Mary taught Betty how to use the cash register at Kress.

While working at Kress, Betty was fired for only a part of one day. She was a very pretty girl, and a boy at the Preston school wanted her for his girlfriend. He stopped by Betty's workstation at Kress one day for a short visit. The next day when she went to work, Betty found her time card had been pulled.

Betty asked about it, and one of the other clerks said, "You've been fired for talking too long to a boy yesterday when you should have been working."

When Betty asked where she could find the manager, she was told he was at the hamburger diner next door. Betty marched confidently to the diner, found the manager, and proceeded to tell him the facts as she saw them and how she wanted her job back immediately.

The manager must have felt like the boys who had torn down Sonny's arbor clubhouse. She immediately got her job back and continued working at Kress until she graduated from high school in 1948 and went to work for the phone company.

During the time Mary and LaMoine were dating, the Japanese army had already attacked Pearl Harbor. LaMoine's brother, Lowell, had joined the army.

Lowell had a 1935 Ford sedan at the time he joined up. This was the car LaMoine drove on his dates with Mary. Frequently, the engine would backfire because the engine spark plug timing was off. More than once on a date, the car would backfire, and the fuel blown out on the engine would catch fire. LaMoine would have to stop the car and throw sand on the fire to smother it.

Sometimes, when they went to a movie, they took Sonny with them. He would sit in the front seat with them since Mary was sitting very close to LaMoine anyway. I could tell from my conversation with Sonny that being included was important to him. LaMoine had become the big brother Sonny had always wanted.

In 1944, LaMoine joined the army after he graduated from high school. Before Mary graduated, they were married.

Mary approached me and her daddy, saying, "I know you won't like this, but LaMoine and I are getting married after he completes basic training and before he goes overseas."

Mary was right about my opinion. The best reply I could make was, "At seventeen and eighteen years old, don't you think you are both too young?"

Even as I said this, I admitted to myself, *If the circumstances hadn't interfered, my Russ and I would have gotten married at the same age.*

Mary's response was decisive and confident. She told me that she and LaMoine had thought it over (as well as young people in love can). Mary answered, "That's what I first thought too, but LaMoine said, 'No, we're not too young at all,' so that's what we've decided."

Mary and LaMoine were married in February 1945. After only ten days, LaMoine left the States to serve eighteen months in the Philippines, rising to the rank of first sergeant.

Mary graduated in May. She complained the school had made a mistake when they printed the graduation card that went in the commencement announcement. It said that her name was Mary Laverne Jones. She happily took every card and added her new name: Neal.

Mary continued to live at home while LaMoine was in the army in the South Pacific. One day, she decided to forcefully give her daddy some family advice that he didn't want to hear.

To put her in her place, he said, "Little girl, just because you're married doesn't mean I won't turn you over my knee and give you a good spanking."

I stayed out of that one—one of the few times I didn't express my opinion.

While he was in the Philippines, LaMoine shipped back some Japanese military rifles and officers' swords. They were packed in wooden crates. Sonny used every excuse he could find to handle these things. They just added to the imagination and glamour of commando games he and his friends played among the boulders in the woods behind our house. He also began to draw pictures of warplanes in dogfights against the German and Japanese fighter planes.

For a social life during the long months LaMoine was away, Mary Laverne and her three high school girlfriends—Colleen, Wilma Jean, and Christine—formed a quartet and sang at school and other social occasions until they graduated.

Even though rationing was in effect all during the war for such things as gasoline, tires, sugar, shortening, butter, meat, and metals, business in Okmulgee was booming, and jobs were being added. Many of the Okmulgee people carpooled to work in the aircraft plant in Tulsa. The Phillips 66 refinery was running at full capacity. The fairgrounds and its buildings were converted to a concentration camp for German war prisoners.

A military hospital was built at the northeastern edge of town for many wounded military personnel. After the war, the hospital buildings were used to open a new two-year college and technical school. It was for men and women who decided to improve their education under the GI Bill. The school also included a two-year college division, which Son attended after graduating from high school.

All of this business activity meant greater gasoline sales and tire repair for the service station. Every Saturday afternoon, cars were lined up for two blocks in both directions from the service station to get gas for the start of the following week.

The gas rationing stamps the station took in had to be glued to sheets of paper and deposited at the bank just like money. The sheets of paper, with little rectangles printed on them the size of the stamps, were coated with water-based glue. A weekly nighttime ritual around the dining room table at our Preston house was for me and the children to help glue the stamps to the paper. We would dampen the paper, stick the stamps on them, and lay them around on the kitchen table to dry.

The war ended in 1945, and LaMoine returned home.

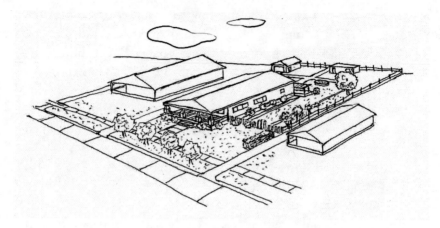

The Move to Okmulgee, Marriages, and Grandbabies

1946 through 1955

It was during the 1946 school year that we moved to Okmulgee. Son had to do another dumb trick in the last hour he went to school in Preston. I had arranged with Mr. Duke for Son to get out of class just after lunch so he could take the bus to Okmulgee to register for classes. The seventh- and eighth-grade teacher was young and inexperienced, and word hadn't gotten to her that Son was to leave class early to catch the bus.

Son was using this occasion to act up in class just enough to warrant the application of a paddle to his behind. What was so bad about it was that he arranged it so it was about time for the bus to arrive.

The young teacher instructed Son to stand at the back row of seats and place his hands on the back of the two seats on each side of the aisle. As she swung the paddle forward for the first lick, Son swung his body forward, and the paddle hit the back of the seat and hurt the teacher's hand. But it didn't hurt enough to keep her from finishing the job, with a few extra licks thrown in.

That wasn't the end of Son's creative, well-planned orneriness. Without saying a word, he picked up his books and walked out of the room. The teacher could see him walk across the schoolyard and down the road to the highway. She could also see him getting on the bus.

She got someone to watch the class and came across the street to the house, telling me, "Mrs. Jones, Sonny has just run away on the bus because I gave him a spanking."

She settled down to some degree when I told her that Son had permission to leave early. I walked back to school with her, and we found Mr. Duke. He apologized to the teacher and me for failing to get word to her soon enough.

After the teacher went back to her classroom, Mr. Duke said, "Mrs. Jones, Sonny's been doing very well lately. This probably wouldn't have happened if I had done my job better. I should have guessed that Sonny would do something different on his last day here. If you don't mind, just one more time, I'm going to ask you to stick with our agreement about his discipline. Don't say anything to him. He will keep wondering when the hammer will fall. That may be better discipline than another spanking.

"Also, I must apologize to you and Russell about another thing. You asked me several years ago to see that teachers gave Sonny extra homework to keep him busy. I failed to pass that on to this new teacher. Take my word for it. When Sonny gets to Okmulgee High School, where the classes are much harder and where he can work at the station every afternoon after school, you're apt to see a different boy."

I took Mr. Duke's advice, although I really wanted to break our agreement and break Son's neck. I thought I might get his daddy to use the razor strap on him. Well, I didn't. I prayed.

As it turned out, Son never got into trouble at the Okmulgee school. He had to study very hard to get his grades up near the level they had been at Preston. God does answer a mother's prayers. Even before Son graduated from high school, he actually thanked us for moving to Okmulgee. He really liked to be good and learn difficult things to prepare himself for college.

We found a nice house that had an extra lot beside the house so I could have plenty of room for a vegetable garden, flower gardens, and a chicken house and barn combination for our milk cow and chickens.

We soon learned that it was better to have milk delivered than to have a cow, particularly since the neighbors complained. Son was very happy to not have to milk the cow any longer. I often wondered if he was the one who got the neighbors to complain. Eventually, it became more practical to buy eggs and chickens for cooking than to raise our own. The barn and chicken house became a storage house, and the fertilized ground around it became part of the vegetable garden and a place for a small fishpond.

The move to Okmulgee was another step in my transition from the old home place. Although we moved closer in miles, we might have moved a million miles away from my dear dreams. Now the closest neighbor's house was only ten feet from ours. We didn't have any air conditioning yet, so our windows had to be open in the summertime. On an area the size of our Preston place, there were now twenty houses. My worst phobia about town life had come true. I felt as if I couldn't spread my hands out at arms' length without hitting a neighbor in the face.

I surprised myself with how fast I adjusted. We had an inside bathroom and running water. A big attic fan brought a breeze through the windows with the flip of an electric switch. Now I had a telephone so I could call my Russ at the station any time I wished. It was close enough for him to come home for lunch if he or I wished. Also, it was close enough for me to walk to the stores and have my Russ pick me up on his way home. He had a shorter workday because of the shorter drive. The concrete paved streets and sidewalks resulted in much less dust in the house. We were close enough to the church, so we could attend Sunday morning, Sunday night, and Wednesday night. And— almost the best thing—there was plenty of room for flower beds that could be watered with a hose, a place for the picket fence I always wanted, and my pick of the nicest neighbors I had ever known, some who became my closest friends.

My Russ had listed all of these benefits when he tried to sell me on moving to Okmulgee, including the better school for Betty and Son, but it's much like a kiss. You don't know how good it is until you've tasted it.

Over the years, my flower beds were far beyond anything I had as a young girl back at the old home place. My Russ had several truckloads of rich, black dirt hauled in. After the dirt was spread around, he built concrete borders around the flower beds to keep the Bermuda grass from encroaching into the beds. This was the first time in my life I had a lawn completely covered with green grass wherever I wanted it. As the trees that my Russ planted grew, the birds of every variety joined me to make my yard a paradise. Some years later, as I realized the true gift I had been given by this yard, I used a small brush and white paint to write a poem on a one-by-twelve-inch plank about four feet long. I used it as a decoration for my garden.

My yard's an earthly paradise,

A haven for my friends and me.

I also have feathered friends.

They're welcome, you can see.

When Son was fourteen years old, he ding-donged his daddy to let him spend some of the money he had saved to buy a Cushman motor scooter. It was legal at fourteen to operate a two-wheeled, low-horsepower, motorized bicycle, scooter, or motorcycle. Several other fourteen-year-old boys his age were riding them to school or to make deliveries for stores. His daddy and I finally agreed. As would be expected, he had several spills until he learned his and the scooter's limitations for going around corners.

I wasn't happy about it because I remembered the two or three times I had to get Son to Dr. Michener's office in Okmulgee when he needed stitches on his head from turning corners too fast in his little red wagon when he was six years old. I prayed.

My Russ taught Son about running the service station. Although he didn't have a driver's license, he could drive any kind of car around on the driveway and onto the ramp of the old-fashioned grease rack. One day when I was at the station, he backed a car up on the ramp just to show off. He said it was because the other end of the grease rack was too dirty. Later, he lobbied his daddy to install an air-operated lift so they could work more efficiently, standing up, rather than having to squat or crawl around under a car to grease the suspension or change the oil.

Son had learned how to measure the gasoline tank levels in the underground tanks and call in phone orders for more gasoline and oil from a Tulsa distributor. He knew how to make monthly inventory and sales reports and how to do the banking. By now, the sign on the top of the station said *Russell Jones and Son*. His daddy bragged on him and told me, "Son can run the station as well as I can. Lots of the improvements we've made are his idea."

That gave me the idea for a California vacation to visit my

family. It had been eight years since we had seen them. I told my Russ, "Papa's sixty-nine, and Mama's sixty-three, and I haven't seen them in such a long time. You said Son can run the station as well as you can. Betty is seventeen, and Mary is close by and would be available for emergencies. Why don't we take a vacation and drive to see my family?"

Son was delighted to have the challenge of running the station by himself. It also gave him a chance to secretly experiment with some things he thought would be an improvement. When we got back home, Son was rewarded by my Russ allowing his changes to stand. There's nothing like the risk of added responsibility for children to grow more independent. It also serves as a test for parents to learn how to back off and place greater trust in their children.

Only a few weeks after our trip to California, Son was taken to the hospital after he collided with a car on his motor scooter. He was on his way to school and just two blocks from the house. Some firemen were on their way home and had stopped to let one of the men out at an intersection. Son thought they were waiting for him, so he went through the intersection at the same time the car driver decided to move forward again. Another six inches between them would have avoided the accident.

Son's right leg struck the car bumper. Neither of them could have been moving at a high speed because the car was barely out in the intersection, and the motor scooter was only a few feet in front of the car. There was only a small dent in the motor cover on the motor scooter. A neighbor girl who lived across the street from our house was on her way to school and ran home to tell me how she had seen Son fly through the air and land on his back.

When I got there, the ambulance had already been called even though the accident was only a block from the hospital. A man who had been walking on the sidewalk when the accident happened was holding Son's head, and a fireman was holding his leg in place. They said it looked like both bones were broken, and the bleeding hinted that the broken bones had broken through the skin. They couldn't tell for sure because the legs of Son's new blue jeans were very tight.

> There was a man I didn't know.
>
> He held Son's head and would not go.
>
> Our Son had been hit by a car
>
> Around the corner, not very far.
>
> Son was on his way to school.
>
> I did not call the driver a fool.
>
> I didn't know who was to blame.
>
> Our Son was young and full of flame.
>
> There was a man just passing by
>
> And saw our Son sail through the sky.
>
> Our Son was hurt so very bad,
>
> The first bad wreck we'd ever had.
>
> This man stopped to lend a hand.
>
> I thanked my God there was a man.

Son was in no pain because of the shock. He didn't complain until, in the emergency room, a nurse took a pair of scissors to cut the right leg of his new blue jeans from bottom to top to limit further injury to his leg. Both bones below the knee were severed, and the lower half of each was protruding through the flesh.

Dr. Maben said the break was far too severe and suggested Son be transported to the bone specialists at McBride Clinic in Oklahoma City. That night, our preacher, Ted McElroy, rode in the ambulance with Son while my Russ and I followed in our car.

After surgery, Son's entire right leg was encased in a plaster cast that held his leg straight. For the first month, Son used crutches and didn't go to school. A month later, we returned to

Oklahoma City to see if the wound was healing. The cast was replaced with a walking cast so Son could return to school.

At the end of the second month, we returned to Oklahoma City, and two windows were cut in the cast where the bone had pierced the flesh to be sure those open wounds had healed. At the end of the third month, the cast was ready to be removed. However, just a few days before we were to go to Oklahoma City for the last time, Son had an appendicitis attack, and Dr. Maben had to perform an operation that would delay the cast removal for two more weeks.

During the month Son had to stay at home from school, he asked Betty to go to his teachers and get enough assignments for each week. Son actually raised his algebra grade during this month at home. He had to have extra tutoring from his teachers and school friends to meet the English requirements before the end of the school year.

His greatest joy after he returned to school was to have Betty carry his books from class to class for him. He liked to brag to the other boys that a beautiful, older, upper-class girl would do this for him.

None of them would believe they were brother and sister. She was dark-skinned with black hair, and he was fair-skinned with very blond hair. This little game didn't last too long before it was obvious that, with the walking cast, he didn't need his crutches.

With the walking cast, he was back at the station, doing everything except checking air pressure in tires. Because of the stiff cast, he couldn't bend his right knee the three months he wore it.

It was hard for any of us, except Son, to imagine how he was going to get to and from school. He had a solution. He talked his daddy into letting him show how he could drive our 1937 Chevy sedan with only one leg.

This was before cars had automatic transmissions. But they

still had a manual choke and manual engine throttle on the dashboard. The gearshift lever was mounted in the floorboard.

Son demonstrated how he could stick his right leg over into the floorboard behind the shifter lever. Then, using his left foot for both clutch and brake, he used the throttle on the dashboard to control the engine speed. When he needed to brake, he put the gear shifter in neutral and braked to a stop without killing the engine.

His daddy was impressed even though he would have to ride the motor scooter to and from work for four months. Well, well. They didn't let me in on the negotiations. Betty voted in favor of this arrangement because she wouldn't have to walk to school.

After his damaged leg was sufficiently healed, Son rode the motor scooter another year without having another wreck.

I found another reason to be glad we moved to Okmulgee when Son had an appendicitis attack. Dr. Maben diagnosed it quickly and got him directly into the Okmulgee hospital. I had to wonder what would have happened if we had still lived in Preston, or even worse, if we lived on a country farm in Lenna. My dreams of the old home place were growing dimmer and dimmer.

Our first grandchild—the first of ten—was born in August 1947 to Mary and LaMoine in Okmulgee. First grandchildren are so very special. Since this granddaughter was born in Okmulgee, we bonded closely. I practiced being a grandmother on Barbara, and she became the main character of many poems.

I openly complained about it when Mary and LaMoine moved to Cushing, Oklahoma, taking Barbara away. I certainly think grandparents should have some legal rights. Surely moving away with a grandchild is against the Constitution. It certainly didn't help my constitution. LaMoine was transferred from Okmulgee to Cushing to be trained as a Safeway grocery store manager. Year by year, LaMoine became a very successful businessman.

The following year, they moved to Stillwater so LaMoine could attend Oklahoma A&M College under the GI Bill. While there, he went into partnership with another young man to build GI and FHA houses, which were much in demand for the returning World War II veterans. They were so successful, they quit school and built houses full-time.

✝

I was one of the few mothers I knew who was overjoyed when her son started driving a car. When Son turned sixteen, he sold his motor scooter and bought a 1932 Pontiac coupe, which was born the same year he was.

In 1949, a year before his graduation from high school, Son was at it again. I tried to use my imagination to list all the prayers I could think of for a seventeen-year-old boy who probably drove his car too fast and was tempted to try many new things. I hadn't thought of putting airplane flying on my list. Son had a friend named Jimmy Boss. They played with each other when we lived in Preston. Jimmy's family had moved to Okmulgee also. Jimmy was one year older than Son and had a job at a private airfield in Okmulgee.

Part of Jimmy's pay was a few hours of free flying time. He had his flying license and wanted to get some time in as an instructor. Son got several hours of flying time in before I got wind of it.

I found out so easily because he hadn't been sneaking around to keep me from finding out. I asked him, "Why didn't you ask for my or your daddy's permission before you started flying?"

His simple answer was, "I didn't think I needed to. The only difference in flying and driving a car is that you have to be six-teen to get a license to drive a car, but you can learn to start flying at any age, without a license."

I found all of this was the truth. I also found another truth. I found Son loved me more than flying. As soon as I asked him to stop, he stopped. I was smart enough to add this to my prayer list because I doubted if I'd heard the end of it. Sure enough! Before he graduated from high school in 1951, he tried to get a college scholarship by enlisting in the Naval Air Force. They turned him down because he had too much overbite. They said that could affect his hearing. Almost ashamed, I prayed, *Thank you, Lord, for our Son's health defect!*

In 1950, Betty married Buck Berry. Buck had already gradu-ated from Okmulgee High School two years before Betty. He worked for a loan company in Tulsa, so Betty transferred to the phone company there. They both worked near downtown and could walk to work together.

I still remember the night they got married. It was the day before her daddy's birthday. Our hearts felt almost as empty as the closet in Betty's room after she had taken all her earthly treasures and moved away. We prayed that their lives together would bloom, and they did.

Betty told me in a phone conversation one evening, "This morning we had a spat, and we walked to work on opposite sides of the street."

That same year, Son graduated from Okmulgee High School and started college at the Oklahoma A&M Technical School in Okmulgee. The school buildings were a military hospital during World War II and were now primarily used for college and tech-nical training for the veterans. It was good because Son could still work at the station and live at home, which pleased me.

He had smaller classes than he would have in Stillwater, and having some war veterans in his classes gave him some mature help he wouldn't have had otherwise. He also got more personal instruction than he would at the much larger campus in Stillwater. I knew the day would come when Son must finish his last two years in Stillwater. I could sense another transition taking place when, soon, all of our children would be married and more grandchildren would be coming into the story of our lives.

At first, Son complained that the competition in the classes was much too stiff because many of the students were men going to school on the GI Bill who had been pilots and bombardiers or women who had been nurses. Most of them were married with children, and they were more serious about their studies than the kids just out of high school. As it turned out, it worked to the younger students' benefit because the older ones helped the younger ones. The math instructor, J.B. Willis, wasn't married and even let them come to his house on certain evenings to help them with their homework.

Near the end of 1952, Son moved to Stillwater. As he drove away, I cried like I would never see him again, although he would be back the following weekend. Only a mother can understand how I felt when the last little bird flew out of the nest.

Also in 1950, Gaines was born to Mary and LaMoine while they were living in Stillwater. They moved back to Okmulgee because, being in the inactive infantry reserves, LaMoine was concerned that he would be called up because of the Korean conflict. He bought a small neighborhood grocery store just a few blocks from our house in one direction and just a few blocks from their house in the other direction. If he was called into active duty, he wanted to have a small business that Mary could run until he was no longer needed or in case something happened to him.

He had a strong sense of responsibility for his growing family. As it turned out, the active reserve was called up, and LaMoine received a discharge. It wouldn't be many years before he owned the biggest grocery store in town. Still later, he would sell his grocery business and open several furniture stores. Every year, he became a more skilled businessman.

I got aggravated at LaMoine when I learned he was investing in the stock market. I felt it was a form of gambling. When Son heard me complain about it, he tried to explain it was a good thing to do because it rewarded investors for using their profits or earnings from wages to provide jobs for other people. Well, I still didn't like it. We kept our retirement money in savings accounts and government bonds, and that didn't feel like gambling.

In 1951, first-class postage was increased 50 percent from two cents to three cents. Mail was delivered twice each day. After telephone service came to every household, and to reduce postage costs, mail delivery was eventually cut to once each day. It was just another transition forced upon me in my comfortable city life.

One really special element in my transition took place one Saturday night in April when Son had his first date with Jerry Ann. Son brought Jerry Ann to the house to wait for Johnny Reynolds and his date to pick them up to go to the stock car races in Tulsa. Baby Gaines was there. Son picked him up and was holding him until Jerry Ann insisted that she have her turn. They weren't there very long, but I saw all I needed to see. She was wearing a white blouse and a gathered skirt.

I watched as she walked from the house to the car.

Her sash, tied in the back, was hanging down just so far.

I thought, *How dainty, how tiny, how trim.*

I felt in my heart God made her for him.

Some may say, "About life you never know."

But God lit a spark and told me so.

Son didn't start dating girls until late in the eleventh grade. He was too busy with cars, the station, and studying. Son never did appreciate my help when I suggested girls he should date. I finally realized that my suggestions guaranteed the girl wouldn't be asked. The next day after he dated Jerry Ann, I knew I was taking a big risk by saying, "She's the one."

Jerry Ann's parents, Jo and Will Forister, moved to Pauls Valley before Son and Jerry Ann started dating. Jerry Ann's daddy was a pipeline welder for the Sinclair Oil Company. When he transferred there from Okmulgee they arranged for Jerry Ann to stay with an elderly church lady until the end of the school year in May.

By this time Son had traded up to a 1947 Pontiac sedan. Son's daddy didn't want to let Jerry Ann get away, so during the summer and the year Jerry Ann was a freshman at Oklahoma University, it wasn't unusual on Saturday afternoons for Son's daddy to fill Son's car with gasoline and say, "Don't you think you should go see that girl?" My Russ kept a photograph of Jerry Ann under the glass cover of the office desk at the service station. Over the next two years Son wore this car out by going to see Jerry Ann most weekends.

Mr. and Mrs. Forister were very gracious and hospitable. After only a few visits by Son, Mr. Forister said to Jerry Ann's mother, "I think these kids are serious." After her first year at college, Jerry Ann got a job in Muskogee with Oklahoma Natural Gas Company working as a clerk. She knew, with a future husband in college for three more years, she would need to earn some money to prepare for that day. Mrs. Forister heard them talking about the money and how they would forego an engagement ring.

This was too much for Mrs. Forister. It was the only time she meddled with Jerry Ann and Son's marriage. She wrote to Son, telling him how much an engagement ring meant to brides. Son wasn't too happy with this interference but took Mrs. Forister's advice. Afterward, he was very glad he did when he saw how much the diamond solitaire pleased Jerry Ann that he had broken their agreement. Son had less than one hundred dollars in his checking account after this purchase. It was time for him to pay his tuition and buy books for his first semester in Stillwater and pay his room and board at the dormitory. Fortunately, he already had a part-time job with the Ford dealership in Stillwater at seventy-five cents an hour. He got by without asking for help. That's the way he was.

In 1952, Betty and Buck's Claudia was born in Tulsa, and in 1953, their Cindy was born there too. Also in 1953, Son and Jerry Ann were married in February and moved into a small duplex in Stillwater, within walking distance from the campus. Jerry Ann went to work as a secretary at a bank. Son kept working at the Ford dealership. Son did the clothes washing and dried them on a clothesline in the backyard of the duplex. Besides cooking supper, Jerry Ann decided her main evening job was to interrupt Son while he studied.

There was one particular behavior where Son fell short as a husband. He hadn't been taught that he should every once in a while take his wife out to dinner in the evening. She had been hinting for several days that it would be nice to go out for a hamburger some evening. It took only one good kicking in the shins one night, as Jerry Ann was reluctantly cooking supper, for her to teach him this important lesson. One of Son's favorite future stories was that, after that lesson, all through their marriage, as he came into the house after each day's work, his salutation was, "Would you like to go out to eat tonight?" I had sympathy for Jerry Ann because he would say this even though he could smell the food cooking.

I prayed a mother's prayer for our three children and their mates: *Lord, we taught our children faith so they will trust in thee. We held their hands to cross the street, but now we need you to guide them. Lord, we've taught them to be brave and not cry from every little hurt. With tenderness and a pat or two, we send them back to play. Today, they need your courage as a shield against the deeper pains. We told them your world is beautiful, that their Maker is everywhere. We've planted your words on their lips so their hearts can be full of song, for we know that only in thee, dear Lord, can they grow big and strong.*

The day of my forty-seventh birthday in 1953, I moped around, thinking of my parents and their aging. Papa would be seventy-six years old in April. My Russ asked, "What do you have on your mind?"

I answered, "Oh, I'm sad to see my parents growing old. Every time I make a trip back to California to see them, I have the fear I might never see them again."

I could see he was thinking what he might do to perk me up. Even though the old home place was fallen down, going back always brought me out of my dark melancholy.

"For your birthday present, why don't we catch a pretty day and go walk around your old home place? The station boys will be out of school for spring break, and we can take all day."

The day we went, we got there early. I impatiently waited for the dawn, before the birds had fully roused to the strong, high, joyful chant of morning song and before the white smoky fog had lifted lazily from the ground. My mind drifted back to our youthful days in Lenna, where I had loved farm living so much.

The little unpainted, tumbling-down house had been empty for years, standing there all alone. To me, it wasn't a forgotten house. In the house were some pictures my brother Troy had put there and forgotten to come back and get. One picture was of Mama and Papa and my grandparents. Another was of my great uncle. I tenderly gathered them and took them home with me.

Flowers still came up randomly around the house, not in the pattern in which Mama's hands had planted them. It was sad to see, and yet it was a beautiful sight to my eyes. I thought, *I can see flowers my mother's hands planted, spreading into the woods, without human eyes to see them and notice whether they are doing well or not.* Then I noticed the pear tree and the backyard gate where my Russ and I had held each other close as young lovers. The pear tree was full of blossoms.

I saw a pair of doves glide down from the deep shadows of the woods. They wheeled about in the sunlit clearing as if to welcome me home. I reached out my hands to them as if to say, "You don't look like wild doves to me. Why don't you fly to my house and live with me in the big city?"

The woodlands were still very much alive because I could hear them breathing. I sensed I could hear in the faraway distance a tremendous haunting rhythm that I carried home with me in my mind. My birthday gift was to relive days gone by.

I said to my Russ, "I wish I could wake up every morning with a million different kinds of birds announcing the coming dawn. Thank you for this birthday gift. It's like a tonic for my soul."

His response was, "Now I think we should go see how much of your nature trail we can find and write another poem about it. We're still young lovers at forty-seven and forty-eight. We're all alone and can do just as we please. You start the first verse like we did the last time we were here."

My Russ and I walked hand in hand.

"Good start, Pearlie! I've got the next line."

In what seems to be a nobody land.

"That's very creative, Russ. The next verse is mine."

We saw where fire had left its mark,
Upon the trees burned very dark.

"That's easy to see, isn't it? Your turn, Russ."

Let's follow the path down to the spring,
Where you listened to the little birds sing.

"You're getting to know me too well."

The old log where we sat before,

"I loved to sit there with your arms around me."

Has crumbled, almost there no more.

"How about, 'My Pearlie can't sit there anymore.'"

The big oak tree still stands tall and bold.

"That's where you carved your name."

For autumn leaves of red and gold.

"That's where you carved my legal name."

We spent the whole day at my old home place. We sat on the old rock horse trough Papa made as we ate our picnic lunch. What a fine, generous man God gave me.

> You're my love forever, my love for all enduring time.
> Just like the bees abuzzin' on a honeysuckle vine.

Please don't ever leave me. The parting would be too blue.

It's not living, my darling, if I'm not close to you.

My love for you is higher than any shining star.

As colorful as the rainbow that glows both near and far,

As passionate as the lightning that strikes in you and me,

And it will keep on striking throughout eternity.

In 1954, Son graduated from college. He and Jerry Ann moved to Tulsa, where he worked as an engineer, designing draw-works for oil well drilling rigs. Jerry worked as a clerk for a company that drilled oil wells. They lived in an apartment for a short time before buying their first house. It was handy having them in the very same town as Betty and Buck.

It was before air conditioning was common in apartments and residences, so Son rigged up a homemade evaporative cooler for their bedroom window. We still had a large attic fan to draw air through the windows. It wouldn't be so very long before my Russ installed window air conditioning. It was amazing. I quickly adjusted to the comfort of a closed-in house on those hot, Oklahoma summer days.

I had more time on my hands now that our children were out of the house. I had a creative urge to do something in addition to my flower gardens and poems. My Russ had built a storm cellar just outside our back door. Its flat roof was our patio. The cellar was cool in the summertime and made a perfect studio for me to make many ceramic figurines that I bought and painted and glazed.

The figurines were mostly small dancing girls, girls dressed in old-fashioned dresses with their beaus in similar fancy clothes, animals, and birds that could be arranged on tables or shelves. Some of these figurines with flat backs, like fish and flowers, could be hung on a wall. The store where I bought the figures had a gas-fired kiln to finish them after I had painted and glazed them. I gave them as gifts to friends and family, the same way I gave away my poems.

I took orders when asked. The bathroom in Jerry Ann's new house had pink bathroom fixtures, and the tile was pink and black. Her kitchen table and chairs were combinations of pink and black. She ordered some black fish for the pink bathroom wall. I wrote a card to her that I would like to make white fish trimmed in gold. I received the following two-cent postcard.

To Pearl's Ceramic Shop:

Dear Madam Pearl,

This is to inform you that I have received your letter of the third of January in which you advise that you prefer to make white fish for the order that I placed with you rather than the black color which I prefer. While I appreciate that your experience probably tells you that white would be prettier, I must refer you to your original order from me in which I clearly specified these sea-going pretties are to be painted black. Due to the present color of our powder room, which is a pale pink, white will not, in my opinion, be suitable. Therefore, please color the fish as originally requested.

Yours very truly,

Smarty

Customers can be such a great trial to an artist. I answered Miss Smarty, alias Jerry Ann:

Some women change their mind every night and day.

There are some who won't. They only want their way.

This certain woman I'm speaking of is a woman indeed.
She wouldn't change her mind, even if I were to plead.
So a black fish she shall have upon her bathroom wall.
Since I can't change her mind, there is no need to stall.
Those fish of blackest black, real dead they're gonna look.
Harrumph! I never saw black fish caught upon my hook.
Of course, I've never seen white fish trimmed in gold.
So, just to get along, I'll do what I've been told.
I love that stubborn woman, so black fish they shall be.
So every time she looks at them, I hope she'll think of me.

Jerry Ann sent me a thank you gift: blue earrings and a dress pin.

Thank you for the lovely gift. You are so sweet and fine.
I wore it on my pink lace dress. Oh, how it did shine.
I wore my new pink hat, the one with the pinkish rose.
I wore a smile in my heart to match my turned-up nose.

During July and August of 1955, our grandchildren total more than doubled from three to seven. Mary had Johnny, Betty had Scott and Skyline, and Jerry Ann had Anne Russelle.

Wow! The twins plus Claudia and Cindy meant Betty and Buck had four children who were under three years old! It seemed Betty's beautiful black hair turned to a stylish, striking white overnight. I was sure her busy days seemed much longer to her.

It was about this time that my Russ began calling me Mother, and I started calling him Daddy when we were at home or around our children. I don't know exactly how it happened. It just seemed natural since that was what our children called us. We wore these names like a title for our most important job.

There's no profession on God's good earth more powerful than a mother or a force more powerful than a mother's prayer. Mothers can't be considered amateurs because they are so handsomely paid.

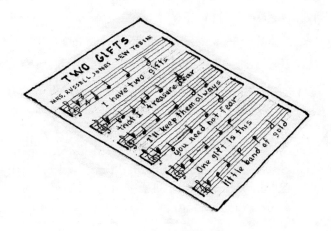

Some of My Most Prolific Poetry Years

1956 through 1962

During this period of my life, I sought to get some of my songs and poems published without any luck. Once I had a poem published in the national magazine *Ideals*, the Easter edition. It was titled "The Night He Was Betrayed."

> Remember the prayer of Jesus the night he was betrayed?
>
> He poured out his soul to God, not because he was afraid.
>
> His heart was heavy-laden, bowed down with deep despair.
>
> His eyes were filled with tears, but no one seemed to care.
>
> Then he heard the angry mob. He saw the torches glare.

Judas betrayed him with a kiss, as he was standing there.

Pilate found no fault in him. But the multitude loudly cried,

"We don't believe he is the Christ. Let him be crucified."

They put on him a scarlet robe and plaited thorns on his head.

They mocked, but he said nothing, as to Calvary he was led.

I eventually gave up on this dream to be recognized by a publisher. However, my soul demanded that I write. I settled for the small audience of family and friends and my Creator, who gave me inspirational thoughts with which I could entertain myself.

I had many poems published in our church's small weekly newsletter. My first one was in January of 1955. I called it "A Soliloquy on Snow." I liked the dignified word *soliloquy* because it gave me license to be transparent and talk to others through my poetry as if I were talking to myself.

When I look out at the snow, so peaceful and so calm,

It seems that heaven has sent me a peaceful, cooling balm.

I seem to hear my Master say, "I'm here for you to know.

I want you to be pure like me, as white as nature's snow."

It seems faith grows stronger as we labor here and wait,

To see that pure, white city as we enter heaven's gate.

May our souls be crystal clear and as pure as falling snow,

And the Lord says we will have his
peace when it's time for us to go.

I felt most prolific when a poem came to my mind about my Russ. My, how I loved that gentle man (in between the few times I was aggravated with him). Here are a few of the good things I had to say about him before I tell about things that aggravated me.

He knew how much I loved nature, so it wasn't unusual for him to call me from the station to tell me to go out and look at a sunrise or a winter sunset. In the cold months on each side of December, it was normal for him to go to work before sunrise and return home after sunset.

Coming home, he drove west up Main Street. One dark evening, as he came into the house, he called from the front door, "Mother, did you see that beautiful sunset that was happening as I was driving home?"

"No. I missed it because I was cooking our supper. Describe it to me as I set the table."

After supper, I sat down to write while my Russ was taking his bath and even before I washed the dishes.

No, I didn't see the sunset. It was heavenly, I know.

The colorful way you described it, I almost saw it, though.

"Flying clouds as soft as pillows were not a glowing red.

They were painted brightest silver"; this is what you said.

There'll be another sunset. You must phone me then.

For the beauty of a sunset will be our nearest kin.

No, I didn't see the sunset hide behind the silver cloud.

Just a little bit of heaven—I would have been so proud.

On his fiftieth birthday, I wrote one of many love poems that I often wrote for his birthdays, as well as for each anniversary, and for almost any casual reason in between.

There's beauty in the forest. The trees are tall and green.

There's beauty in a meadow. Wildflowers can be seen.

There's beauty in the sunlight. The sky is blue above.

There's beauty in the home when it's lighted by your love.

As a token of my love for you,

May I write what I know is true?

If I could only write one line,

It would be, "I'm proud you're mine."

Your views of life are of great worth.

They mean more to me than all the earth.

Let the stars peep from up above,

And tell the moon we're still in love.

Do you see now what you mean to me,

Why you're the sugar in my tea?

You're why I'm still in love.

I really appreciated my Russ as I began having health problems that required many visits to doctors in town and specialists in Tulsa. Some visits resulted in expensive operations. But he never hinted about any concerns about the mounting expenses. I could tell when he was worrying about me because he would get quiet and melancholy. Then, after a short time, he would snap out of it and say positive and encouraging things about my health. This was when I knew he had gotten consolation from his prayers.

On one particular trip to a doctor in Tulsa, the news wasn't very good, and we were both in a contemplative mood. Betty and Buck and Son and Jerry Ann were all living in Tulsa at that time.

Fortunately, the Lord had provided that we would visit Betty and her little children on the way home to give us something to laugh and be happy about.

The bright sun was setting as we drove south from Tulsa to Okmulgee. My Russ was quiet, and so was I. That's to be expected when you leave a doctor's office without answers to the questions about what it will take to resolve a problem that has persisted for several months. Too often, I didn't get significant relief from other remedies, forcing me to turn to surgery.

It was another time when our faith was being tested. We weren't so much into asking for a miracle from God. We were primarily asking for strength to accept the reality of the Creator's natural risks. My Russ escaped into a contemplative vein, and I escaped into my own world of the poetic confidence of hope. I sat in the passenger seat looking toward the western sky, mentally writing the lines with care to see if there was a supernatural message in its setting.

I watched the sun sink peaceful and westward bound.

The sun was going down. Darkness gathered all around.

As the nighttime shadows made their repose,

With the shades of night drawn to a close,

Far beyond the purple, radiant glow,

The sun is shining bright. We know.

As we see it sink, we'll see it rise

When morning sweeps the eastern skies.

It makes no difference if it's night or day;

The sun keeps shining all the way.

By that time, we had reached Preston, and I asked my Russ to turn off and drive around the school past our old Preston house. I quickly reviewed God's providence over those ten years since we had moved to Okmulgee, and within the next seven miles, I finished the poem.

So this is how my mind did roam,

As we drove from Tulsa to our home.

I turned toward my Russ with a smile of cheer,

"Thank God my dear husband is so near."

The next day, after a good night's sleep, I realized the value of living only one day at a time. I knew it was possible that I had an illness from which I might die. But I told myself, *You've already had more happiness than one life or any wife could expect.*

My Russ left for work that day without even saying, "Time to go," so I knew my job for the day was another love poem to make light of my supposed health problems.

> If I could use the clouds to write across the sky so blue,
>
> The thing my pen would write is how much I love you.
>
> If I had the gift of David and could play a tune or two,
>
> The only tune I would play is how much I do love you.
>
> I really can't put it into words. There is no need to try.
>
> But one thing I can say for sure: I'll love you 'til I die.

When I read it to him, the last line caught him by surprise, and he didn't know how to take it until he saw the devilish look on my face.

His response was, "If you're trying to make a joke, it's not very funny."

I replied, "Why waste another day worrying about something that will probably turn out fine?"

I was rewarded with a little grin and a long, tender hug in his lap.

I did have the first of several operations. In the long run, I realized my health problems were more difficult for my family and friends than they were for me. I tried to treat each operation and trip to the doctor with as much good humor as possible.

> Getting ready for operations is like
> getting ready for a dance;

You dress just right, as if you might
not get another chance.

The nurse gave me a too-short
gown, tied with a little bow,

Then said, in a bossy voice, "Your
false teeth have got to go."

I refused, so we chewed that rag for quite a spell.

I argued, "Without my teeth, I don't look too swell."

She had no time to mess with me,

So to the doctor she went to see.

The doctor said, "She's very proud, so let's just take it slow.

But I'm just as proud, so she must
learn they've really got to go."

With a sleeping pill in his calm way,

He stole my teeth that very day.

Three days later, things came to light.

I found out then who won the fight.

I've told this story so you can learn,

When, for your dance, it comes your turn.

Grit your teeth 'til your face turns blue,

Or I predict they'll take your teeth too.

During those three days they kept me doped up to kill the pain. As it turned out, I didn't need my false teeth after all. It was a waste of time for anyone to come from Okmulgee to Tulsa to see me during that time. Of course, my Russ and Mary did. They told me about my lack of hospitality during their boring visit with smart-aleck comments like, "Why, Mother! The reason we brought you to the hospital was to get your hospitality fixed."

I returned, "Well! Please accept my apologies."

You came to Tulsa to see me. The way I acted was a sin!

Sleeping with my mouth open wide and didn't ask you in?

I'm sure you will forgive me. Don't make so big a deal.

I said to them, "I sure do hurt." They gave me a little pill.

The next time I'll do better when you decide to call.

If they offer me some little pills, I just won't take them all.

To visit me in Tulsa was almost a full day's job, so I got a lot of cards. I asked Mary to put my thank-you note on the church bulletin board.

Here's a big thank you for the pleasure your cards bring.

Amid my aches and pains, each was not a little thing.

The shots the nurses gave didn't bring one smile of cheer.

But every card and note tells me why you're all so dear.

Many cards I received, some serious and some so funny.

For me, both kinds of thoughts were exactly on the money.

So with these lines, I thank you, 'til you have time to call,

When I can say it to your face, I love you one and all.

Of course, I had to write a really special thank-you note to my wonderful, patient husband of over thirty-five years.

To the end of time, I'll love you.
To me, you've been so true.

I've never seen a single soul I could love as much as you.

Through all my aches and pains piled high,

I've never heard a single sigh,

Nor a grumble as you work each day,

As bill after bill with grace you pay.

I smile when you say, "Money doesn't measure wealth,

For in addition to God we each have our health.

We have love and children too. How
can we be much gladder?

We've more blessings than we've had
pains, so money doesn't matter."

✝

Now, here were some things about my Russ that aggravated me. I didn't say he was perfect. I said I loved him beyond reasonable proportion in comparison to some of his sorry ways.

Always picking and teasin'

Surely there must be a reason

To stir me up and make me mad

When you could easily make me glad.

If I act aggravated, like maybe I would cry,

Why do you tease me so? Tell me the reason why.

I'm 'tween a rock and hard place, bewildered and so blue.

Ah, what the heck. Here's my secret. I like to tease you too.

To get my way, I had to understand him and manipulate him. I didn't always get my way, and that was even more aggravating. My mister had some big problems that I constantly either had to change or learn to live with. He tended to pout when things at home, work, or church weren't going the way he wanted them to.

One time he pouted over a man who moved in across the back alley from our house. This man saw me working in my yard and flower beds. If I was trying to lift too large a load, he would offer to help, and I would accept. His name was Rufus. I told my

Russ about this for two reasons. First, just so he wouldn't hear it from some other neighbor or from Rufus himself. Second, I wanted him to feel just a little guilty for not doing more of the yard work. After all, he only worked over ten hours each day, six days each week. My Russ would pout a little each time I told him that Rufus had helped me, even though he knew he could trust me completely.

One summer afternoon, I washed bed sheets and hung them on the clotheslines in our backyard. The clotheslines were sagging and needed to be tightened. My plan was to leave the sheets on the lines to encourage my Russ to tighten the clotheslines while I fried chicken for supper.

When he drove the car into the garage, I had just finished wringing the chicken's neck and was holding it by its legs with its naked, bloody neck in full view. He couldn't miss the fact that I was preparing his favorite meal for supper. I said in my most charming tone, "I sure would appreciate it if you would tighten the clothesline wires."

I suppose I had already decided he might say he was awful tired or some other familiar excuse.

I didn't know if he was teasing, joking, or pouting. So when he responded, "Ah, just let Rufus do it," I snapped.

Holding the chicken by its legs, I whacked him on the back of his head and shoulders several times with the bloody end. When I got through with this angry display, I had not only covered his head and shirt with blood but had speckled the clean, white sheets with my crimson wrath.

Both of us were so astounded we just stood there speechless for several seconds.

My Russ was the first to speak. "As soon as I wash up and change clothes, I'll tighten your clothesline for you while you cook supper."

All I could think to say was, "Don't hurry because I've got to rewash these sheets before I can start cooking."

It was a very quiet supper and evening. I sat at the kitchen table that evening after washing the dishes, trying to decide my next step. My Russ was in the next room acting like he was reading. We always made it a policy never to go to bed angry with each other. I think better with pencil and paper.

I know there are none so deaf as those who will not hear.

You must give me an answer now. I need your voice, my dear.

Or tomorrow you might forget and turn your back on me.

If you go, I'll love you still. My heart would go with thee.

If up to now, you won't forgive or even forget somehow.

I wonder about my life and how lonely I feel right now.

If we don't forgive each other for things we say or do,

I'd search for my other half and always look for you.

I'll love you forever if you forgive me or not.

But I know you will forgive, and that means a lot.

I'm ready to make up with you. I hope you will agree.

Tomorrow, we must forget tonight and let be what will be.

I handed this poem to my Russ and went in another room to get ready for bed. When I returned, he swept me into his lap, and I could tell the curtains were closed on that little drama. We made up that night!

It was a few days before we were able to laugh about it with each other. Fortunately, Rufus didn't live across the alley very long.

Another aggravating thing about my Russ was his habit, and finely developed ability, to turn a deaf ear to things I really wanted him to hear and respond to. My church friend Rosey Haworth had the same problem with her husband. We had a conversation about that. Then I wrote a poem to try to make sense out of this strange illness that has crippled most husbands.

I gathered a few thoughts together—
in fact, all I could find—

To understand an illness that attacks my husband's mind.

It seems for my best thoughts, he turns on his deaf ear.

Even with my outside voice, my Russ just doesn't hear.

Like when watching TV, leaned back in his sleeping chair,

In a moment, there's silence. He doesn't know he's there.

But if I turn off his program, he wakes up mighty fast.

What's expected of a wife? How long can patience last?

Then in the middle of the night, his snoring rest is deep.

If I could turn on my deaf ear, I could get some sleep.

Why, with this old deaf ear, were our husbands born?

Must wives with gentle words be treated with such scorn?

We know the answer when they hold us in their arms.

We can get their attention with our many other charms.

I must admit I used my charm, humor, and wit very regularly to get my way. It was as if I had this imaginary key ring with various kinds of keys that I used to open magic treasure boxes when I wanted something from my dear Russ really bad.

Sometimes I had to use stealthy means to get important things accomplished. When I decided my Russ needed a new suit, he kept putting me off. At this time, LaMoine owned a large grocery store, where I bought our groceries. I arranged with LaMoine to overcharge me three dollars each week when I bought groceries. I would squirrel away this amount each week until I had enough for the suit I had picked out.

I gave the new suit to my Russ as he was dressing for church one Sunday morning. We were a little late, and I told him we didn't have time for him to ask questions about it.

Oh! He looked handsome in his new suit with the new tie I also filched out of the grocery money. He got so many compliments from the ladies at church that he never asked where I got the money.

Smart man! I hated to lie to him to avoid revealing my source of funds, but I would have. I learned a trick Jerry Ann used on Son. She told me on one of our visits, "I never lie to your son without a good reason."

As hard as I tried to improve my Russ, I had to confess to him that I really didn't want him to change too much. After I realized I couldn't change him, I realized I also couldn't change myself if he wanted to remake me. Still, at fifty-five years old, I knew we had the love of all loves.

There were things about my Russ that I called aggravations that did nothing to diminish our love affair, which society calls a marriage.

In 1961, on our thirty-sixth wedding anniversary, I composed my annual poem to him, plus several others.

From January to December, will you love me a lot?

Will you love me if I'm pretty? Will you love me if I'm not?

I'll try to give you courage so you will bolder grow.

And if you're feeling gloomy, I'll be the first to know.

From January to December, to make our days more bright,

And to make each day different, I'll try with all my might.

I want to keep your love shining as brightly as the sun.

Then I'll whisper to myself, "I am the lucky one!"

My life's a path of sunshine. The whispering shadows say,

"You were the lucky one when you stole his heart away."

I wanted you for myself alone. You meant the world to me.

I looked into your heart. Only happiness could I see.

It's never been necessary for me to write a book.

I remember every word you say and just the way you look.

I'm not the very best of thieves, and I need help each day.

So I'm glad you understood when I stole your heart away.

✝

A week before my fifty-first birthday, I went by train to California to do my part by helping Mama take care of Papa. I stayed there for two months until it seemed he was getting better.

I missed my Russ as much as a rose would miss the dew. Before I left, I left several poems for him to find at various times. I pinned one on his chair in the living room. I hid another in his Sunday shoes, one between the pages of his Bible, and several in various other places. It was my little way of reminding him of my love and that I was there with him.

He looked so very alone when the train pulled away from the railway station. I know he waved to me longer than I could see him, for my eyes were filled with tears. Knowing my Russ, I'm sure he was crying too. I would have cried more if I had known how long we would be away from each other. I made the expensive long-distance phone call to let him know I had arrived safely.

I knew he shouldn't get too lonesome while I was away because Mary, living in the same town, could have him over for supper. Son and Jerry Ann and Betty and Buck weren't far away in Tulsa. My brother Troy still lived not far from our old home place in Lenna.

I wondered why my Russ was slow about writing to me. Then I got an airmail letter the last week of March with two letters. He sent the first letter to the wrong box number, and it was returned to him. He addressed the second letter with only the route number in care of W.L. Logan.

By now, I had flagged down the postman several times and

asked him to keep his eye peeled for a letter from Oklahoma with my name on it.

The second letter from my Russ was written in green ink and was dated later than the other, which was written in blue ink. I read the most recent one first.

> Dear mother wondering how you are to day fine i hope i am cold and damp it has been raining all day Shure hope it continues for we need it how is mom and Dad Mother you know I ask you had you got my letter when i talked to you Sunday morning well i got it back to day i must have got the wrong Box Number on it i addressed it Rt 1 Box 1424 the address Mom had on her letter but guess they will all come back i wrote you Sunday and mailed it Sunday night Sent it air mail in care of WL Logan so you Should get it every one at home is OK but i Shure woud love to see you and have you home with me every one has been asking me when you was coming home i told then Soon i hope well mother will close and work some more So by for now and i love You Dad

The first letter was twice as long. I read both of his letters over and over.

> Dear Mother have just finished eatting dinner and i cant call you i will just write you I Shure do mis you hope you are feeling good hope Mom and Dad is Still feeling better Troy called me about a hour agoe to See if i had heard from you i told him you called and that Dad was quite a lot bet-ter i wrote the Tulsa kids to let them know you made the trip OK i Shure was glad to hear from you i think the trip was longer for me than it was for you Seamed like you was on the road so long guess i was just anxious to hear from you how is every one Else out there hope every one is fine i went by to eat Supper with Mary last night and Johnie he took me in his room and Shut the doore and he open the

dresser wher his clothes were and got his cap and coat and
wanted me to put them on him and take him out to play So
i did when Mary called us to Supper he dident want to go
in the house at all but eny way he come in the house with
me and Soon as Supper was over he took me to the doore
and wanted to play some moore but it was dark So he had
to Stay in he is quite a little guy we had a dust Storm blow
in from Mexico last knight the dust was So thick an the
ground this morning you could See the tracks of car gow-
ing down the Street the Sky has been full of Dust all Day
now don't say eny thing i have your house all closed up Ha
Ha i beat you to it it Shure is nice and warm here to day
Just like Spring i got a card from Jerry Ann i will Send it to
you So you can See Russelle is Still up to her old tricks well
Mother let me know how Mom and Dad gets along and
give your mama a big hug for me tell them i Shure wood
like to See them and you to hope this finds all feeling better
So by for now and i Shure do love you Russell

Papa passed away July 6, 1957, two months after I returned
to Okmulgee. Mama lived another five years. My family buried
him in the beautiful hills of California where he loved to stroll.
Papa and I were very close from the time I went hunting with
him as a child to the day I spent with him before returning to
Okmulgee.

I mentally sensed when he had passed on. I rushed to the
phone to call. Then I looked at the clock and decided to go
outside to the patio and wait a while. My first thought was a
desire to hold Mama in my arms and comfort her. It wasn't long
before my Russ came out, patted my hand, and said, "Mother,
your family called." I looked at him, big-eyed and afraid, even
though the Lord had already spoken to me.

I found comfort by allowing my mind to wander back to
the old home place where, in our loving Creator's natural world
on a farm, seeds must be buried before they can be resurrected
in the glory of their stalks of grain that are needed to sustain

human and animal life. The more I remembered, the less afraid and more confident I became.

My memories took me back to my childhood near the steep hillside where Papa and I walked together. I could see Old Limbo Creek, where I played hour after hour, where we learned to swim and dive off the oak tree limb. I saw the old boat we paddled up and down the crooked stream. I saw the orchard Papa tended so tenderly and the valley behind it. I recalled the bluebirds building their nests in the trees, the sandstone horse trough Papa made, and the deep well he dug where Mama lowered milk containers down in the well to keep the milk cool. God in heaven only knows how many times she raised and lowered the milk container.

†

It was Thanksgiving Day, a year and a half later, before I felt like going back to look at the old home place. It was a good thing I had mental pictures of what it looked like before my family moved away twenty years earlier. The weeds had grown so tall where the house once stood. I didn't think the dusty road in front of our farm had changed much with the passing of time, except dust clouds rose from behind the cars rather than from a horse-drawn buggy or farm wagon.

However, there was one thing that hadn't changed as I worked through my grief. The kinds of birds that I heard on this Thanksgiving Day visit were the same ones that sang to me in my Okmulgee backyard. In my mind, I drew pretty pictures of these childhood memories of the old home place.

I experienced the start of a second touch from God during those five years between Papa's and Mama's deaths. I learned again that human death is as natural as the song each bird has written. It's as natural as the dog's bark, the cat's meow, the hen's cackle, the rooster's crow, the crow's caw, the duck's quack, a geese's honk, and whatever it is the seagulls and squirrels do. Death comes as naturally as tears of both joy and grief.

It's natural for God to spiritually hold our hands or carry us as he walks through each day with us. It's as natural as it was for Papa to use those strong, muscular hands to lift me up to sit on his broad shoulders when, as a child, I went hunting and trapping with him for food and fur pelts.

In nature, I knew God as my friend and my Creator. I felt close to nature around a country farm and the things that grew there perennially, with the broad sowing of a farmer's hand or a young maiden's flower bed. I knew I was part of his nature because I was made from the dusty clay of the earth God modeled on the sixth day of creation, to which I would return when my physical self died.

I also knew I was as high as the glorious heavens God uses to model the glory of our resurrected bodies in the colorful blasts of a sunrise or sunset, with all the colors blended together, as in a rainbow that allows the colors to be their individual selves.

The touch of the Master's hand upon our eternal souls is as real as his sensual and natural touch upon our communion with him in earthly things we can see, hear, smell, taste, or touch.

I learned another very important thing in this chapter of my life. Through God's Word and his Holy Spirit, I can possess God's own righteousness the same as our father Abraham did. This truth reached out and grabbed me one day as I studied the Bible. God counted Abraham as "righteous" because he believed. I said to myself, *I can do that too!*

There is a window in my heart. It opens from inside.

Through it, I talk to my Lord and in his Word abide.

I open the window every day to
receive new spiritual power

To do good deeds to ones with needs each and every hour.

I'm glad my heavenly Father says in his book so true,

I have his own righteousness to share with each of you.

So I challenge each of my friends, if you will take a dare,

Open the window of your heart. The
window's name is prayer.

✝

By the end of 1962, all ten of our grandchildren had been born. At that time, our children ranged in ages from thirty to thirty-five. I was amazed at how wise and brilliant our children became. Like my sisters, they made fun of me for primping so much. Then they claimed I was inconsistent because I spent my grocery money on beauty products but wrote my poems on scraps of paper. Or they made fun of me because I washed and reused aluminum foil for cooking. I would try to explain it to them, but they're too smart to understand. So sometimes I wrote a poem to them on the worst scrap of paper I could find just to see what they would say.

One day, when Mary came by for a visit, she noticed a grocery list I had made on the back of the envelope of a letter from Mama. I was in the kitchen making a snack for us when I heard her laughing real big. I asked, "What's so funny?"

She replied, still laughing, "I'm reading your grocery list. Ha, ha! Does Daddy know you're sneaking around buying hair tint, nail polish, and perfume out of the grocery money?"

I grabbed the envelope out of her hand before she could see that I also had some birdseed on the list. I scolded her by saying, "You're entirely too nosy. And don't you say a word about this to your daddy because he likes me to look pretty just as much as he likes my cooking."

After lunch, as she was going to her car, she looked over her shoulder and, with another laugh in her voice, she asked, "Are you and LaMoine still padding your grocery list by giving you cash to buy clothes for Daddy? I think I'll stop by the station on my way home and tell Daddy about your money-laundering schemes."

There was a broom on the front porch. I grabbed it and made like I was going to beat her. We always had fun together.

As soon as Mary left, I rushed into the house to find the worst piece of scrap paper I could find and dashed off a poem to her and mailed it across town so she would get it the next day. I titled it, "My Children Laugh at Me."

My children often laugh at me, but it doesn't matter at all,

'Cause I had to be careful when they were growing tall.

Life taught me to save and not to waste the things we had.

Had I not learned soon enough, for them it would be bad.

I had to learn very early money doesn't grow on a tree.

I had to learn by working hard; few things in life are free.

I can't wait for that day when they take the saving path.

I'll sneak around in their kitchen and have my little laugh.

Jerry Ann was a recycler too. I noticed she reused aluminum foil and even table napkins. We got to talking about reusing such inexpensive things, and I told her about my children laughing at me. Jerry Ann gave me her merry laugh and beamed. "Well, Pearl, this just proves that we will always be soul mates."

During this phase of my life, which I called some of my most prolific poetry years, I did more and more communication with my children and my Lord and his creation than at any other time. My Russ and I talked daily about how blessed we were with our children and their faithful spouses, who we also considered to be our own children. This poem was published in 1961 in our church newsletter for other parents to consider.

Our children are gifts from God,
the richest blessings of all.

Don't try to mold them alone. If you do, they might fall.

Like flowers of beauty, like the weeds too fast, they grow.

Teach them to find our God, because they need him so.

God has only loaned them, a priceless gift to hold.

But this we must remember: God gave to each a soul.

It's true we make mistakes in judgment and in deed.

Since we truly love the Lord, he'll
help when we're in need.

Don't expect them to be perfect, for that's not an easy role.

Pray for them, and in his time, he'll watch over their souls.

A mother's prayer is the greatest protection a child has.

Bless the homes of our children, for
they are gifts from thee.

Watch over them day and night; from sin keep them free.

When storm clouds sweep around their humble home,

When their burdens are heavy, don't let them walk alone.

If in doubt they grow weak, give them more faith to pray.

Show them your peace to make storm clouds roll away.

Lead them by thy loving hand so they will never roam.

In thy calm and perfect way, please
bless their humble home.

Our children gave me plenty of quality attention all through
each year. Since we and Mary lived in the same town, we saw
much more of her and LaMoine than we did Betty and Buck or
Son and Jerry Ann. We ate together more often and knew much

more detail about each other's business, particularly the older we got. We were good friends too. I remember going to their house on my fifty-fourth birthday.

Thank you, Mary,

For the soft pink rosebud and the fresh-smelling perfume,

And the lovely dinner served in your dining room.

And loving thoughts in a card you sent my way today.

For mother and daughter, I won't have any other way.

Of course, I felt important. I'm sure that you could see.

Who has a better friend than you, who God gave to me?

My relationship with Betty Loyale had its own unique qualities. She was the little, brown baby I had asked God for the first time I saw my Russ's baby sister Lena Loyale as a baby. It was she who got me started on this story of my life by asking me to write about my life, my family, the old home place, and things she hadn't seen firsthand. Following her marriage to Buck, we were separated by distance in miles. Most of their married life was in Austin and Houston. However, we did spend enough time with them and their children to maintain that precious, close family feeling.

Thank you, Betty, for the lovely card, written in soft blue,

In four little words, you said, "Mother, God Bless You."

You are wishing many blessings will come along my way.

My darling, with you, he blesses me each day.

You say you ask every day God will keep me in his will.

If that isn't what he decides, of you I'll be happy still.

God blessed my every need—contentment all life through.

He gave me a most precious gift when he gave me you.

Son was a gentle mixture of both me and his daddy. Because he and my Russ spent so much time working side by side at the gas station, they were very close. It was difficult for them, most of the time, to know whether they were playing the roles of father and son or boss and employee. How that boy loved to work! He was a good worker at the station and a good student in school.

Son's hard working was something he and I had in common. We also shared the artist's gift of creativity. I noticed this when I would find good drawings of cars and airplanes. To encourage him to be a good student when he was in high school, I bought him a desk with a study light and decorated his room with the best masculine flavor I could imagine. The only thing he rejected were the frilly curtains I got for the windows.

I don't have to make any excuses. It's a well-known fact that mothers are partial to their sons. Even he admitted that we both spoiled him and gave him much more independence than we did the girls. I guess that was his way of saying, "Keep it up, Mother and Daddy." I almost always sent a poem to Son on his birthday.

On January the fourth, nineteen hundred thirty-two,

God gave us another boy, and that little boy was you.

You were a blond with dark brown eyes.

Your build was slender as you grew in size.

Happy birthday to you, Son, our wonderful boy.

You aren't just a son but a big world of joy.

May your joys be doubled as coming days unfold,

For we think that you deserve the best that life can hold.

You are my bright sunshine. You
made your dad's heart glow.

On your twenty-ninth birthday, we wanted you to know.

Not all my poems to Son were complimentary. After all, I'm a mother. When I sense that one of my children needs a few gentle hints, I must get it out of my system. Son gave ample opportunity for this. Even he admitted he was twenty-seven years old before he realized how immature he was. As his mother, I wouldn't have put it in such strong words. However, if that was what he had found out about himself, I had to take his word for it.

Son was very ambitious to get ahead in his career. Just before I wrote the preceding poem to him, he told us he was going to change jobs because his employer was too "status quo," whatever that meant. I think it meant his boss wasn't letting him try out every new idea he had. So I wrote him a subtle poem.

Stand tall, my Son. Stand tall as the tallest tree.

And don't forget, my Son, God has given you to me.

Look for the best in everyone as you walk in the crowd.

Be humble, gentle, and kind, yet, my Son, be proud.

If you need strength to overcome
some weakness that you feel,

Seek for a deeper faith from God, for God is really real.

As you grow older, Son, you will never know it all,

So do the best you can, and stand tall, my Son. Stand tall.

✝

During those years, to satisfy my artistic bent, I painted more ceramic figurines, flowers, and birds. I sent some of them to our children and filled many shelves in our house with them. Some were made flat on the back so they could be hung on a wall like a picture. Betty and Mary seemed to like them. But Son wasn't into what he called "whatnots" and "knickknack dust catchers."

I made a little doll face for Jerry to hang on her wall. Son knew if he encouraged me I would have their bookshelves and walls covered with ceramics like my walls were. So he took the little doll face and hid it.

I got a letter from Jerry Ann. She tried to smooth over Son's ungracious behavior. At this time, she was five months pregnant with Ryan.

Tuesday morning

Hi,

My silly Russell has me all fixed up with a mess of typing this morning, and I'm sure not in the mood for it. But then I'm not in the mood for anything else either.

Don't you come to the doctor in Tulsa this Thursday? I can't tell if two weeks have passed or not. If you come, I'll be looking for you and Dad for supper. Okay? And I won't go to any trouble either—just plain stuff.

Those soup bowls I got for you are $2.10 each, and you owe me for seven. But I'm not worrying about it, so why should you?

I went to the doctor yesterday. Everything seems okay. He said we really couldn't be sure until the baby starts moving, which might be sometime this month. Julie started after three months.

Julie has been brushing her teeth for quite a while, so I'd better go see. Here is a poem I wrote to tell you about your sorry son.

The little doll face is put up and hid.

We just couldn't love her, so that's what we did.

Now we know you worked hard on that sweet little look,

But Son wouldn't have her in a shelf, cranny, or nook.

So she just may be pining for her maker so fair,

Or for a new home where they'd treat her more square.

So, if you should know of a right, homey place,

We'd be glad to give back the little doll face.

Oh! The little doll face is put up and hid.

We just couldn't love her, so that's what we did.

As soon as I received Jerry's letter and after I got over my aggravation at Jerry's sorry husband, I whipped out an answer to him so I could have the last word.

If I were an artist, this is what I would do.

I'd paint, on cheap paper, pretty things for you.

It wouldn't be ceramics for my Son to hide away.

That's too much work and not enough pay.

I'd paint on cheap paper so you could let it fall

Into the wastebasket, and that would be all.

But please tell me now. What must I do?

I've painted more ceramic for your Christmas too!

Ha! Ha!

✝

Mama died in July 1962. I went to California alone for Mama's funeral. Ten months before her death, I had a great urge to get a copy of my birth certificate. Since I was born at home, out in the country, there had been no opportunity for a doctor to order one. Here I was, fifty-five, without proof I had been born.

I was told at the courthouse to write a letter to the State Bureau of Vital Statistics and ask for a form to get a delayed birth certificate. If I had a living parent, I would need them to sign an affidavit attesting to the place and time of birth.

I mailed the form to Mama. I received the form back from her. She attached a note that said, "To my dear daughter, Ida Pearl Logan Jones. Attached is your excuse for being born. I guarantee you are the genuine article. There is no mistake. I've never seen anyone like you. Your loving certainteed mother, Mary Logan."

I didn't realize how very much Mama's death would sadden me. Knowing how much I loved and depended on my Russ, after the funeral and before I returned home, my tumbling mind began to imagine what life would be like without him. Such thoughts as:

I wouldn't want to live.

When the sun went down, I wouldn't be able to sleep.

I'd be lost in this world.

My dreams would tumble down.

My heart would be heavy.

I would want to run far away.

My heart would weep.

I would no longer be complete.

I mailed this list to my Russ. I had to tell someone who could help shoulder my deep grief.

Not only did I make my lonely grief known to my Russ, I turned to my garden, where I could talk to and listen to the birds and flowers. My starting place was another garden where my Redeemer had to talk to our Father God when he was suffering grief for me.

At the Mount of Olives, near the path over the hill,

There used to be a garden. I wonder if it's there still.

For today my mind is searching in a lonely sort of way,

Searching in the garden where my Jesus used to pray.

And I often wonder why, the perfect one, in deep distress,

Suffered for me, a sinner, so I might find his sweetest rest.

I can finally see him now when no other help was nigh;

Birds and flowers never left, remained with him close by.

As I let my mind listen, it seemed I heard him say,

"I'm ready, oh my Father, if this cup can't pass away."

In my garden, with my Bible and prayers, I now understood in a deeper way that sometimes God tests the worthiness of our faith as part of his growing process. I learned that every season has its own unique tests for God's creation. I began to see and hear some things in my backyard garden I had never seen or heard before. Flowers can talk. The leaves on trees whisper to each other. The dew is a healing balm on growing grass. Rain baptizes gardens with God's saving grace.

Yes, birds can talk. My backyard was my best therapy, and my conversations with the trees, flowers, and birds reminded me of my dreams as a little girl. It was the Lord's way of telling me that he knew my storybook before I ever wrote it. He knew the months when my backyard dream would blossom into a time of healing, growth, and completion.

As a little girl, I dreamed of a very pretty white house with a white picket fence and a gate for my children to swing upon. I saw crepe myrtles standing in a long row as a background for other flowers throughout the growing seasons. In front of the crepe myrtles, I saw foxgloves, touch-me-nots, zinnias, and violets planted by me and God's birds. I imagined marigolds, pansies, irises, tulips, roses of Sharon, hibiscus, daisies, and cannas.

I saw an apple tree with a bluebird house hung in it so I could listen to their velvet voices each morning. My dream was dominated by a giant magnolia for my grandchildren to climb and a wisteria vine and a lilac bush with blossoms for me to smell. This dream exactly describes our Okmulgee house and yard.

There was a large holly tree at the corner of the house, making a striking sight when the berries turned red. Against one fence was a redbud tree with reddish pink blossoms in springtime. The butterflies were so tame they would flutter around my feet. From dawn until twilight, the birds were full of mirth.

I felt closer to God here than at any other place. Although the flowers talked and the birds sang, I was awed by the silence of the overall beauty. My Russ and I called it our paradise as we grew older and had more time to sit and enjoy it, even in the depth of an Oklahoma winter.

Nature lost hold and fluttered down,

Spreading a carpet on the ground,

Sending a winter wonderland

With the touch of God's own hand.

So with this touch of splendor

In the passing of December,

Nature put on a lovely glow,

Changing the landscape with its whitest snow.

Our cottage roofs are snowy white,

And Nature trimmed them oh so bright.

It felt like magic in the night

On our city, peaceful and quiet.

In this touch of splendor, I'm completely lost in dreams.

I'm filled with inspiration—at least that's the way it seems.

The King of kings of earth and skies,

The true artist of this paradise,

Sent this touch of splendor

With the passing of December.

I recovered from my deep grief over Mama's death. I knew I was almost back to normal when one day, as I sat on the patio, I caught a little boy in my backyard stealing my apples. I suppose the Lord sent him.

I said, "Come here and let me talk to you. Did you steal some apples from me the other day?"

He twisted the sack he held in his hand and said, "I don't believe I was that boy."

It sounded like an admission to me.

I took a different approach and asked, "Have you ever been in my backyard before?"

He answered, "Yes, but I knocked on your back door. I wish we had a backyard like this. I dreamed once we did."

Well, I gave him all the apples he could carry and invited, "Stop by for a visit any time you wish."

He always knocked on the back door and asked after that.

Second Touches

1963 through 1974

This chapter of my life I called Second Touches because I'd grown even closer to my Russ, our children, and their families; to the events in our great land; and, most of all, to my Creator, God the Father, Christ, and the Holy Spirit. I continued to write a great number of poems during this period of time, and I shared them with anyone who gave the slightest hint that they enjoyed them.

A symbol of this second touch was a crucifix Sonny bought for me one of the summers when he went to the Stamps Quartet music school in Dallas the first time when he was in the eighth grade. I wanted him to become a song leader in church someday, so I also convinced him to take voice lessons after we moved to Okmulgee. I hung the crucifix on the wall of my bedroom, and it seemed to serve as a frequent reminder of the freedom I had received from the ransom Christ had paid for me as I observed the second touch that Son was also experiencing.

My youngest grandchildren were now old enough to visit and correspond with me. Sometimes they included little pictures they had drawn. The oldest ones were now sending poems they had written and were asking advice about deeper things that touched on how to live a good life.

I've used autumn as a signpost for each year in this chapter of my story about the thoughts of my soul.

✝

Autumn 1963

While standing at my window, the leaves began to fall,
Tumbling from the cottonwood standing up so tall.
Some, dressed up in gold, were waltzing through the town.
Some of them fell drowsy like, asleep upon the ground.
As I walk through autumn leaves, rustling 'neath my feet,
It's like the sound of music; its rhythm is so sweet.
Next morning I looked out, every tree was standing bare.
Mother Nature was working, whirling leaves through the air.
At once, my heart was frozen. I heard the sad wind cry,
"Old Man Frost walked through our
town. Winter's drawing nigh."

It brought me double pleasure when I saw creativity spring from one of our children or grandchildren. Mary was becoming a much better artist, and her latest oil paintings were taking on more of a professional look. In 1964, Mary started taking art lessons from a professional artist. Mary had an art show of her work in the Oklahoma capitol building and won a competition for the cover of the Okmulgee County phone book, which showed a rendering of the Creek Nation Council House Museum in the Okmulgee city square.

Being a parent is a big responsibility.

> While they are in your hands, you
> must teach them each day.
>
> Take them to the church where Christians sing and pray.
>
> You must teach them to work, but give them time to play,
>
> And tell them to be thankful for each and every day.

I know I made many mistakes, as mothers always do. My children did not expect me to be perfect. That's why I wasn't afraid to hold my hands up high so God could give me all the love I could hold in my arms. Parents can't be perfect; however, all can make time to mold their children into the image of God. Only he can turn our limited time on earth into blessings for our children and grandchildren.

What Son did when he was about thirty-five I considered to be a good page in his book of life. Even though he and his daddy had worked very close to each other up until Son went away to college, they maintained a formal relationship by shaking hands with each other when they met and when they parted. Son always hugged his sisters and me when we met after being apart for a time.

Then one day when Son and his family came from Tulsa to Okmulgee for a visit over the weekend, my Russ met them at the front door, and Son gathered his father in his arms with a strong hug. I was standing behind my Russ, and I heard him say, "That feels really good." So from then on, handshakes were out and hugs were in, just as naturally as if that had always been their normal greeting.

The Bible talks a lot about knowledge, wisdom, and under-standing. The Bible says, "O, Lord God of Abraham, Isaac, and of Israel, our fathers, keep this forever in the imagination of the thoughts of the heart of thy people, and prepare their heart unto thee" (1 Chronicles 29:18, KJV).

To me, this means that we are to honor the concrete thoughts of knowledge, wisdom, and understanding as one way to know God's heart and mind. And we're to honor imagination as an equally effective way to see God's dreams for us in living color, directly and supernaturally from his mind as we study the Bible.

God gave me his thoughts when I started my dreaming as a windblown country girl. It soothed my heart to wander through God's thoughts and dreams as they came alive in the images of my imagination. Imagination can be an unending source of fun. Without the reality of knowledge, wisdom, and understanding, nothing can be done right. With imagination in everything, there is a picture or image of hope. I would have liked to have had more book learning, but I wouldn't want it if the price of the tuition was my imagination from God's heart and mind to mine.

Using God's creative mind, I could sense simple things like drinking spring water from a gourd dipper and stepping across Old Limbo Creek on exposed rocks. I could fly with wild geese winging overhead, being led by a gander, making their honking sounds. I could smell rich, beautiful farming country surrounded by flowers and shady nooks. God's imagination reflected into my mind was like the echoing of songbirds as nature's supreme reality from which the dreams and hope-filled imagination of heaven were painted. My imagination knew exactly where my freedom lay.

Autumn was a signal for me to prepare for our family to get together for Thanksgiving. We had a pleasant Thanksgiving family dinner with turkey, my own special cornbread dressing, cranberry sauce, hot rolls, mashed potatoes with brown gravy, chocolate pie with meringue topping for Son, pumpkin pie for my Russ, and mincemeat pie for Buck.

We had such a good time together I composed a poem and made handwritten copies for each of our children as enticement for them to return for Christmas.

> The nativity scene is placed in the Council House Square.
>
> It's on display for the whole town to share.
>
> A lifelike scene, hay covering the ground,
>
> Joseph, Mary, the babe in the manger, who wise men surround.
>
> As people stand watching, every face is aglow,
>
> Some wearing holly sprigs with a touch of mistletoe.
>
> Like all others, I'm in a hurry. Christmas is so near.
>
> I haven't wrapped the presents for those I love so dear.
>
> Christmas means more to me than shiny lights of gold.
>
> Just to have our children home and my grandkids near to hold.

✝

Autumn 1964

Roscoe, my Russ's younger brother, who worked at Ball Brothers' Glass plant, found some really beautiful jagged, transparent-blue glass waste that gave one of my flower beds a unique appearance. Each time he found a piece of waste glass that was unusually beautiful, Roscoe brought it to me, and I would find a place for it in this special flower bed.

Listen to the sweet music of autumn.

See the fleecy clouds sail overhead.

The flower bulbs have fallen asleep

Beneath the blue rock bed.

I heard summer whisper, "Farewell."

And to it I said, "Goodbye."

Then I saw the changing colors

Like a rainbow against the sky.

God drew the curtains on summer.

Now autumn sounds fill my ears.

And the soft fall rains are falling

Like a hundred million tears.

At fifty-eight years of age, I still enjoyed being outdoors as spring made its appearance. As a child and a young woman, I enjoyed walking barefoot in a freshly plowed field. Now, I took off my shoes and walked in our small vegetable garden after my Russ plowed it with a hand plow or in a flower bed after he or I used a shovel to turn the dirt over. As I plowed my feet in the fresh-turned soil, under the blue ceiling of heaven on a spring day, I felt closer to God.

Every year, when we first turned the dirt in the vegetable and flower garden, robins appeared to join in the annual fun. Being a good neighbor to my bird friends, I sat at the edge of the garden and let them have it to themselves.

"Cheer up," say the robins on each garden-turning day.

"It's time for us to do our work, or do we call it play?"

They hopped along beside me, hoping to find a worm,

Alert and ready to do their part each
time they see one squirm.

I could almost touch them as they put on their show.

I love them for their trustful ways. I think that they know.

With their day's work completed,
they bless me with a song.

I listen to each joyful note the blessed whole day long.

Each morning I hear them again.
They sing with all their might.

So happy they can hardly wait for every dawn's new light.

As I played in the soft dirt with my feet, a young cat walked up to me, rubbing her soft fur against my leg. She walked with me to my back porch steps and sat beside me as I washed my feet. Being neighborly, I gave her a dish of milk to drink and talked to her as she drank it. Early each morning, she would come back for more, and I would oblige. She stopped coming after a couple of weeks. One morning, she gave me a big surprise. She brought three baby kittens for me to see. They gathered around the dish of milk until they had their fill. Then, by some signal from their mother, they licked their little paws and followed her into the back alley and disappeared.

As that young mother cat walked away with her children, I had a feeling I would never see them again. It was as if God had provided this other mother as a connection between the fresh dirt and how he leads his plant, animal, and human children in their individual walks through life.

One of the few things that could spoil my outside yard in summertime were the pesky flies, particularly when they came into the house when the door was open the least little bit.

I could write about one pesky fly
enough to fill many books.

I hate those pesky critters; I don't even like their looks.

So here's a little story about a pesky fly.

I swatted at him all evening as he kept whizzing by.

When I shut things down that night to rest upon my bed,

He kept buzzing all around and kept lighting on my head.

Then I turned off the lights to rid myself of him.

I asked myself the question, "Could a fly cause me to sin?"

When next morning I made breakfast,
that pesky fly was there.

Then I remembered I hadn't said my morning prayer.

"Oh, my Lord," I said as I opened the ice box door.

"I pray the fly will disappear, and I'll see him no more."

That moment he flew into the fridge.
I said, "That's really cool."

I suppose my prayer was answered by praying like a fool.

Oh yes, I found that frozen fly. "Now,
I like the way you look.

I'll write your *biografly* in the flyleaf of my book."

I should have felt ashamed to expect so much help from my Russ with the yard work after he worked almost twelve hours six days a week at the gas station.

However, he did make enough time to take me fishing at Okmulgee Lake, the reservoir for our city water system. He always took me with him when he went fishing. He would take his fishing tackle, and I would take a book to read. He asked me, "Why do you bring a book when you go fishing with me?" So, I explained.

There are two kinds of fishermen: some
who fish, some who don't.

And if they aren't going to bite, I'm
one of those who won't.

You've cussed and discussed from our house to the lake,

"Why do I buy a license for you if a
book you're going to take?"

Well, fishing can be lots of fun, but only if they're biting.

But just to sit and hold a rod—I don't find that exciting.

I'm as smart as the dumbest fish who
can never find my hook.

I might as well play it safe and take myself a book.

Yes, there are two kinds of fishermen,
like my Russ and one like I.

So until you reel in a batch, I've got better fish to fry.

✝

Autumn 1965

Autumn is in the air again, with gray clouds in the sky.

The leaves act very restless as the breeze dances by.

The sky is blue behind the gray. I sense an autumn thrill.

Scarlet trees are edged in gold on each and every hill.

Magnolia blooms have their pods, turning orangey red.

The squirrel in the old oak tree is making its winter bed.

The birds aren't near as loud. The songs are soft and low.

Remembering, after autumn breezes, icy winds will blow.

One day, my Russ put on his work pants, and they were full of holes. Some of the holes were made from getting battery acid on them, some were torn places, and others were just thin from wear. The previous day, I had taken time out to entertain myself by writing a poem that he had apparently noticed on the table and decided to read it.

I've got no worry. My life is at ease.

I'm happy-go-lucky. I do as I please.

No job to go to, no one bossing me,

I'm as happy as any human can be.

Bad timing! My Russ showed me his pants and said, "You let my pants be ragged and worn because you're feeding your artistic ego and writing crazy poems."

I just gave him a pretty smile and responded, "Do you want to change pants, or do you want me to pin up some of those torn places until I can get around to it."

He shook his head back and forth, looked up at the ceiling with his eyes, gave me his I-give-up smile, and said, "It's six o'clock. Time to go."

That evening, when he got home, I handed him a big stack of freshly mended work pants with a poem pinned to the top. He read it and smiled, and I knew I had won again for a little while.

The time has come for you to go.

Now take good care, for I love you so.

There's a nip of winter in the air.

Wrap up real warm. You know I care.

Do your work well, but hurry home.

I'll be waiting here where we're all alone.

Tomorrow will be your time to go,

But for tonight, I love you so.

Actually, my Russ and I got along very well, even though I pleaded with him to mow the lawn until I was black and blue in the face. He called me a slave driver. We both had our way of wiggling out of things. I know my ways were the most conniving. He still said I was the apple of his eye. I know that's true because when I got up really close, face to face, I could see my reflection in his eyes. Every day, he said, "I love you." We both knew how badly spoiled I was.

My Russ was seldom sick enough to stay home from work. But this year he had to check into the Okmulgee hospital near our house. He had a hernia that had to be repaired. They didn't have phones in the rooms in the hospital. This happened in February, cold and windy. The hospital was only four blocks from the house. I could visit during the day, but it was lonely at night without my Russ. Guess what. I wrote a poem and mailed it the four blocks as a surprise and get-well card.

This evening, the birds are singing.
I think they sing for me.

They know I am lonesome, as lonesome as can be.

This house is far too quiet when you aren't at home.

Get well soon, my Russ. I don't like it here alone.

I'd rather pick up the things you string here and there

Than for you to be away—that's how much I care.

Of course, when you come back
home, I'll be as sassy as ever.

But for you to be gone, my Russ, it's
not my wish. No, never!

In 1965, we happily celebrated our fortieth wedding anniversary.

Autumn 1966

Each time we went back to see what was left of the old home place, it took several weeks to get it out of my system. But each time as we drove to our modern and convenient Okmulgee home, I could, as an adult, see the great contrast in human comforts. Logically, I knew that the best days I could remember about the old home place had to be rationalized to the many advantages of living in town. But as an imaginative dreamer, I had to yield to my fantasies about my youth.

Eventually, I began to learn that it was of little value to go back there very often because all of my visual memories were no longer a reality. So I made an agreement with my shadow to go there for me on cloudy days or at night, when she wasn't doing anything anyway. We had been together for so long she knew the best memories to relive and wouldn't even be noticed. Unlike me, Mama never yelled at her when we did something naughty.

Little hope was held for me when I was just a child.
I was young and noisy and drove my parents wild.
My shadow was always quiet—never spoke a word out loud.
She stayed close beside me, never lost in a crowd.
If I could float on a lazy cloud or curl up in a chair,
It makes no difference where I am; my shadow's always there.
I could climb the highest hill or sleep beneath a tree.
I can't hide in a single place where my shadow can't find me.
She doesn't gripe if it's cold or hot, never makes a sound.
She never gets in my way as she sort of slips around.
She loved the quiet of our country farm, as quiet as falling snow.

She loved the whisper of the wind when clouds were hanging low.

We watched neighbor children grow. To us, they were so sweet.

To see them scramble, run, and hide with those little, dirty feet.

Each day, we love it more and more. It holds a peaceful charm.

Although we're growing kinda old, we love our country farm.

We each still have our playmates. Russ is the name of one.

Our husbands are so much alike. That's why we have such fun.

✝

Autumn 1967

Jerry Ann and Son frequently brought their children to Okmulgee for weekend visits. At that time, Julie was nine years old. Since she was five or six, she'd made it a habit of going into my flower beds to pick a flower bouquet for me. One particular weekend, there were no bright-colored flower blossoms. I noticed Julie in my backyard walking around and looking around as if she didn't know what to do.

I saw the autumn bouquet from shrubs growing wild.

I thought, *Lord, how beautiful is the mind of a child.*

With colors of the rainbow, she pressed a leaf still green,

Kept moving leaves around 'til the scarlet could be seen.

With nature in her veins and willingness to share a part,

A bouquet of leaves

Made by her hands
To melt her grandma's heart.
Her mother said, "She's just like you."
It couldn't help but show.
For I too love God's nature gifts
From spring to winter's snow.

✝

Like other Americans, I was impacted by the nation's conflict over the Vietnam War as it was brought home to us by the dead bodies of the military personnel. I had a good friend, a black lady named Letha Tarkington, whose young son was killed in South Vietnam combat in 1967.

A whitewashed shed in Vietnam at
the end of a muddy road.

Medics worked around the clock to
lighten our soldiers' load.

Helicopters dropped to a primitive
path. Marines in an operation.

Tending the dead, carrying wounded
to the whitewashed station.

A Red Cross flag unfurled overhead.
Trees leafless and bare.

Hospital odors float through the shed
on the faint breeze in the air.

Our Letha's son lay on a stretcher,
a pillow beneath his head.

Two other youths with serious wounds
lay beside him on a bed.

Outside, a half-dressed sergeant ate
pork and beans from a can,

His wounded buddy bleeding. "Thank
God for brave, young men."

✝

We went on vacation to the Texas hills with Betty and Buck and their children in September. They lived in Austin at that time. Our cabins were surrounded by a pasture with a background of bright cedars.

We enjoyed looking at the horses as they grazed in the pasture. The twins, Scott and Sky, rode these gentle, white horses while Grandpa led each one around by its mane. Their faces were happy and full of smiles.

We slept well that night listening to the quietness of the mountains. The next morning, there was a fine mist in the air. The river below the cabins sang nature's tune as we got closer to it.

Small boats were provided for us. We had much fun as we raced down the river in the boats. Buck and Scott rowed one boat, and my Russ and Claudia rowed the other. We stopped at a place where the kids could go swimming. Sky went swimming with her wristwatch on. It wasn't waterproof, so her grandpa had to work on it to dry it out so it would keep ticking.

All three of the girls failed to bring their sweaters. As the evening grew cool, Grandpa's sweater was wrapped around them since it was big enough to keep out the cold until we got back to the cabins. For dinner that night, we had steaks and all the trimmings.

Our last night there, my Russ and I strolled near the river. The shadows were deep and still as we watched the sun's last golden rays hide behind a green hill. By the time we reached our cabin, the stars were out. We felt much richer than we had before we went to this beautiful place with our children. As we stood there with our upturned faces looking up at God's glory, my Russ said, "Perhaps someday we might come back to this peaceful place."

✝

In the latter part of 1967, my body was giving me signals again that something was wrong. If I worked one hour in the yard, I hurt for another hour, and if I worked two hours, I hurt for two hours. I started out trying to rake leaves by myself but soon learned that I couldn't get it done. First, I called a man and paid him twelve dollars to finish it for me. Next, I called the doctor.

I told the doctor it felt like my food, rather than going all the way down, was gathering in a pocket and causing me pain. The doctor thought I might have a tumor and took X-rays. He said he didn't find a tumor, but based on what I was feeling and what he saw on the X-ray, his diagnosis wasn't certain. He asked me to go to a surgeon in Tulsa to get another opinion.

We went to the Tulsa doctor. He scheduled me for surgery the next week. When we got home, Mary had a hot supper ready on the table.

I dreaded going through another surgery. It forced me to think seriously about the realities and risks involved and the consequences resulting both from a successful surgery and an unsuccessful one. I turned to my one dearest friend, to whom I always turned when I had no other place to go.

Help me, precious Lord Jesus. Please
hear my humble prayer.

Comfort me with your presence, for
I know that you are there.

I've read that you have said: "Call on me, for I am near."

And at this very moment, Lord, my mind is not so clear.

I feel my heart's in prison when I know it should be free.

Draw nearer to me, Lord Jesus, for I'm in need of thee.

As usual, this dreaded operation went fine. We returned to the doctor for my final exam. While he waited for me, my Russ went to a flower shop and bought a single, beautiful, pink zinnia blossom for me. It thrilled me. It lived on for two weeks and two days. After it had lived its time and lost its pretty glow, I pressed it between two heavy books so my Russ would always know how much I appreciated it and him.

Operations always drew me closer to the Lord and to my Russ. They almost always demand a poem for the record.

God made it possible for me to reach that sweet home someday.

I know I want to go, for my Father has paved the way.

He sent his Son to die upon the cruel tree.

And I must go through my Christ if I'm to be set free.

My days are still lingering. I do not know how long.

But I will follow Jesus, for it's he who makes me strong.

I'll always love you, my Russ. You know I always will.

'Til the last rays of sun hide behind the darkest hill.

You've always meant so much to me, and you always will.

When God calls one of us in death,
we'll love each other still.

Autumn 1968

The other day, I thought for sure spring will never come.

Dry leaves drifted oh so high, I got
out and raked up some.

Then the north wind came with rain, sleet, and snow.

I asked myself the question, "Where did the summer go?"

I claim I seldom question God, for
I'm sure that he knows best.

Why does he test my patience and let me have no rest?

Finally, the leaves break forth. I hear the songbirds sing.

I see them build their nests. With them, I welcome spring.

Oklahoma is a state with four clear, distinct seasons. I called it the four seasons state. I thought God designed each season just a wee bit too long so we would be more willing to welcome the next season back. I imagined the Lord must have laughed at me when each year he played the same joke on me by making each season so long my patience would be tested over and over.

Autumn

Autumn rains made me feel so lazy. Sometimes, after my Russ and I had our breakfast and he had gone to work, I would sneak back into bed for a last nap. I listened to the softness of the rain and quietly said to myself, "Why not take another nap if you have nothing better to do?"

Winter

The soft, fall rains could quickly change into sleet or snow. In Oklahoma, we could have rain one hour, then sleet or snow mixed in, followed by a covering of rain that froze into one large ice-skating rink. When Son was fourteen years old, he would carefully drive his motor scooter to an open space in the front yard, gun the engine with the front wheel turned fully right or left, and spin it around and around. My Russ and I also had our own brand of spinning around if we had to walk on one of these icy surfaces.

Confidentially, I'm not sure of my little, old self at all.

I was so busy being very careful I gave myself a fall.

I had no confidence in my Russ, and he had none in me.

I slid around on our back steps, and
he slipped beneath a tree.

Why we hold onto each other, I see no reason at all.

We slip and slide around, and sometimes we both fall.

He can't help me or I him. We must
stand on our own feet.

I guess that's why I lost my hold and fell upon my seat.

Spring

I awoke this morning early to a mild, golden dawn.

I saw a robin feeding upon a dewy lawn.

I think spring is here again. The birds are singing loud.

I'm filled with peace and serenity. I
can't help feeling proud.

As a child, the waters murmured,
cascading around the bend.

God was sending me new colors. Who
could have a better friend?

The trees are swaying to and fro.
Flowers unfold in the sun.

In every shape and hue, I counted every one.

I saw tall, slender pines that have withstood the cold

I hear the chatter of the squirrels. My, how they can scold!

Tiny wildflowers are blooming in my yard on every side,

Their pastel colors showing off, so
small but with such pride.

I feel the sun's warm, golden rays
filling my heart with cheer.

I'm happy spring is here again. The winter was so drear.

Summer

In Oklahoma, barefoot children had a different kind of plague: sand burrs or sticker burrs. In town, the burrs didn't grow if grass was kept cut short. However, there were always alleys or lots that weren't mowed where they patiently waited to snag a barefoot child. Sometimes, there was no other course of action but for a child to limp to the closest neighbor for help.

While I was out working in my backyard one day,

I saw a small, unhappy lad, but he wasn't at his play.

He was standing in the alley looking up at me.

He wasn't a lost child. I could plainly see.

He touched my heart, making not a sound.

There he stood all alone with tears streaming down.

I said, "What's the matter with you, my sweet?"

He bravely answered, "I got stickers in my feet."

My Russ was truly a man for all seasons. He worked outside in all kinds of unseasonable weather. He was as predictable as each season. His customers knew he would be there to service their cars in all kinds of weather. The young people in his Bible class knew, every Saturday night, he would be faithfully preparing a Bible lesson for the next Sunday morning, being faithful in season and out of season.

I didn't say he was perfect. This was the forty-third year I had been working on him as a married woman; I knew he ran a successful business. But around the house, I would have fired him if God hadn't been on his side. I didn't plan to give up. He kept reminding me, "I really planned to be a bachelor."

Five years we courted. It seemed only a year.

Add forty-three more, and life is still so dear.

Forty-three years, and add one more day.

I'm still trying hard to have my way.

He's a man for all seasons, more precious than gold.

Perhaps it's our season for together growing old.

Autumn 1969

I enjoyed looking at the beautiful work of artists who painted pictures of autumn. I liked to gaze at their tree-filled pictures. But I enjoyed the autumn pictures God painted best. Not only were they three-dimensional, but you can imagine walking right into them as deep as you wished until you disappeared into the background. Then, if you imagined you stayed a few weeks, when you came back out and glanced back, the scene you saw before had changed to another season.

God has returned to paint the trees

With every color the rainbow shows.

So, I'll agree this is the time

For this year's autumn to strike a pose.

God's brush and palette are hard at work.

With a rosy glow, he colors the leaves,

Brushing in a restful whisper,

With a soft and stirring breeze,

A fall with clear, azure skies

And a russet, fiery-covered hill,

And a brisk, cold, autumn evening

When the snow brings winter chill.

Oh, autumn in all its splendor,

Glowing brightly in the sun.

I'm thankful to my Creator God

For the masterpiece he has done.

I grew spiritually as I studied my Bible and wrote poems about the role of Christ as the Messiah, Christ's role on the cross, God's role in Christ's rise from physical death, the role of Christ the King as he sits on his throne in heaven, and of my own role on his return when the dead in Christ and those believers who remain will meet him in the clouds of the air. Something spectacular happens to God's children when the Holy Spirit reveals the reality of these truths to them.

His grief-stricken friends stood round about,

Watching and hearing the wild mob shout,

"Release Barabbas. Let him go.

Jesus is guilty. This we know."

Early in the morning, they led him away

To a place called "The Skull," on that awful day.

The cross was too heavy for Jesus to bear.

So Simon was forced to carry it there.

On the cross of shame, they nailed his hands,

The only Savior in all the lands.

Suspended between heaven and earth,

Showing each of us what our soul is worth.

One criminal made a humble plea.

"When you enter your kingdom, remember me."

With a solemn promise, great and wise,

"Today, you'll be with me in paradise."

By noon, darkness fell all around.

The angry mob stood there spellbound.

Laughs of scorn had turned to tears.

They stopped their shouts. There were no cheers.

Stricken with awe, a Roman soldier said,

An innocent man now is dead.

What happened to the crown of thorns as they took Jesus down?

I have always thought, *It took root in the ground.*

There are shrubs, when they touch the
earth, that take root and grow.

What happened to the crown of thorns? We may never know.

Were it not for the empty tomb, I would be forever lost.

There's no question in my mind; Christ paid an awful cost.

Fastened upon Calvary's tree, he suffered, bled, and died.

Between two sinners upon their cross, our Christ was crucified.

Giving up the Holy Ghost, he slowly bowed his head.

For my own sin and shame, the Son of God was dead.

The angel at the tomb then said, "Come see where he lay.

He is not here. He came alive before the stone was rolled away."
How beautiful is the thought, *There was an upper room.*
And how glorious is the truth, "There is an empty tomb."

We have God's own promise we will live with him on high,
Far beyond the brightest sunset, where our souls will never die,
With our earthly tabernacle folded beneath the sod,
For each of us who've done his will, our spirit dwells with God.
God will keep his promise if our faith and trust remain.
Then on resurrection day, we each shall rise again.

The Bible is a living book. God meant it to be heard.
I've respected it and pondered it. I believe its every word.
I accepted his invitation. The door of my heart opened wide.
Today, I know the prince of peace since Christ has come inside.
He called me out of darkness, before his face so bright,
Though evil darkness is all around, the Bible is my light.

When our grandchildren came to spend some time with us, we always took them to church on Sunday morning, Sunday night, and Wednesday night. I used all of these visits as opportunities to supplement the good training they were getting at home. I often sent them poems and letters in between times to keep our bond secure. To see how well they were reading, I would pick out stories from the Bible for them to read to me.

I can't sharpen a pencil keen enough to mark a line fine enough to more clearly tell the truths the Bible reveals. God says what he means and means what he says. We can't touch him with our hands. We can't see him with our human eyes. But we can easily see him through our God-given eyes of righteous faith.

God sent his Son to carry my cross. Heaven is just a breath away. I pray that when God opens the Book of Life for me, I will hear laughter coming from it.

✝

One day, in a melancholy mood, I failed to look for my God in the natural events taking place around me.

To get my mind back into focus, just a few days later, it seemed God sent one of his most powerful birds on a Sunday afternoon to speak to my heart and get my creative juices flowing again. This beautiful hawk flew directly into the glass of our back door. It lay dead or dazed. I wanted to bring it into the house, but my Russ said, "It's dangerous to bring that hawk into the house."

Yesterday, a beautiful hawk flew down and hit our door.

This graceful falcon of the air lay helpless on the floor.

The red-tailed hawk was lifeless. I
thought that it was dead.

I tried hard to revive it. It lay with its wings outspread.

Its beak was brightest orange, its
plumage a reddish brown.

I've seen it many other times winging its way over town.

I caressed it with tenderness, brushed
its feathers with my hand.

I whispered low, "Lord, let it live. It
belongs in nature's land."

I seldom touch God's living birds. I've only held a few.

I laid it on some autumn leaves to see what God would do.

A sweet repose came to my heart as
the falcon took its flight.

I watched the graceful falcon as it
winged its way from sight.

I tried several times to get this poem published. I thought
since God had delivered the bird in a timely way, he could also
deliver a publisher, but it didn't happen. I was so surprised when,
at supper, after I showed this poem to my Russ, he prayed that
God would someday let it be published.

This was our forty-fourth year of marriage, and it got better every year. We'd never in any year doubted our love for each
other.

Each day, I observed you closely. I
could read between each line.

I knew the day was coming when
God would make you mine.

I already knew my feeling. I was willing just to coast,

Until I heard from your own heart
the words I wanted most.

I guess you were speechless until that moonless night.

The moon refused to shine, and the
stars turned off their light.

It must have given you courage, for
you whispered in my ear,

"You are the only one I love, and I always want you near."

Remember, we were very young.
They laughed at you and me.

But after forty-four years together,
I guess our friends can see.

Autumn 1970

Autumn did bad things to my lungs and my breathing. I hadn't heard a lot about allergies at this time. Therefore, I tried various remedies, including some awful-smelling stuff called Bengay. I rubbed it on my chest. I would use it during the day and take a bath before my Russ came home so I wouldn't smell so bad. He tried some one time when he had a cold and declared he couldn't wash the stuff off.

He asked me one September, "Pearlie, do you know how I know autumn has arrived each year? The inside of the house starts to smell like Bengay."

He said, "The stinkingest woman I ever smelt.

When the sun shines on you, I hope you melt."

Turpentine, kerosene, and Vicks VapoRub

Sent me hurrying to the old bathtub.

My Russ says it makes me stink.

I know he's right. That's what I think.

I know he has a right to scoff.

That's why I try to wash it off.

Autumn's here, and I'm in pain.

I'll need to use Bengay again.

When I marry another feller,

I'll marry one without a smeller.

Mary bought some perfume just in time

To save our marriage, her dad's and mine.

That night when my Russ walked in,

He asked, big-eyed, "Where have you been?

You're all dressed up, perky and bright.

Are we going out tonight?"

I said, "I only want to look my best,

So you won't gripe. I need my rest."

He said, "Thanks to Mary. She saved my life."

I said, "For one night only, I'm your sweet-smelling wife."

We had really great times together, although I had many complaints. I felt obligated to tease him with a poem. But we still loved each other deeply and competed with each other to do and say loving things. We just had our different ways of teasing each other.

He often told me I was mean. There was a time this year when I had every right to be mean. I hurt my back while working in my garden and was forced to wear a back brace for several weeks. The doctor assured me that the more consistently I wore it, the sooner I could get rid of it.

Why explode and be mean or make a little scene.

It won't help a little mite just because this brace is tight,

Or suffering agony and despair

Just because the brace is there.

It feels like a clinging vine, clinging to this back of mine.

Mine is a special case, for I'm allergic to a brace.

Now, I must tell the truth. I'd used every trick I knew to keep from letting my Russ find out about too many of my failings. But there are some things you just can't cover up.

I started out this morning with a heart full of song.

Suddenly, something happened, and
everything went wrong.

First, I burned the biscuits—two times in a row.

I didn't tell my little man. He didn't need to know.

Then I overcooked the sausage and
burned it black and blue.

I quickly cooked some bacon and also burned that too.

I'll keep my big mouth shut. This I will never tell.

I hope I get away with this, though I know he can smell.

I could overdo the most mundane things, such as a grocery list. I didn't show this list to my Russ because I was sure he would view it as a waste of time. Perhaps, my children, when they read this book, will be kind to me and understand because they have received a measure of my desire to express myself in some artistic form. Perhaps they won't find it a waste of their time to enjoy it.

I must get a few potatoes, green onions,
and cooking onions too.

A can of Folgers coffee—no other brand will do.

A bottle of Crisco oil and a small sack of flour,

Salt, pepper, and Borateem and suds called Cold Power,

Tomatoes and tomato juice to brighten up my table.

I drink this and orange juice too when my ulcer says I'm able.

I want some pure cane sugar and good, old-fashioned bread.

A package of rolls to bake; my husband must be fed.

A box of Parkay oleo and a juicy cherry pie.

We really live it up when we eat. I will not tell a lie.

Sausage, bacon, ham, and eggs, and one pound of real butter.

Wow! When I paid the grocery bill,
I felt my poor heart flutter.

My Russ was sixty-five years old this year. He wasn't completely ready to retire, but his body told him that twelve-hour days were too much for him. He started assisting the high school vocational training classes by providing a boy with a job each day during the afternoon. He began coming home for lunch and a short nap.

I was so accustomed to him working long hours each day that I had to remind myself that it would be better for him to cut back on his work hours than to retire.

Each day after our lunch, he would fall into his chair, and almost before his eyes were closed, he would be fast asleep.

As he was taking one of his naps, I realized I would be sixty-five the next year. Perhaps I should talk to him about my own retirement. What better way to reveal this decision to him than with a poem? I knew he would tease me for even considering such an idea, but it was my nature to speak my mind.

You may be inclined to scoff at my plan to retire,

But I'm not trying anymore to set the world on fire.

Tease me and call me lazy. You won't bother me at all.

I'm well equipped to sit in the shade
until long shadows fall.

I'm making ready to receive the blessings I have earned.

Stop teasing me, my Russ. I'm really not concerned.

You're making a grievous mistake if
you don't want me to retire.

It's a beautiful chapter in my life,
which you could help inspire.

It's just a new challenge to meet, painful for you, I see.

Stop teasing me, my dear, and sit in the shade with me.

Autumn 1971

Mother Nature's moods are changing.

She's dressed in colors of fall.

The flowers that were so pretty

Aren't standing near as tall.

For, once again, it's autumn.

Oak leaves are turning brown.

With every whisk of the breeze,

The leaves are falling down.

Vacation days are over.

Children are back in school.

And things are far too quiet

Around the swimming pool.

The insect songs are louder.

They make a concert rhyme.

I often ask the question,

"Do they know it's autumn time?"

I enjoyed watching the younger children on our block excitedly run to school each day. There was a certain charm about living near a school so I could hear the children happily yell at each other during recess and lunchtime.

We thanked the Lord for our children and grandchildren. He graciously gave us three children to raise. He kept one for himself, to welcome us to heaven. We prayed for them every day.

Thank you, Lord, for our children and
one we didn't get to keep.

We never worry about his soul, for in
God's arms he gets to sleep.

You know we're proud of the others
given to my Russ and me.

And when we pray to you for them,
in your thoughts they will be.

May they remember the things we
taught about your only Son.

May they learn that the way to you,
his way, is the only one.

May they not forsake the Creator,
tempted by enchanting sounds.

We've tried to set an example until their faith abounds.

My Russ and I learned very soon that we weren't fully complete without our children. We learned to include our children in our marriage. We agreed it would never be my Russ and me, but with our children, it would be "we."

As I look on my life's work, it's not one bit small.

We have two lovely daughters and
a son, handsome and tall.

Now, in my latter days, I've a life I don't regret.

I've done the best I knew to do, so there's no need to fret.

I knew what was required of me, and
this has meant so much.

I haven't walked my life alone; I've
felt my children's touch.

I did not need worldly pleasures. I
had pleasures of my own.

I am a wife and mother and the keeper of our home.

Autumn 1972

Near the end of each summer, I always became impatient for autumn. Knowing my impatience for each season's change, the Lord provided a particular flower blossom to signal me that I must wait just a little longer. This special flower has several names. It's called a resurrection lily because its foliage dies back, and you would conclude it is dead. Then, near the end of summer, its pink blossom appears on a long stem declaring that it has arisen from what appeared to be seasonal death. It's also called a surprise lily because when its foliage dies you forget the plant is there until, overnight, it's there to surprise you. It's also called a naked lady because its blossom appears on a long, skinny torso without any foliage to clothe it.

> Today, I saw a robin. I heard a whippoorwill call.
>
> I felt a soft wind blowing. Oh! Surely, this is fall.
>
> A canopy of fleecy clouds, above my magnolia tree,
>
> The fragrant scent of naked ladies drifting on the breeze.
>
> The sun was warm and mellow, the sky a deep, deep blue.
>
> The birds were busy on the wing with many things to do.
>
> I sensed leaves were turning. Soon scarlet would appear.
>
> I know by all these natural signs autumn is almost here.

Kristy Dawn was our first great-grandchild. She was the daughter of Mary's first child, Barbara. Within two years, Kristy Dawn was a big girl. We knew this because she started carrying a small purse. Son's sixteen-year-old daughter, Julie, was visiting me the same day Barbara dropped Kristy Dawn off for a short visit. Kristy came into the house with her new purse under her arm.

Julie and I told her how much we admired her purse, and I asked her if I could look at it. I said, "Kristy, your purse isn't very heavy. What do you have in it?"

Kristy flashed her blue eyes at me and answered, "Mama says what a woman has in her purse is a secret."

Julie responded to Kristy as one young woman to another.

"Kristy, Grandma and I agree with you. What we women carry in our purses is nobody's business but our own."

Julie played big-girl games with Kristy all morning, and we had a tea party for lunch as each of us set our purses beside our chairs.

After our lunch, Kristy was feeling tired and took her purse with her as she curled up on the living room couch for a much-needed rest. Julie and I peeked around the kitchen door to watch as she unzipped her purse and took out her pacifier.

Julie was giggling as she said to me, "No wonder her purse was so light."

I answered, "I need to learn a lesson from Kristy. She only carries in her purse what she really needs."

Autumn 1973

We went back to the Austin hills this year. This time I went, as an artist, to make word sketches for poems. I used these notes when I got home so I could enjoy the challenge of putting the visual images into words to replay and enjoy all over again.

Before going to Texas, I did research about the flowers I remembered from the previous trip. I got books from the flower gardens that Lady Bird Johnson set up in Austin, Texas. Armed with a list of flower names, my goal was to roam the nature trails near the cabins we stayed in on our last visit to find as many different flowers as possible.

There I strolled on nature trails, where
God planted every tree.

He filled them with sweet music, on
wings of birds born free.

The manmade part of this scene was
a beautiful sight to me.

Bubbling water, winding in and out,
was enjoyable as could be.

There was a little, log cabin. Memories
rushed back from long ago

When I was a little child, remembering
things I used to know.

Standing at a cabin door, two ladies did there reside.

We talked about their cabin, and they
showed me things inside.

They told me where to find flowers,
more than I could ever name.

More than I had on my list, gift-
wrapped in autumn flame.

God's timing is so perfect, giving me new trails to roam.

My mind's at peace. I feel released
and ready to go back home.

Autumn 1974

At sixty-eight years old, and not in excessively good health, my body began to give me signals that I was in the third quarter of the game of life. My mind didn't agree with this reality. After all, my imagination could transport me to any stage of my life, even to the part that would be lived in heaven. In my fantasies,

I could do physical things I'd always done, and I could do them when I wanted to without the interruptions of responsibility.

I'm living in my autumn years. Time is slipping by so fast.

But this is no surprise to me. I knew youth couldn't last.

My life has never been my own, yet life has been so sweet.

I'm waiting and longing for the time
I'll kneel at Jesus's feet.

When my time has slipped away, I'll fantasize no more.

No autumn years and wintertime—with him forevermore.

My Russ and I began to experience short-term memory problems. We wrote more notes to ourselves and to each other as our natural way to help each other without feeling offended. My Russ began to start more sentences with, "Don't let me forget to—." He always wore a military-type service station cap to work, so that made a good place for me to write reminders to him.

I would jot down a note and put it on his working cap

While he was very busy taking his afternoon nap.

I knew I had to write things down
where we both could see.

He was as forgetful as I, and I was as forgetful as he.

As he got up to return to work, he found my helpful note.

He said, "If you run for mayor, you
will surely get my vote."

I stopped getting as many compliments as I once did. The poems I sent to friends and family got fewer responses, and less often people told me that I was pretty. It surprised me to learn how egotistical I had been all my life. Then I found, with my

self-confidence about my looks and skills, I had to more frequently pat myself on the back.

I pat my back every now and then. It doesn't hurt at all.

I give myself a compliment so my ego doesn't fall.

Contented? No! I'll never be unless
I'm on top of every list.

That's why I pat my own back—
or else I might get missed.

When I feel very important, I let my ego bloom.

Who would pat as tender as I? I'm
best qualified in the room.

After a pat or two, I'll see I might look the same as before.

And if my ego will permit, I'll pat myself some more.

I'll splash it on good and thick. Every
day will be like spring.

I'm sure most ladies will agree. Our
own pat won't hurt a thing.

Johnny, Mary's younger son, was nineteen years old this
year. He had, some time before, asked me to write a few things
to him, personally, about life. I took this request as if it were a
school class assignment. It was as good for me as it was for John.
I did a lot of Bible research and discovered things about myself
I hadn't known before, or at least hadn't admitted. I even put it
in a three-ring binder so he and I could refer back to it every
now and then if we wanted to be reminded of a sentence or two
that seemed to fit our own life goals.

This is what my report to Johnny said.

Johnny, it was last year when you asked me to write to you
about life. After two operations and very much pain, known
only to me and God, I will try to put into words what I've been
thinking deep in my heart these past few months. I've learned

we need great courage for the big sorrows of life and patience for the small ones. The true test that this is working is when we go to sleep each night and sleep in peace, knowing God is wide awake with each child of his on his mind.

Johnny, I've heard people say, "I wish I had never been born." What a sad thing to say. To me, life on God's good earth is precious. Not once have I been unhappy that I was born. If we allow it to happen, life has a way of teaching us that we need faith in Jehovah's watchful care (James 1:17, Genesis 1:26, Genesis 2:7, Matthew 10:28).

Life is a School Room

God expects us to keep learning, from the cradle to the grave.

Just lean on God's precious word and pray you he will save.

(2 Timothy 2:15 and 3:15–17)

Life is Happy Love

I read this from a church newsletter. "Keep your heart away from hate and worry. Live simply. Expect little. Give much. Sing often. Pray always. Fill your life with love. Reflect sunshine. Forget self. Think of others and their feelings. Do to others what you would have them do to you. Love God with all your heart and soul and strength. Love your neighbor as you love yourself. These things are links in a golden chain of contentment. Don't pull tomorrow's clouds over today's sunshine."

Life is a Dressing Room

We must clothe ourselves in the spotless, white holiness of
Christ. He will sanctify and cleanse us with the washing
of the water of his Word, that we might present to him a
glorious church family, not having spots or wrinkles or any
such thing on our clothing, but that we and the church will
be holy and without blemish

(Ephesians 5:26–27, Romans 12:1–2).

Life is Moral Consistency

The fortunes of life are so random and unpredictable. We are
constantly called upon to adjust ourselves. The blessed person is
the one who can do this. Sometimes situations can't be changed
for the better. But we can improve the bad situation by changing
ourselves to fit life's realities. For a simple example, if I'm caught
outside in a big rainstorm, there's no need to fuss about it. I can
choose to accept it and start looking for the sunrays behind my
back to make a rainbow in the cloud in front of me. God expects
us to be predictable in random, unpredictable times.

The world's full of frequent change but not God's Word, my
friend.

He'll never change one jot or tittle—not even at the end.

With each deed, there's a beginning. Each task will have an
end.

But when I stand before God's Son, I want him for my friend.

Life Is What We Make It in the Room of Our Minds

Look at each day on its own. In each day of your brief life,
live the virtues and realities of your existence, the blessing of growth, the glory of action, and the splendor of all
beauty. Yesterday is but a dream. Tomorrow is but a vision.

Live today in a mind that is full of positive and confident thoughts. Johnny, the measure of a real man is in the room of his thoughts. "For as he thinketh in his heart, so is he"

(Proverbs 23:7, KJV).

Live one day at a time. Look not into the chasms of night.

Use God's Word for a window to let in your mind-room's light.

Don't be afraid to relax, as with God you spend some time.

Get God's perspective on your life. Meditate with the divine.

Search his Word with vigor. Find from his Word what's true.

Then, give yourself to others, and he'll give words back to you.

Life Is Described by Our Feelings and Actions

Let me speak of what I've observed about you, John. I've seen a heart as big as a large, golden moon and as tender as a baby's touch. That's why you carefully brought home cats, dogs, birds, rats, and what have you. Remember that beautiful sparrow hawk with long wings and black eyes? Remember how you nursed it back to life and when you released it to fly away the jaybirds fought it in the air as it escaped that savage gang of thugs?

Remember the gray kitten with the broken back? It couldn't even crawl. I doubt if it would have lived if it hadn't been for you. I've seen love in your heart and a forgiving spirit since you were a little boy. I've praised you to your face for your honest ways and the feelings you have for others who are less fortunate. I'm proud of you, John. I'm glad you belong to me.

When you do something you are proud of, dwell on it just a little while. Praise yourself. Relish the experience. Those feelings aren't wrong. It's exactly what God did during the creation days. Genesis 1:31 says, "And God saw everything that he had made, and behold, it was very good" (KJV).

Life Is Happiness

Happiness isn't the impossible dream for which everyone reaches. Too few of us have mastered the art of being happy. We're not born with the secret. Happiness is one habit we must learn and practice, first in our minds and then in our daily actions.

If we've learned we must get rid of bad habits, surely we can decide we can add good habits into our lifestyle. We know we do things that make us feel bad. We can either ask forgiveness for these actions or say, "I couldn't help myself." Therefore, the key to life must be to decide to do things that aren't morally bad and that make us feel good.

This should be easier for you, John, than for most people. The beginning of happiness is to do things for others. By helping others, we help ourselves. As a small boy and a young man, you have demonstrated this over and over until it became a habit. I was happily thrilled when, just before Christmas last year, you and your Grandpa Jones studied the Bible together. That's my kind of happiness.

Life Is a Clear Conscience

A guilty conscience lashes at the soul like a whip or like the splashing waves hit the shore, with unrest and turbulence. Our conscience has the power to make us happy or unhappy. We can't sleep well when our soul is disturbed by the horrors of guilt. It's like trying to sleep on a pillow of thorns. I read somewhere that there is no pillow as soft as a clear conscience. A sick conscience makes us sick in body, soul, and spirit—the very things the Bible writer in 1 Thessalonians 5:23 prayed that God would keep perfect in us until the day Christ returns.

Life Is a Seed Time and Harvest Time

Whatever we sow, we will reap. For every idle word we speak or sow, we must give an account on the day of judgment. By our productive words, we will be justified or reap a good harvest. And by our unproductive words, we will be condemned or reap a harvest that rots on the vine. John, your grandpa has held this policy over my head for the many years of our marriage. I know he is mostly teasing me, but when I read them directly from Christ's mouth, I know exactly what they mean. My response to your grandpa is, "You just want me to be quiet so you can take a longer nap."

Life Is a Target of Satan

Satan is the angel of death and the champion of lies. He is always lurking in the shadows of our minds to destroy our faith that Christ is "the way, the truth, and the life" (John 14: 6, KJV). He's our biggest enemy. Watch for his attacks. He prowls around like a hungry lion to find those he can tear apart and devour. Stand up to him because he's a loser, just as he lost when he tempted Christ after his baptism by John the Baptist. As a Christian, you are already a winner. Don't let that liar tell you any differently.

Life Is a Race

Even though we are certified children of God, we must every day run fast, carrying the torch of God, in the race against sin. Satan is a crippled, fallen angel and a loser in everything he attempts to do as long as we keep our eye on the finish line where Christ is waiting to congratulate us. He is "the author and finisher of our faith"

(Hebrews 12:2, KJV).

Life Is the Gateway to Heaven

As faith-filled believers, we have passed from death into life in the here and now. The Bible tells us about our eternal life in the present tense (John 17:3). "This is life eternal, that they may know thee the only true God, and Jesus Christ, whom thou hast sent" (KJV). Life is all of these things rolled into one and more.

It matters not what life brings.

Learn to smile and think of pleasant things.

Have the courage to take a stand,

And never question God's command.

Since I used autumn as the theme for this chapter of my life, I scanned this chapter to see if there was a facet of autumn that I might have left out. Then it seemed the Holy Spirit found a poem at just the right time that I had written in October 1966. Knowing that the garden of Eden in the wonderful creation story of Genesis is often called paradise, my mind demanded to know if the garden of Eden experienced the seasonal changes of the vast geographic area surrounding it. I imagined it did.

Autumn is a wonderful season. It's like a fall bouquet.

The goldenrods are blooming up
and down my life's pathway.

The trees are dressed in yellow, golden
brown, and scarlet too.

With tree arms stretched in glory,
moist from the morning dew.

Erect are the surrounding mountains
beneath the mellow sun.

R.F. Jones

The garden of Eden; Eve, Adam's wife;
and Adam, God's first son.

I think I've found the secret of charm and grandeur too.

God showed paradise in Eden with
a smile for me and you.

The Last Years
with My Russ

1975 to Mid-1979

So many threads of gold were woven in and out of my life. The brightest golden thread was my Russ. In December 1975, we graciously celebrated our fiftieth wedding anniversary. The party was at the house where Mary and LaMoine lived in Okmulgee. All of our children and grandchildren were there. By the middle of 1979, my Russ would precede me to heaven. Maybe my poems, during these four and one-half years, will reveal how precious the golden threads of these few years were to us.

I and other people who knew my Russ well must have had a premonition that our time was short to be with him. It was as if we needed to make our expressions of appreciation before it was too late. Mary wrote him a special Father's Day note and included it with her gift.

Dear Daddy.

Happy Father's Day! I can't find words good enough to tell you all the deep feelings I have for you. I just feel so very blessed to have a dad such as you. You are just so very much a part of us—the way you think, the way you act, the things you love, and the things you hate. I feel so close to you, for I have been privileged to be much like you are in many ways. I believe your personality is a strong one, for it passed through me and shows up in my children. It's especially strong in Gaines and will, I am sure, show up in generations to come.

So on this Father's Day, it is easy to see that it is you who have given a gift so that this small gift I give you can only be worthwhile because these shoes will caress your dear feet that have left footprints worth walking in. Thank you for walking in Christ's footprints and showing me the way.

First in Christian love.

Second in daughter love.

Your Mary

My Russ had many young high school boys who worked for him at the station in addition to Son. One of them was Lloyd Hodges. He was a church friend of Son's who was one year younger than Son and graduated in Jerry Ann's high school class. Lloyd tended to have the wanderlust and enjoyed the freedom of moving from one part of the country to another. He liked to sing. He sang the tenor part in the gospel quartet that Son sang in with two other boys from the church. My Russ was like a father to Lloyd, so he often wrote to us to maintain the connection.

Dear Jones,

Hope all is well with you and yours. My situation has changed. I'm on the road to California and then a good chance at a job with the Alaska pipeline. Keep your fingers crossed for me, as this may just be my chance to get well financially. Someday, I want to buy a little piece of land somewhere and establish a peaceful little area to call my own, a place where I can be alone and think my own thoughts and live my own life.

Well, tonight I'm camped high in the California hills near Mount Shasta, and my heart and my mind are at peace. My little camper is cozy and warm, and the coffee pot is handy. So I said to myself, *No time like the present to send friend Jones a note.* You said it all when you spoke of feeling a closeness to me like that of a brother. I feel it too, and I'm glad you said it.

Wherever my wandering feet take me, and regardless of the distance or time between our letters, I'd like you to know that I'll always be in touch sooner or later, and my feeling will be the same.

I'll forever be mindful of that time I needed you and you were there. Losing my mother wasn't easy, and it was good to have you and Mrs. Jones there to comfort and strengthen me. Thank you both. Always stay happy and healthy and be good to each other.

Your friend, Lloyd

✝

I began to write to my sister Bertha more often. She was my best poem fan, so I wore her out by sending a poem with every letter so she would write back to me to tell me how good it was and how much she enjoyed it. It was now over forty years since our family had moved to California. Other than Troy—my oldest brother and my Russ's boyhood friend—Troy's second wife, Olga, and their children, I was the only close part of my Logan family who remained in Oklahoma. All the others were in California, emigrants of the Dust Bowl days. Bertha became my primary source of family news after Mama died in 1962. Bertha and I also wrote to each other about our faith and things that happened in our individual churches. I particularly liked to brag by saying, "This poem was published in the church newsletter."

I've found peace with my Savior, peace
I couldn't find anywhere.

His love dwells in my heart when my
heart is filled with prayer.

I feel the power of his presence. I never feel alone.

I've found peace with my Savior, and
someday I'm going home.

I look beyond the stars to that home I long to go,

When from this life I pass and leave this world below.

For there's a city built on high. Its
streets are paved in gold.

Its walls are jasper with gates of pearl.
Its beauties are untold.

Someday I'll live beyond the sky and
soar through outer space.

But in this life, I won't attain this
heavenly, wondrous place.

Only those who do God's will can walk that heavenly way.

They'll enter through the gates of pearl
when dawns that perfect day.

Bertha and Floyd, her husband, sent us a Christmas card every year. She always included family news in it. I don't know why people send Christmas cards if they don't include some personal things about themselves. I usually just sent a letter after Christmas telling how we celebrated the day with family.

Dear Sis and Floyd,

We got your newsy letter and Christmas card Monday. We surely were proud to hear from you all. I had begun to worry if I had written or just thought I had. I'm not too sure about anything anymore. We had a nice Christmas. We ate a noon dinner with Sonny's family, and then we ate supper with Mary's family. At Son's home, it isn't so noisy, but Mary has this music piped to every room in the house. I'd go nuttier than a bat. As with every Christmas, Russell gained too much weight, and now I have to take some abuse for helping him get his weight down again.

Dear Sis and Floyd,

I enjoyed your newsy letter so much I've read it at least six times so far.

I worked in the yard and cut down so much excess growth it took two truckloads to haul it off. At first, Russell wanted to kill me. I know he must have been thinking how big my doctor and hospital bills have been these last few years, but he would never lay that on me. Our yard sure looks different. I didn't tell Russ, but I doubled my pain medicine for a few days because I hurt enough for two people. I thanked the Lord that he let me do what I set out to do. Poor, patient Russ. I really take advantage of him and the Lord.

Russell had to get a different man to work for him. He has certainly had a hard time getting good help lately. I don't know how long he can continue to keep the station open because he's not physically able to keep it open twelve hours, six days a week. His is the only station in town that closes on Sunday now. Most of his customers know this, so Saturday's always a very busy day.

I finished my seventeenth quilt top today. I have a quilt top for all the kids and grandkids now, so I can take it easy until I think up a new project. I have a place to send the quilt tops to get them quilted. My eyes got so bad it worries me. I don't have enough sense to know I overused them working on the quilts.

✝

Dear Sis and Floyd,

Here it is, August 3, 1978. I know you are thinking of Mama today as I am. I don't remember exactly how old she would have been today. I think it would be ninety-four or ninety-five, the best I can remember. I still miss Mama and Papa so much, even though they have been gone this long.

> I think of my daddy. Oh, how I fill with pride!
> I was a constant shadow, walking by his side.

He came home from the fields, sometimes very late.
I ran so fast to meet him and opened wide the gate.
I also think of Mama with her long, black hair.
Her busy hands working hard, her arms always bare.
I still hear her singing as she molded daily bread.
I can hear her scold us when we sat on her feather bed.
Daddy gave me courage. Mama gave me song.
I can't wait to see them. Maybe it won't be too long.

I'm turning back many pages, sixty-five years or more.
I was raised in the country with no rugs upon the floor.
We drew water from a well. With a
broom, we scrubbed the floor.
When I was very young, this used to be my chore.
I walked to school and Sunday school,
three-quarters of a mile.
The sand and dust was so deep, sometimes I'd rest a while.
I shall always be grateful for the old rock well nearby.
I'd go there to wash my feet and wait for them to dry.
I wore calico dresses with no trimming, I recall.
And yet I felt so proud that I held my head up tall.
I used cornhusks for paper, and with
strings I'd roll my hair.
I put buttermilk on my face to make my complexion fair.
When the milk dried on my face,
I could hardly bat an eye.
It seemed to work wondrously for my
Russ looked as I walked by.

Sis, do you remember when I was just a child that I claimed a big tree near the house as my own? This was the tree near the spring, on which I carved my name, "Ida Pearl Logan." The day we were married, my Russ took me back there and used his pocket knife to add the name *Jones* to it.

When I was a child, I claimed a tree.
It grew near our home.

I used to slip away for hours and play there all alone.

Once while playing there, I roughly carved my name.

That was a long time ago. Today, it's not the same.

But I still see it in my mind, growing older every day.

And yet my mind is very young, so
it still goes there to play.

✝

Dear Sis and Floyd,

I hope you and Floyd are feeling better. I've had quite a time this past month. The doctor here in Okmulgee told me to go back to the doctor in Tulsa. The doctor in Tulsa wanted me to go to the hospital. I told him I didn't want to go the hospital if I could take the medication at home. I awoke this morning with breathing problems. Poor Russ. I feel so sorry for him. I'm a walking doctor bill.

Dear Bertha and Floyd,

Russ has a real nice fellow working for him now. He says it's so nice to have someone he can trust and who shows an interest in the business. Now, three days each week, he doesn't go back to work after lunchtime. This is a beautiful day in the spring of 1979. Russ got the newspaper and went out on the backyard patio to read it. It was really too cold for him to enjoy himself. I watched him as he laid the paper down and seemed to be thinking serious thoughts. After about thirty minutes, the cold drove him back into the house. He commented as he passed by me. "You know, Pearlie. If this man who's working for me now ever decides to quit, I think I'll know it's time to shut the station down." Sis, if this man continues to do well, the Lord willing, we might come to visit you this summer.

The Lord wasn't willing. My Russ was gone by summertime.

Bible study was a pleasant way for me to visit with the Father, Son, and Holy Spirit. Being a Bible student was to me more important than being a Bible teacher because too many Bible teachers stop learning. Individual Christians should have their own, individual, creative way to learn about their Creator.

Son was a good Bible student. He told me once how he had set the book of John to poetry. I had also been doing a similar thing in my daily Bible study. Looking at every word in a Bible verse and choosing words that rhymed forced me to look deeper into the Holy Spirit's thoughts. It helped me learn more new insights into the mind of Christ and into the Word of God than I would have found by any other way.

I want to go to heaven someday, to be there with my King.

I want to see all God's angels, to hear them sweetly sing.

I want to walk God's golden streets
and stand before his throne.

I want to hear my Jesus say a loving, "Welcome home."

I want to kneel at his feet and look upon his face.

I will hear him say, "Well done, my
child. You have won the race."

When I started on my journey, I was a lonely soul.

Then I met King Jesus and gave him full control.

I know where I'm going and where I'm going to stay:

A beautiful place called heaven, not very far away.

God goes with us on our journey to set our spirits free.

He guides us in our search for that sweet eternity.

Once I got a real good look at the heaven of the Bible, it was much easier to see some of heaven on earth. Once I accepted, "We have the mind of Christ," as the apostle Paul claims (1 Corinthians 2:16, KJV), it was easier for me to think like he does. Once I knew we have eternal life, as the apostle John says, "We know that we have passed from death to life," (1 John 3:14, KJV), it was easier to accept the spiritual fact that I didn't have to wait until heaven to start living the eternal life.

As I studied my Bible each day, I realized an overwhelming need to meditate and pray. If I was to meet him over there, I must hear him whisper hope and peace to me here as I connected my prayers to my Bible reading. I had learned to expect the scripture I was reading to speak to the question I had or the problem I needed him to solve. I did my best praying when I took time to set my prayer to poetry.

I want you, blessed Lord, to lead me all the way,

Not hurriedly, nor too slow, but steadily, Lord, I pray.

I want to make the road shine brightly
with my candle lit by you

So I can aid the saints of God in everything I do.

If you will light my candle and make it burn more bright,

If you will light my road ahead before my heavenly flight,

Then I will be more confident if you are walking near.

Please make my candle burn more
brightly so I will have no fear.

I even wrote a friendly letter to God one day as a prayer when I realized my prayer time was becoming too inconsistent.

Dear God,

I'm sure you think I've forgotten you. Here I am. As usual, I'm having to apologize for not letting you hear from me more often. I really do think of you every day, and I know I'd feel a lot better if I talked with you more often about what is on my heart and on my mind.

Dear God, you would be surprised how our great grand-children are growing. Kristy Dawn will be seven years old her next birthday, and Heather Marie will be two and one-half. Oh yes! I almost forgot. Our granddaughter Anne Russelle gave us a new great grandson named Luke. You probably didn't know about that since I haven't been communicating with you regularly.

Speaking of growing pains, I've been having some of my own lately. Our three kids are getting really old. Mary is fifty years old, Son is forty-five, and our Betty is some-where in between. The worst thing about it is that they are self-sufficient and don't need me in lots of ways like they once did. As you probably know, with me as an example, it really is hard to take when they act like they don't need you anymore. I'm learning how to handle this rejection to some degree, but I sure do need your help.

I must confess I haven't been obeying you as well as I should. Your Word tells me to have faith in you and not to worry. I worry about so many things I can't do a thing about. I worry my children don't talk to you often enough even though, if the truth were told, I'm not being a good example. I sure would like to have your help on this.

I know you will forgive me for such inconsistent reliance on you. It makes me feel much better to share these things with you.

My dear God, my dear friend, I can't close without thanking you from the bottom of my heart. Thank you for the many, many blessings you have allowed me, for my wonderful husband, our three children, grandchildren, great grandchildren, our many Christian friends, and good health. Thank you for your earth and the special joy each season brings.

Thank you for the material wealth you have given to us and our children. Please forgive me when I take your generosity for granted.

Most of all, dear Father, I thank you for constantly assuring me in your Word that you are in control of the universe you created and always will be. It fills me with great joy that I will see your face one of these days.

I will close now and will try very hard to talk to you and your Son more often.

All my love forever.

Your daughter in Christ,

Pearlie

The Bible is all about love. Its title could be, as the scriptures say, "God is love" (1 John 4:8, KJV), or, "For God so loved the world, that he gave his only begotten Son" (John 3:16, KJV) to shed his blood on the cross for me. I never questioned the Bible when it said love was greater than faith and hope, but I often pondered to know the depth of that truth. Here I was, seventy-two years old, and I still didn't understand it as fully as I would have liked.

In mildest weather, I often went out to our covered patio before sunrise. For me, flowers always reminded me of heaven at early dawn. I could feel God's presence in the magnolia blooms with their lemon smell and big, waxy leaves.

On a particular spring morning I was having these kinds of thoughts after Heather Marie, at three years old, had spent the night with us. When Heather awoke, she came looking for me. She crawled up on my lap and said, "What are you doing, Grandma?"

"I'm looking at the trees and flowers and listening to the birds singing. I'm thinking about watching you play among the flowers so I can look at you and listen to you too."

Heather wasn't one to stay in someone's lap very long, even in the early morning. She jumped out of my lap and started running around the lawn in her sleeping gown. Heather was like a falling tree when she ran. She had no more than started until she was there. As I watched her, I imagined what it would be like to watch her run and play in the garden of Eden. In my mind, I began to see other children running and playing with Heather, in and out of Eden's flower beds and blossoming fruit trees. Then, in my imagination, I saw a child who could have only been our baby Francis crawling around on the grass as other children leaped over him as he laughed with glee. Watching Heather playing was as if the Lord had made it clear that he had taken the garden of Eden up into heaven as a playground for little children he had taken "before their time." This impression gave me great comfort.

Heather was running in circles, flapping her arms up and down. "Look at me, Grandma. I'm a bird." I called to her, and she called back, "What do you want, Grandma?"

"Come and sit in my lap again. I've got a special secret I want to tell you."

She bounded around the flower beds and, with expectant eyes bugged out and a big smile on her face, commanded, "I'm here now! Tell me your special secret!"

I hugged her up close and whispered in her ear, "Heather, you are a jeweled flower in God's hand."

Her response was, "Okay. Let's eat some breakfast. Being a bird made me hungry."

✝

It was in this chapter of my life that Betty asked me to write the biography of my life. It started out harmlessly like this.

"Mother, why don't you write an autobiography of your life? I think it would be real interesting for the family to read."

My reply was quick and a bit haughty. "So you think your Daddy and I aren't going to live much longer."

Betty did that thing she did with her head, tilting it back and forth sideways, and, with an equal mixture of good humor and a pure statement of fact, she answered back, "Well, you're not getting any younger."

I wanted to give another sharp retort, but I thought, *Now, Pearl, you've been writing some little things recently about growing old gracefully. Here's your chance to practice it to see if you really want to make a habit of it. Just think about it. Here's an excuse to play around the old home place again, write in some really flowery sentences, and have a captive audience to read it. Maybe some of your family will say it's so well written it should be published.*

So I answered, "Dear, sweet Betty, that's the dearest thing you could ask me to do. Back home when I was a young girl, I sought peace in the placid hills and fields around Lenna, hills with lovely, green hollows and sweeping prairies. Each day, the birds filled the air with previously unsung melodies from misty dawn to the dusk of evening. In spring, the birds trilled and twittered fearlessly, only silenced by a heavy rain. I remember watching the clouds build into the great, soft shapes of a castle floating through the sky until it was scattered by a mischievous puff of wind. Oh, Betty! This is going to be such fun!"

About that time, Betty held up her hand and, with the body motion this time of holding her head very stiffly, with her chin against her chest and her shoulders doing an up and down dance, she spoke very authoritatively, "I didn't ask you to tell your life story to me. I asked you to write about it."

I cut back at her, "Well. You sound just like the publishers I send my stuff to. Are you going to reject my story before you ever read it?" *Back up Pearlie,* I said to myself. "I'm sorry, Betty. I know you're just teasing me. I so wished to get some of my things published and become famous. I got myself all emotionally worked up over your request. Rejections are no fun, but I can't stop writing. Thank you for encouraging me to entertain myself by doing this for you. It will be fun."

"That's what I had in mind, Mother. I promise to be your best literary fan and read every word as if I were playing beside you as we walk across the soft, green meadow, tuned with the clear, ringing notes of a bob white, singing from the pink, wild roses blooming on a rail fence as cowbells on a distant hill sound like fairy wind chimes. Ha! I can do that too. If you want me to, I'll be your editor."

"Now you're making fun of me. Keep it up. I like to be teased. Now, get out of my way. I've some serious remembering to do. Let's see. How should I start it?"

Sweet memories of a little garden where I used to go and play

As I gathered sweet wildflowers that bloomed along the way.

There in this lovely garden, in my own secret realms,

The stars came out to greet me as I slept beneath the elms.

How awesome were the flowers. But oh, my child, how brief,

For seasons change so quickly from buds to autumn leaf.

Yet the stars were always with me, full of wonder and delight,

As I strolled in my garden on a warm, summer night.

I had finished my memories and sent them to Betty when Son and Jerry Ann came down from Tulsa one weekend. Son noticed the leftover small pieces of notes I had made and read some of them. He asked about what they were, and I told him they were just notes or thoughts I hadn't been able to find a home for yet.

He said, "Mother, some of these are really good. If they're original, you should put them together into a small book called *Pearlie's Proverbs*."

I thought, *I wish these kids would leave me alone. Are they ganging up on me now?* I wondered what bright idea Mary would have for me next. I told Son that I had written many pages about my life for Betty.

Son's casual remark was, "When do I get my copy of this story?"

This was long before every household had a computer and a copier ready to use at a moment's notice. I was still in the old-fashioned mode of a lead pencil and ruled pads of paper. I could have used a typewriter, but I thought better and was more accurate with a pencil in my hand.

The next week, as I was gathering up the scraps of paper, I jotted down some of "Pearlie's proverbs" just to see what they might look like.

Pearlie

Your face is for others, not for you to see.

Yesterday is today's memory. Tomorrow is today's dream.

I said, "Why can't birds get along and not fight?
They have the whole world to live in."
Daddy said, "Why can't people get along and not
fight? They have the whole world to live in too."

Be alone in your thoughts, and dwell
in the solitude of your heart.

The greatest teacher is the heart. From the heart the
mouth speaks. The sound of laughter comes from the
heart. The sound of music comes from the heart.

Life is such a mad race

Lived at such a rapid pace.

Not going anyplace. What a disgrace!

Abraham Lincoln wisely observed, "Most people are
about as happy as they make up their minds to be."

A run in your hose, a stopped-up nose,

Can make you miserable, I suppose.

Life is too short to be wasted on
unhappiness and selfishness.

Nothing hurts a woman more than to have
a live secret and a dead telephone.

Little by little, I am learning,
While the wheel of life is turning,
To stop and think before I speak
And let my thoughts play hide and seek.

Learn to have a sense of humor.
Put Mr. Worry on the shelf.
There's always something to laugh about,
Even if it's only about yourself.

Life is so hurried and hectic for people like I am who
don't have a regular job to go to each day. We have to
run like the dickens to catch up with the day before.
The author of *Alice in Wonderland* said something
like "running fast to stay in the same place."

Frogs have it made. All they have to
do is sit in the mud and sing.

Supreme Court Justice Clarence Thomas said he
had a bust of his grandfather in his office with the
words, "Can't is dead and I helped bury him."

That little old word *can't* will surely get you down.
It fills your heart with misery and makes you wear a frown.
But if you keep on trying, there will surely come a day
You'll never say, "I can't," and work will seem like play.

Too many of us are victims of worry sickness. We worry
about the future and fail to enjoy the present. We worry

about what will happen and what has happened. It's not
worth it. Why don't we just make up our minds to live
each day as a holiday and enjoy it one day at a time?

Procrastination is a terminal disease.
It's fatal to procrastinate,
Until you find it now too late
And then blame it off on fate.
To put to right a big mistake,
The forgiving gesture you meant to make,
The habit you vowed to break—
Tomorrow just might be too late.
Not what we have but what we use.
Not what we see but what we choose.
Not what's nearby, not what's afar,
Not what we seem but what we are.
Not what we take but what we give.
Not as we pray but as we live.
These are the things that mar or bless,
The sum of human happiness.
These are the things that make or break,
That give the heart its joy or ache.
These are the things that make for peace
Both now and after time shall cease.

If you want to be loved, you must practice love.
If you want to be trusted, you must
prove yourself to be true.
If you want to be glad, you must learn to give.

Must I lose love to really know what love means to me?
Must I be blind to really know what it means to see?

You can cure your worst frown with your sweetest smile.

When your work is hard, rest if you must, but don't quit.
Success is failure turned inside out,
For many a failure is turned about
Because the winner stuck it out.

Life has its disappointments. There's
no reason to be one of them.
A new broom won't sweep a room
clean unless someone uses it.

Christians don't have a part-time job.
Full-time Christians don't get two weeks off with pay.

A river filled by little streams, frolicking over waterfalls,
Murmurs and hums upon its way
and won't ever stop to play.

"The fear of the Lord is the beginning
of wisdom" (Proverbs 9:10, KJV).
The Lord's Word is a pillow of
comfort under my aging head.

A cool head and a warm heart will serve you well each day.

Don't we show trust in our Creator
each time we plant a seed?

Why don't we trust him on other things we do?

Even tiny quails leave tracks when
they walk across a dusty road.

You can't walk with Christ and not walk with God.

If you're an unhappy Christian, doesn't
that seem rather odd?

Make the next season better by thanking
God for the present one.

The most important thing a father can do
for his children is to love their mother.

I finally had to learn to take a more lighthearted approach to the many publisher rejections I received. I should have decided long ago to stop sending poems and songs to publishers, but I decided to try one more time by mailing four songs I thought might be good enough. The worst part of this kind of decision is the waiting and hoping after a few weeks.

I had learned that the results would be obvious as soon as the letter carrier stepped upon the porch to deliver the mail. If there was an acceptance, a letter would arrive asking permission to keep the poem or song for possible consideration. I didn't get many of these. If the letter carrier placed a big package in the mailbox, the same size I had sent off, I knew it was a rejection with the return of my work. From much experience, I learned the sound of rejection very well.

I heard the mailman drop mail in the box,
So loud it sounded like he delivered some rocks.
I said to myself, *Nothing else could it be,*
But my four little songs coming back to me.
Sure as the moon shines up above,
There were my four songs that only I seemed to love.
I said to myself, *Happy I should be,*
To be writing songs for nobody but me.
I said to myself, *Happy I should be,*
That these silly old songs aren't feeding me.

✝

Growing old gracefully was one of my goals in life. My body clearly told me I was growing old at seventy-three. My hair had turned white. Wrinkles were showing on my face, and my biceps were begging to hang down no matter how much I used my arms in the garden.

When some young woman would, with a sweet voice, ask, "How old are you, dear?", I would sometimes answer, "I say to all who think I'm old and past my prime, I'm not so old. It's just that I've been young a very long time."

Then, if this younger woman asked, "What's the secret of staying young, honey?" as she looked me up and down to evaluate my lacy dress and practical, old lady shoes, I would fire back, "Oh, I've found that dreams never go out of style."

Then, after deciding to leave a more graceful impression with this young thing, who's trying her best to be kind to me, I use a genuinely friendly tone to add, "I want to stay busy and dream dreams as long as I have breath. I've never known a busy person who was miserable and really seemed old to others."

I've always thought it was wonderful to see people grow old gracefully. I've never seen it fail. If one is happy, relaxed, and in good spirits when they are young, that's the way they will be when they grow older. But if they are crabby, quarrelsome, and hard to get along with in their younger days, they'll grow more that way in their older days.

There are two psalms that the Holy Spirit has provided to encourage God's children when they are feeling old or useless.

I have been young, and now am old; yet have I not seen the righteous forsaken, nor his seed begging bread.

Psalm 37:25 (KJV)

Those that be planted in the house of the Lord shall flourish in the courts of our God. They shall still bring forth fruit in their old age.

Psalm 92:13–14 (KJV)

✝

When Son and Jerry Ann visited me one weekend for my seventy-third birthday, she gave me a big bottle of pink lotion. I couldn't believe how wasteful I was with it and how quickly I emptied the bottle. I suppose I thought it might remove some of my age wrinkles. I sent her a thank-you poem.

The pink lotion was wonderful. It made me feel so fine.

I poured it on so thick because you said 'twas mine.

I must have been wasteful. The lotion just went way down.

I felt like a wasteful queen wearing a waster's crown.

I've tried to make it last by spreading it so thin.

When the pink lotion is gone, what will I do then?

Use Vaseline Intensive Care or some other kind?

Or wish for an early Christmas to ease my poor, old mind?

For his gift, Son wrote a poem on twenty pieces of paper cut out the same size as dollar bills. There were two lines of the poem on each of the pieces of paper. He put dollar bills of various denominations between each poem sheet, so by the time I got to the last line of the poem I had quite a sum of money. I thought, *I'm making more money on Son's poems than I do on my own.*

Once each year, we have this problem
That comes in March, the windy season.
How do we give a gift of money
Without giving some logical reason?

We thought about giving you crutches
For the next time you climb a tree.
But since you're enrolled in Medicare,
You can probably get those for free.

We thought about an electric shocker
To keep our Daddy Russ awake.
But you'd have to wake up to use it.
That wouldn't be handy, for goodness sake!

We considered giving you a monument
For putting up with us so well.
But we couldn't find one big enough;
The Grand Canyon isn't for sale.

There's no way to repay you
For the things you've given us.
You've given us so many things
That give our lives a buzz.

You've given us a saucy mouth
That hasn't helped a lot.
But you've given us a happy smile
That helped when we got caught.
You've given us an ornery streak,
And we won't give it back.
Because it makes us more like you,
With funny wit, sharp as a tack.

So take this sum of money.
Decide to spend it or to save.
But after seventy-three fun-filled years,
Don't you think you should behave?

Julie, Ryan, Russelle, Mark (Russelle's husband), and Son signed it. Jerry Ann included a note with her signature. "I'm the one who took him off your hands."

✝

At the end of May 1979, my Russ closed the gas station and was completely retired so he could be at home all day long. This was when the convenience stores came into existence, selling both gasoline and groceries, including beer. The idea of selling beer was so foreign to him that he decided it was time for him to get out of the business.

He had already ceased being a full-time elder a few years before this, although church people kept coming to him with their personal burdens. He did most of his pastoral counseling in the informal atmosphere of the gas station. Work at the station six days a week and listening to the problems of church people and customers probably contributed to the burden on his heart.

Less than two weeks after my Russ closed the station, while he was mowing the lawn, he had a heart attack. I called an ambulance to take him to the hospital. Next, I called Jerry Ann because Mary and LaMoine were on vacation in Colorado. Betty still lived in south Texas, and Son was in Seattle on an important business trip.

Jerry Ann came from Tulsa the morning I called her. She planned to stay with me as long as necessary. She brought a bucket of plums with her to help keep me busy between hospital visits by making some plum jelly. Since I never learned to drive a car, she became my personal chauffeur and listener during those few traumatic days.

I told my Russ all the things Jerry Ann had been doing for me. During one of her visits with him, he took her hand, and by way of a compliment, said, "Jerry, you're quite a trooper."

He said a similar thing to me as he was rushed to the hospital in an ambulance. He said, "Mother, they've been working on me like little troopers."

His condition was deteriorating quickly, so we called Mary and Son to let them know. Son arrived late at night. A wise nurse, who knew us and knew that his daddy wouldn't live much longer, took Son aside and told him, "Sonny, you need to go talk to your Daddy and tell him everything you need to say to him."

The next morning I asked, "Daddy, did you see Sonny last night?"

He answered, "Yes, I saw Son last night."

Later that day, he went into a coma.

Early the next morning, we got the call that my Russ had died. That morning, when Mary and LaMoine got back to Okmulgee, they came straight to the hospital, not knowing they were too late to talk to him once more.

I didn't remember very many details about the funeral. I was pretty much in a daze. A year earlier, we had selected a gravestone and a gravesite near the main entrance of the Okmulgee Cemetery. We had bought a burial policy from the funeral home even earlier. For such a humble man, I was surprised and pleased that my Russ had picked a gravesite that everyone entering the cemetery had to drive by.

The funeral and burial were on a Monday. Because he was a well-known businessman in town, his picture and an obituary were on the front page of the Sunday *Okmulgee Daily Times.* All day Saturday, I sat with his body as family and people from town and church came to the funeral home to pay their respects to him and to encourage me.

I was a little bit surprised, a little bit jealous, and a little bit proud that so many attractive women came by and told me how well he had taken care of their cars. I told Son about this, and he said he wasn't surprised at all because Daddy was a handsome man and gave all of his customers very good service. Then, he added, "And when I worked for him until my third year of college, I helped."

Among his friends and customers who came to pay their respects were African Americans, whom he respectfully called *Negro* and *colored people* back then. Also, there were full-blood Native American Indians. One was an Indian rancher named

Bunch Miller. His two sons sometimes took Son with them to rodeos on Saturday nights when they competed in calf roping and bulldogging. Okmulgee was the capital of the Creek Nation.

There was a black farmer from as far away as Boynton, who my Russ and Son addressed as Mr. LaGrange.

The black owner of the tire shop next door to the service station came by. My Russ insisted that Sonny address him as Mr. Carol, though George and Son were close friends.

The owner of the black funeral home came. His business was on the street north of the gas station.

Some ladies from the segregated black church wept as they viewed his body. My Russ taught their ladies' Bible class for a while on Sunday nights when they were without a preacher.

The church people who came by told me how much they appreciated his leadership as a church elder for thirty-six years and how much they enjoyed his Bible teaching on Wednesday nights.

I kissed my Russ goodbye. His lips felt like an angel's wings brushing my lips, and I remembered his saying to me, "Mother, be careful with the savings. If I should go before you do, I think you will be well taken care of."

Even though I had Jesus beside me, my children to help me with practical matters, and church friends praying for me and visiting me, I felt lonely. I was comforted knowing my Russ was drinking from the crystal fountain that flows from the river of life from the throne of God. I was comforted that he would stand beside the river, under the fruit trees, holding our baby in his arms, when I joined them. I knew someday God would send one of his strong angels to carry me up the stairway to heaven and through the gate to heaven as God held it open for me to go in and hold my family members in my arms again.

Grieving for My Russ

Mid-1979 through 1981

The week before my Russ went to be with the Lord, he taught a Wednesday night Bible lesson at church. He talked to us about the Bible being like a mirror for us to see ourselves as we really are at any given point in our Christian walk. He said, "If each of us is truly faithful and filled with God's own righteousness, we can look in the mirror and see that our burdens aren't as heavy as we thought." He continued. "If we really trust God, we can fall asleep at night and know if we don't wake up in the morning, we would be safe with God."

As usual, I turned to my writing to put my lonely, grieving thoughts into perspective. I knew I had to take one of two choices. I could shrink into myself and wait for the day God called me home, or I could prepare myself to walk on for many more years until that glad day arrived. Since my Russ had gone to great lengths to provide money for me to live on, he would expect me to plan for the long-term for the remainder of my time on earth, knowing it's only a tiny fraction of eternity as a measure of time.

Within a month after the funeral, I had written a nine-page letter and hand-copied one for each one of our children. I felt compelled to tell them what was in my heart and mind, hoping that my openness would help them speak to me more openly about their feelings.

I reminded them of the love we have in our hearts for each other and the love we will have in all of our tomorrows as we help each other to adjust to live this life without our dear, sweet Daddy. I reminded them how so very much their daddy loved them.

A day didn't go by without him telling me how abundantly he loved me. I would have felt stranded with no purpose in my life without the Lord and our children.

Daddy's death didn't shake my faith. I said to myself, *God will keep his arms around me, and I will carry on. Besides, Daddy is with the Lord and looking down on me every minute of every hour.* I knew this was true because God's Word says we will be around family in heaven. For example, in the book of Genesis, Moses writes, "Then Abraham gave up the ghost, and died in a good old age, an old man, and full of years; and was gathered to his people" (Genesis 25:8, KJV).

Being without Daddy was like climbing a mountain. Burdened and drained of energy, it was hard to continue. So God gave me a whole church, a fellowship of believers to strengthen and encourage me.

Although Daddy was gone, he still lived on whenever we thought of the Christian deeds he did while living. Heaven's files bulge with all the good deeds Daddy did while working for the Lord, even after a long, hard day's work. Daddy let religion be his everyday practice. Consistency in Christian living was his way of life and his way of thinking. I never heard Daddy say a bad word in his whole life.

I always wished I was as good a woman as Daddy was a man. I'd heard him tell many people who he was trying to lead to the Lord, "After you become a Christian, your life won't be your own because you've been bought with the price of Christ's death on the cross."

My flesh was so weak when I thought about having to live without Daddy. A deep sense of loss washed over me. There would be no more sweet talks. The best times of all were when Daddy and I sat on the backyard patio on rare evenings and talked about the past. More often, we would sit at the kitchen table after supper and talk. Oh my! There were so many things I needed to ask Daddy that I didn't know how to do.

I prayed that our children would remember all the things their daddy stood for. No one stood between him and God. He cherished lofty ideals and beautiful visions about heaven. Now his dreams had come true. He now had a lot to sing about. I really loved to hear Daddy sing at church as I stood beside him.

Daddy and I often looked at the stars and imagined, "If the bottom side of heaven is so beautiful, imagine what the top side looks like."

Some of the things my Russ failed to teach me were how to write banking checks, how to balance the checkbook, how to keep track of the Medicare papers, and how to pay the income taxes.

Son said, "Don't worry about balancing your checkbook, trying to figure out the Medicare papers and doctor bills, or filling out your annual income taxes. I can do that when Jerry Ann and I come down on weekends. We'll set it up so your Social Security check and monthly interest from your savings account go directly into your checking account. We'll see how well you can live on that amount and then decide if or when we need to take any principal from your savings account."

Mary laughed real big and said, "I can help you learn how to write checks. I'm really good at that." Then she laughed even bigger and spoke with a bigger laugh in her voice, "And when Betty comes home from Texas for a visit, she can help you write checks too. She's even better at it than I am."

I was alarmed about all this talk about financial freedom. All I could say was, "Daddy told me to be careful and I think you will be well taken care of." This turned out to be true.

The very God of the ages was with me after I lost my Russ. My heart was so heavy, but I made myself go on in a quiet voice. I had known of God's greatness for a long, long time, and I knew he cared for me personally. I was sad, but the sun still shined on in a world that was unbelievably beautiful. I was seeing God's provision for my needs.

I ached with homesickness, like heavy snow falling on me, as I carried the trash out by myself, a job my Russ had always done in our last years together. For my healing each night, I breathed a special prayer, speaking the greatest truth of all: "Jesus loves me." And through these nightly prayers, I became aware of my commission to share this love with others. It was as if Christ said directly to me, "How can you be a Christian and not give of yourself?"

Although I feel so lonely and my heart is very sad,

When I think of Daddy's deeds, my heart grows very glad.

I learned to give time a chance. Time is a great healer. I learned to live again and laugh again. I could finally clean the headstone of Daddy's grave, arrange some flowers from my garden, and say, "Thank you, Lord, for this beautiful day." The birds sang at the cemetery just like they did in my garden. I grew more reconciled. I was still lonely, but I had peace in my heart. The Prince of peace was making each day more peaceful.

I then knew more about death than I had ever known before, and I wasn't afraid of it. Though in my youth it seemed so far away, now I knew it really wasn't very far away at all. Of course, life has its limits. I might live another year, five years, or ten years. As I had been told by people older than I, "Life goes faster the older you grow." So I decided I had to hurry because Christ had given me a mission to fulfill.

Our grandchildren were a great part of my healing process. Ryan was working on an engineering degree at Tulsa University and drove down to see me sometimes. We had a lot in common since we both had an active imagination and liked to make words fit together.

When Ryan came from Tulsa to visit, we would have a quiet lunch together while we had a nice conversation. We shared our vivid imaginations, and he would ask me about things I had gotten published. He had aspirations of being an author someday. I told him, "If it wasn't for our weekly church newsletter, I wouldn't have had many of my poems published for the public to read. I guess if it hadn't been that your grandfather was an elder, I wouldn't have even gotten many of those published."

We laughed about this. I gave him the best advice I had learned. "I've concluded that most successful authors have to know someone on the inside who will vouch for them to get most publishers to consider their work."

Ryan and I went out into the yard to look at my flowers and walked over the concrete driveway he constructed. Son sent Ryan down to dig out the dirt, pour concrete, and smooth out a driveway when Ryan was in high school. I was a little peeved at Son for not coming down to help him.

As it turned out, the concrete truck came and dumped its whole load inside the wooden frames Ryan had formed and drove away. It was too big a job for one person to spread it, so I and Mrs. Gray, my neighbor across the street, had to hurry and help spread it. This didn't appear to be one of Ryan's most pleasant memories. But I thanked him again for it.

Ryan asked, "How're you getting along without Grandpa?"

I used the driveway pouring as an example of how I felt. I told him, "I keep telling myself there is a light at the end of the tunnel. Life has been good to me, and it will be good again. It's like our experience with the driveway. I accept the fact that things will go wrong occasionally and even overwhelm you. But if someone like you shows up at just the right time to carry some of the load, I can always make it to the next day."

Until then, he hadn't realized how much his visits meant to me. Fortunately for me, frequent visits from friends and family helped make me a stronger person. I wouldn't say I never got angry. I also wouldn't claim to be an incredibly sweet person, because I knew I wasn't. I was very nice, though—not all the time, but often enough to be given the benefit of the doubt.

I continued answering Ryan's question. "Most of my life is behind me now. I'm not as sad as I was. I'll never get over losing Daddy. I can't put back the clock of time or the calendar of days. But I can begin again, at this time of my life, even if it's nothing more than sending a poem in the mail as an encouragement to someone who is going through something like I have lived through. It could be that my best poems are in front of me."

I thanked Ryan for coming to visit me and to see how I was getting along without his grandpa.

Back to My Old Self

1982 through 1989

Jo Forister, Jerry Ann's mother, lost her husband, Will, the year before I lost Daddy. She visited me and told me that it had taken her almost three years to recover from her deep grieving when Mr. Forister died. I hadn't quite reached that point yet, but her visit gave me hope.

Daddy was like an ancient oak when it came to the faith he had in God and in his role as a church elder. He would say to me and to himself as well, "Elders who aren't humble and who rule with force and hardness will scatter the sheep. Elders who function only as decision makers, while totally neglecting their duties as a shepherd, can never have the full confidence of the congregation."

He loved to hear God's truth proclaimed by a preacher. He didn't care if a sermon was long, as long as God's Word was being preached. This is the way he lived until his last breath. I had heard him pray, "Lord, give me a peaceful hour to depart and be with thee."

I once asked Daddy what advice he would give to a young preacher. His answer was a gem: "The most important thing is to be yourself. Don't try to be or sound like someone else. Second, live faithfully, so you may gain the confidence of the congregation. Don't ever think you are better than they are. Study your Bible and learn as much as you can about the 'Thus saith the Lord.' Above all, live righteously, and don't let others upset your mind. Be ready to suffer as Christ and the apostles did."

Daddy suffered more than I ever would have in his place. As a church leader, God tried his faith many times, and like Job, he never found it wanting.

Daddy had many friends from many races who fondly remembered him. Everywhere I went around town, people said how much they loved him and what he did for them to cause them to live a more faithful life. He also did that for me all the years of our marriage.

I met a lady in the grocery store one day. She had a bunch of dill in her hand. So I asked, "May I smell that? I love the smell of dill when I can dill pickles in jars."

She lifted her eyebrows as if she had been searching around the store for me. She exclaimed, "You're just the person I need to talk to. I don't know exactly how to make dill pickles."

"If you will give me a phone call, I can give you my recipe," I offered. I wanted to offer her a way out in case she was only trying to be nice to a lonely, old lady who wanted to visit with people in a store.

She asked my name and phone number. When I told her my name, she threw up her hands as if I had given her a gift. "Oh, Mrs. Jones, I'm so glad to meet you. I knew Russell for a long time. He was always so kind and helpful to me. I hope you don't misunderstand if I tell you I loved him."

"I don't mind at all. Thank you for making my day."

I hadn't been able to dispose of Daddy's clothes and shoes

yet. Just to think about doing this made me feel blue. I decided to practice by throwing away his medications.

I threw away Daddy's medicine,
almost more than I could do.

When I took it to the trash, it made me feel so blue.

In the cabinet, it left a vacant place
where it had stayed so long.

I gazed at it for many days, willing it to make me strong.

I'm going to keep the shaving cream,
like he left it in the bowl.

The lather had once foamed and then
dried up and turned cold.

Nowadays, I need an angel to kindly quiet my mind,

To guide my faulting footsteps and
stretch these ties that bind.

The silver cord has been severed.
Daddy's voice is quiet and still.

Even though the tears of grief are
falling, this is our Father's will.

He now has sweet serenity no mortal life has known.

We know his soul is rejoicing, wearing a robe of his own.

The silver cord is broken. Hush. Hush. Let us not cry.

He'll meet us that great morning,
when Christ comes in the sky.

I pictured Daddy smiling at me at times. Other times, I thought I heard him telling me to hurry so we wouldn't be late for church. One day, when he was alive, as I was dawdling around, probably on purpose since he was hurrying me, he pitched a quarter to me and said, "Here. Call a taxi cab when you get ready."

I loved him more and more each year we lived together. I didn't claim we didn't have our differences. During his last year, he seemed more nervous and would get upset over little things. He would always say he was sorry when he hurt my feelings. Sometimes I would forget that he was getting more sensitive and I would tell him about something he did that I didn't like. He would listen until I ran down and then say, "Mother, you have always been the sassiest little thing I've ever known."

†

The telephone company had a TV commercial that said, "Reach out and touch someone today." I gave it a try. I thought, *A little long-distance phone visiting with my California family will help cure my loneliness.*" However, when Son was going over the checkbook to balance it, he noticed the big phone bill and asked if it was possible they had made a mistake. I confessed, "I guess I reached out and touched too many people last month."

On this particular visit, about six months after Daddy had passed away, Son spent the night with me. After supper I said, "Let's not watch television tonight. Let's just talk."

He could tell I wanted to talk about Daddy. "Okay. Tell me how you're doing. I'm real proud of the way you're getting much more like your old self."

"I'll never be my old self again until I'm in heaven with my family and Daddy and the baby. But seriously, you kids have been a great help, and I'm adjusting very well. That doesn't mean I don't sometimes step out of the kitchen and walk to his chair in the living room to tell him something or ask a question that only he can answer. Sometimes I try to imagine he's just gone to sleep watching television and I will talk to him later."

Son replied, "Oh, I catch myself doing the same thing. It's not just that I would like to talk to him sometimes. It's just a natural reaction to actually pick up the phone to call him and realize I can't do it anymore. Sometimes, I walk by a mirror and see him because my walk is the same as his."

I told Son a funny story on myself that I had been dying to tell someone. When he chuckled, I heard Daddy's laugh. "That's why I like to say funny things that make you laugh—because your chuckle is just like his."

I said to Son, "I know I'm doing better because, more often now, I try not to inflict my grief on others. I'm also thinking about my plans for the future. So I feel like that's a good step forward too. I plan to live in this house until I can't live alone anymore." I was actually fishing for some good response from Son since he knew what my finances were.

"You don't need to worry about that, Mother. Daddy has taken good care of your finances, and you're doing a good job of not spending more than is coming in. Why don't you revise your plans to say you're going to live in your house, even if we have to pay someone to stay with you if we can't take care of you?"

That was exactly what I wanted to hear.

Son decided to get us off that subject. "Tell me what you've been thinking about writing next. We're all needing to receive a good laugh in the mail. I think it's time to put your imagination to work again. Do you want to practice on me the way you used to practice on Daddy?"

"Well, I've been thinking quite a lot about heaven lately. I'm really looking forward to it because clothes won't get dirty there, and food won't have to be cooked, and dishes won't have to be washed. How's that for a start?"

"Sounds good to me because when Jerry Ann was going to college, the kids and I would have to jump up from the supper table and clean up the kitchen. But you're a very active person. Surely you'll want to find a job to do."

"I hadn't thought about that! Yes, I will need to find something to do. Let me put my imaginer to work. Let's see. The clouds will surely get holes in them that will need to be darned.

"I'm like Liza in John Steinbeck's book *East of Eden*. Tiny Liza was a hardworking, Bible-reading wife and mother all her life. She couldn't imagine 'how even the Elect could survive for very long in the celestial laziness which was promised.' Surely there will be some 'weary angel wings that will need to be rubbed down with liniment.'"

I asked Son, "Do you suppose there will be cobwebs in the corners of the mansions? Liza said, 'Even in heaven there would be cobwebs in some corner to be knocked down with a cloth-covered broom.' I also don't know if I would want to go to heaven if there weren't cobwebs that need to be knocked down with a cloth on the end of my broom."

Son yawned and said, using Daddy's repeated phrase, "I think I'd better check it to you, Pearlie, and go to bed."

"This has been a real good visit," I said, trying to think of a way to keep him up a little longer. "I think I'll stay up a while and work on these new ideas now that you've stimulated my imagination. Why don't you have another piece of chocolate pie and sit in Daddy's chair and eat it while I jot down a few notes I can finish tomorrow?"

Son's visit got my creative juices flowing again. My wide-awake dreams came more often. Also, I spent more time writing to Betty and my grandchildren. Mary and LaMoine were in Okmulgee, and Son and Jerry Ann were in Tulsa, so I saw their children often. Eventually, Russelle and her husband, Mark, moved to the Dallas area, where Mark ran an accounting business. Russelle helped him part-time.

My second poem after Daddy passed away described how I liked to record things I saw and imagined in my daydreams.

> I love to sit in peaceful solitude, within
> the shadow of lacy shade,
>
> And feel such gladness in my heart
> for all things God has made.

Butterflies sway on colored wings.
Lovely fairies dance in the rain.

Birds light on swinging boughs to feed
their young in the spring.

The drowsy beauty of a summer day or an unrippled stream

And gentle winds rustling in the trees.
This is how I love to dream.

I saw fewer and fewer young women who were willing to remain at home to raise a family. This seemed to come from wanting more material things than their husbands could provide. I had never been embarrassed when people asked, "What was your occupation before you retired?"

I never replied, "Oh, I was just a housewife." I don't care whom I was talking to. I would just fling my shoulders back, lift my chin a noticeable level, look the questioner in the face, and say, "I'm a wife and a mother, and I don't ever plan to retire." Then, when I realized how haughty and proud this sounded, I added in a more conciliatory tone, "I can't think of a higher calling than to be a full-time mom."

This always meant my children never had to come home to an empty house. I was there to see my children off to school in the morning, when they came home at noon for lunch, and when they came home from school or home from work after school when they were older. I could confidently say, "Motherhood is one of the greatest honors and one of the greatest responsibilities. It helps to know the good Lord gives us mothers all the help we need."

I got back to paying more attention to my neighbors, hoping to not be a lonely, old widow to them. I walked across the street to take a piece of cake to my friend Ilene and caught her in an awful mess. I had phoned to say I was coming over, so she said, "Good. Bring enough for yourself also. I'll make some popcorn so we can have a vegetable before we eat the cake and call it lunch." When I knocked on the door, she opened it, and I could hear the popcorn popping.

My friend Ilene lives across the street.

Most of the time, she keeps her house real neat.

She put the popcorn on to pop but didn't put on the lid.

I'll give one guess for you to know
just what the popcorn did.

We heard the popping sound. She turned and ran in there.

Orville Redenbacher's corn was scattered everywhere.

I don't think my friend Ilene will do this anymore.

She'll hold the lid on really tight and
not answer her front door.

This incident reminded me about a time when I was a new bride at our house in Preston. I grew vegetables in a garden each year. I learned that people learn from their mistakes. That's why I've learned so much in the fifty-seven years since then. I had a neighbor named Mrs. Cotton. I liked to be the first one among my neighbors to harvest new potatoes each year. This is where I learned, "Pride goes before a fall." I also learned a way not to clean new potatoes.

I experimented with the cleaning of my new potatoes by rubbing them with dry white sand. I didn't rinse them off. I made a batch of mashed potatoes. Before serving my Russ his supper, I took Mrs. Cotton a bowlful of mashed potatoes. Then I proudly served my husband his dinner. The potatoes were so gritty we couldn't eat them. The most embarrassing thing was to have to run up the dirt street and tell Mrs. Cotton how very stupid I had been. She gave me a chuckling encouragement, "Well, live and learn. When I give you some of my new potatoes, I promise to clean them with water."

I soon had another poem published in the church newsletter as I began to feel more like my old self.

Christ came with flying footsteps, eyes
aglow, and voice so sweet,

Kneeling on the turf beside us and
laid his pardon at our feet.

Wide he flung the massive portal
leading to our home on high,

Far from the darkening shadows where
our soul shall never die.

In strong arms, he'll clasp us to him,
whispering, "Have no fear."

We'll hear his voice inviting, "Come
little ones. The path is clear."

All night long, the wind moaned eerily, and I had trouble
sleeping. Of course, I thought of Daddy and his comforting
arms around me when I couldn't sleep. My mind wanted to go
to work. By morning, the wind had stopped, and a fresh, dawn-
ing peace surrounded me.

Our lives should grow dearer as we start each day anew,

If we walk close to our Master, each
day, the whole day through.

When the silvery, winter shadows hide
the stars from us at night,

We won't wander off the path, if God's our guiding light.

He has led us very gently toward the hill of Calvary,

So we can walk with our Master and be forever free.

Tears may come, but God's clean wind
will dry them on our face,

As we walk with our Master to reach
God's heavenly place.

✝

Betty's boy, Scott, whose twin sister is named Skylene, came to stay with me for a few months in the summer. He would later become a public school teacher as was Jerry Ann and his sister, Claudia, who was at this time thirty years old. Scott was now twenty-five and hadn't quite found himself. He was an excellent artist. Since there was no car in the garage and the weather was mild, we set up a studio for him there.

As Scott worked in his garage studio in the cool of the morning, I sat with him, and we visited as I made afghan lap robes for each of my grandchildren.

As we worked, Scott said to me, "Grandma, you are the most straight lady I have ever known."

Not knowing the secret language of his generation, I took it as a compliment. "Your grandpa would have loved to hear you say such nice things about me."

While Scott was staying with me, Mary had to take me to Tulsa for a neurology CT scan. It was painless except for having to lie very still for a whole hour.

Scott asked what the scan was for.

I told him, "They were taking a very detailed picture of my wrinkles for scientific study."

He said, "Ah, Grandma, I want to know the truth."

I confessed, "They think I might have a problem with my lungs." I tried to lighten the subject by laying some philosophy on him. "Let's not worry about it just yet. I can tell you for sure that my photograph does tell the worst and the best about the journey I've traveled since 1906. Old people's wrinkles of age are the maps of life portraying the joys and the sadness of each event they've experienced along the way."

I also confessed to myself, *This scan might be the first sentence in the story of the remainder of my life on earth.*

After Scott returned home to Texas, I got a letter from his twin, Skylene. We called her Sky, a very fitting name for her.

Dear Grandma,

As I sit on my bed, I'm gazing at the beautiful squares in the afghan you made for me. It's so beautiful. Thank you so much.

As I was looking for stationery to write to you, I came upon all of your past letters to me. One dated October 2, 1977, when Scott and I were twenty-two years old, drew me to read it again. The poems, "Autumn Day" and "The Christ I Know" were enclosed. I still love both of them.

I also love you and think about you so often. I will always cherish the support and kindness you have always had for me, even when you thought I should act differently. That's pure, true love.

With all my love,

Skylene

When I thought of my youngest grandchildren and the youth of this period of time, I had the deepest sympathy for them. Each decade in America, it seemed they were faced with greater dangers and problems than we faced in the gentler days of my youth.

The youth of my day knew the satisfaction of simplicity that youth of later generations had no way of finding. I was glad I lived in what was called "the good old days," although I was thankful for many of the modern conveniences and improvement of medical services. I felt they were the best of times and may never be as good again.

I wished every living soul could have had as good a life as I had. There were ups and downs, but there were more ups than downs. The key for me was to live for God, knowing he lived in me day by day and feeling secure that if he should call me in my sleep I would be ready to meet him. This was my prayer for all generations to come.

✝

In 1983, I went to Texas by passenger jet. It was my first time to fly commercially. LaMoine had a single-engine, private plane in which he had taken me for a ride one time. Betty and Buck had arranged for me to fly from Tulsa to Houston for a two-week visit and for the June wedding of Skylene and Dennis. Because of poor health, I had been staying with Mary and LaMoine at their lake house on Lake Eufaula for a few weeks.

LaMoine wasn't feeling very well on the Sunday I was to fly from Tulsa, so Son and Jerry Ann met us in the town of Leonard, a very small town south of Tulsa. Son and Jerry took me the remainder of the way to the Tulsa airport and waited with me until it was time for me to board the plane.

I had dressed in some of my finest clothes for the trip. When I got in the car, Jerry Ann said, "Pearl, you look like you're dressed fit to kill."

My revealing answer was, "I feel like I'm dressed to die."

I was nervous about the flight. I believe the correct word is *scared.* As we waited, before the flight was called, I thought to myself, *Pearl, as many poems as you have written about flying to heaven, isn't it a bit inconsistent for you to be such a scaredy-cat? Don't you want to see what it's like to see what heaven and earth look like from thirty-five thousand feet up?* I thought a little while longer and answered myself back. *But Pearlie, it's not the same. When you fly to heaven, you'll be carried by an angel. There can't be any flying safer than that.*

After the wedding, another high point of this trip was the trip to the Gulf to play in the ocean and the sand. Cindy and her two-year-old, Josh, went with us. I tried to use this trip to redeem the time with Betty and her family since I missed out on so many things because of the geographic distance between us.

It was such fun to walk along the deserted strand of beach with my child, my grandchild, and my great grandchild. The sky blazed with a fiery sunset, and the evening fog looked like a fuzzy pink blanket rolling over the ocean as a flock of seagulls glided overhead.

Suddenly, I was held fast by a sense of great beauty. My skin tingled, and my whole body glowed inside. I stopped walking for a minute and let this wonderful feeling wash over me like the incoming tide.

From a practical point of view, I was concerned with the rising tide and the darkness, thinking of what we might step on with our bare feet. I felt like a child as I plowed my feet in the deep, powdery sand.

Early the next morning, I returned to the beach alone, strolling up and down. I waded out into the water, standing still, and allowed the waves to lap up around my feet. At times, there would be a gust of wind that would send the waves a little higher. I was struck by the beauty of the rising tide and the restless sea that never sleeps. As the others came to join me, the sound of the ocean harmonized with a lot of laughter ringing out from among all of us. It made me feel all aglow and happy to be alive.

When my visit was over and we were doing our goodbye hugs, I said to Buck and Betty, "Tell Skylene and Dennis how much I enjoyed their wedding and how much I enjoyed meeting Dennis's family and friends. Tell them I will always remember this time I spent with them, just in case I never get to do this again."

When I arrived back in Oklahoma, I went to Mary's lake house. It was the Fourth of July. Their children had come down to watch the fireworks on the other side of the lake. I was so glad because I needed chances to tell and retell about my trip to Texas.

After the holiday week, I went into my own room at Mary's house and kept my door closed. LaMoine had picked up all of my mail the post office had for my Okmulgee house. Some of it was a month old. There were newspapers, bills to pay, and several letters that needed to be answered.

In 1984, I wrote this poem about our children, who were all in their fifties by this time.

The sweetest voices this side of heaven,

Are the gifts God gave to Daddy and me.

When I hear them calling me Mother,

My heart overflows with glee.

These voices of my children,

Calling, "Mother, come and see."

I whisper, "Thank you, Lord Jesus,

For giving them to Daddy and me."

In my old age, they are a blessing,

Running my heart over with joy.

Thank you again, dear Father,

Two sweet girls and a precious boy.

In 1986, I got two letters from Skylene. One was in June, and the other was in November, after Betty and Buck, Sky and Dennis, and Scott and his wife, Ginger, had come to Okmulgee for a visit. Buck's parents, the other grandparents, lived only a few blocks from me.

June 25, 1986

Dearest Grandma,

Thank you for beginning your letters to me, "My dearest sweet one." It makes me feel special, which I assume is what you have in mind. Are you feeling well? Last when we talked by phone, you were having the preacher and his wife over for pork chops. I hope you enjoyed their visit. Dennis is coming home for lunch today. Chicken salad. I always loved the big gatherings after church when we were with you for a visit. Those are the best memories of my childhood when I got to see my grandmas and grandpas Joneses and Berrys. This sure has gotten mushy somehow. I just like to remember and share nice thoughts with you. I'm working at a medical lab run by a husband and wife team. They gave us their chickens because we live outside of town. Their neighbors were complaining. So we now have six layers and one rooster. I just reread your last letter to me. I get a real nice, secure feeling from them. Your love means so much to me, even though most of it must be long distance. Well, my sweetest Grandma, I better let you go. I will write more in the future. My phone bill got entirely out of hand, so I will be writing more. Dennis sends his love. Tell everybody there hi for me.

All my love,

Skylene

November 26, 1986

My dear sweet Grandma,

I'm happy to have such sweet thoughts of you and sweet memories of Grandpa Jones. You worked so hard this Thanksgiving to make sure everybody had what they needed. I know you didn't feel good at times, but you kept smiling. I do admire you so. All your children are independent just as you are. In turn, all that you are has been passed down through your children to us grandchildren. Dennis and I love you so much. I know

Grandpa is so proud of you. Please don't be sad ever. I know you well. If I can ever comfort you, I hope you will think of me. Thank you for sharing your love with Dennis and me.

Your Skylene

Ryan was continuing to come down from Tulsa to visit me. He was twenty-four years old, had graduated from Tulsa University, and was working as an engineer at the aircraft plant in Tulsa. He would soon transfer to St. Louis, where he would find his bride, Carol, a tall, pretty, red-haired lady who was a perfect match.

My brother Troy died in 1986, leaving me without any Logan family in Oklahoma except Olga and their children. They had their fiftieth wedding anniversary the year before. After the funeral, I visited what was left of the old home place. Enough was left to refresh my memory of the joyful times when I pestered Troy and my Russ to let me play and climb trees with them.

The Lord and I had conversations to remind me not to make an idol of my images of the old home place. Fortunately for me, I convinced him that it remained an outlet for my creativity. As my Creator, he should know that. We reached an understanding.

Between 1985 and 1991, Anne Russelle and I had considerable correspondence by mail. Her letters were short and newsy about my other Texas great grandchildren.

April 27, 1985, Lewisville, Texas

Dear Grandmother,

I hope you are feeling well and enjoying all the green

trees and blossoming flowers. I sure am. Mark is putting up a new fence on the back of the yard and a flower bed the length of the fence. I am looking forward to it. We had a revival at church that has been nice. I took Luke (eight years old) for a much-needed haircut. Kirby is getting fat and spoiled. I'm loving every minute of her new life.

Kirby was born March 8, 1985, one day before my birth date. That was close enough to make her special to me.

July 24, 1987, Lewisville, Texas

Dear Grandmother,

We are well. Luke and Mark are putting together a model airplane. Two-year-old Kirby is trying to help, and that is causing quite a bit of trouble. I enjoyed spending the weekend with Julie and new baby Jordan. Jordan looks like her Daddy Jeb. She is smiling and cooing now. Most of the time she is fussy, but we enjoyed her anyway.

In 1988, two of my three California sisters traveled by bus to visit me in Oklahoma. Bertha, Mae, and I decided to make pillows for our living room sofas as we each talked about our children. It so happened I had bought the material before their arrival as the entertainment for one of the days they were here. We mostly acted silly, as sisters are prone to do, as we poked fun at each other. With much laughter and bantering back and forth, I had to compose a summary of our personalities on this fun day.

There are three little sisters, and they love each other dear.

There's another sister, Blanche, and
they wish that she were here.

Blanche lives on Gold Run Mountain.
The pines grow stately tall.

The echoes ring from hill to hill and from the canyon wall.

Sister Mae is very quiet, very calm, and very still—

Until a needle pricks her finger;
then her voice is very shrill.

They worked on sofa pillows, heads bowed intently low.

When Sister Bertha completed one,
her eyes would proudly glow.

And sister Pearl, the feisty one, who
primps and preens all day,

Acts like someone's coming. That's why she acts that way.

It takes the other sisters to keep sister Pearl in line.

But after the teasing is over, they still think she is fine.

Then with pillows completed, the too-short day was done.

The little sisters laughed and said,
"Haven't we had loads of fun?"

By 1989, my production of poems had greatly fallen off. I couldn't concentrate as well. My thoughts had more trouble finding their way from my brain to my pencil. I wasn't physically able to work in my flower beds as much as I would have liked. I don't know why I expected so much from myself at eighty-three years old.

The fact was that I couldn't get up and down without help. I had only two choices: all the way up or all the way down.

Son and Jerry Ann came to visit me one warm and sunny weekend to help me clean grass out of the flower beds. All I could do was sit on the ground and scoot along on my bottom to pull up clumps of grass or dislodge them with a garden trowel.

It was glorious. We worked for short periods of time and rested for long periods of time. By the end of the day, I was plumb tuckered out.

This exercise and its stimulation did more than clean the weeds from my flower garden. It also pulled up the weeds in the garden of my mind, opening my mind again to my love of nature and the sights and sounds of God's creation that had been my major entertainment for so many years.

In the following weeks, my mind wandered into the makings of some poems I could send to my friends about how the world was so beautiful. I wanted to walk slower and enjoy more of it before the day rushed into each night. Many of my friends didn't love nature as much as I did and didn't completely understand the way I felt. Some thought I was an incurable nut with a terminal illness. Well, whatever I had, my friends could use a big dose of it.

Stop and listen to the patter of gently falling rain,

Falling, softly falling, upon my window pane.

If you stop and listen, you'll hear the sweet birds sing,

Each song in perfect harmony with
whispering sounds of spring.

Colorful buds burst forth. The breeze rustles the leaves.

Stop and thank your Creator for precious gifts like these.

Stop and count the richness in fresh-turned garden sod.

Stop and sing your praises. Rejoice with our *living* God.

The songbirds sing for me. They look for food nearby.

I work in my flower garden as around me they do fly.

They build a comfy nest, which I'm so fond to see,

Hopping in my flowerbeds, giving
contentment's peace to me.

They make my day more happy. They aren't afraid of me.

They sing to me as I feed them beneath my apple tree.

They pay me back with songs sung the whole day through.

They make spring so beautiful and summer prettier too.

This poem reminded me of a white, snowy day when I ran out of birdseed food for my birds. Daddy had brought a fifty-five gallon drum from the station. The top of the drum was waist-high, and there was a rim around the circumference that made a big bowl to hold the birdseed, allowing the birds to hop around on it as they picked out their own favorite kinds of seed. In winter, I kept it close to the back door so I could add seed without going out into the weather.

That was in January of 1979, less than six months before Daddy died. The tire ruts in the snow-covered streets were several inches deep. Daddy had come home from the station, carefully and slowly driving his big blue Buick through the snow that was continuing to fall. Before he could get his coat off, I took him to the backyard and counted out several male and female cardinals that were flying around and lighting on the empty birdseed drum. As I was pointing them out to Daddy, one bright red male cardinal flew to the drum and seemed to look directly at the back door, asking, "Does anyone in there see what's going on out here?"

Daddy looked from the bird to me and said, "Is this a hint from you birds for me to go back to town in this awful weather to buy birdseed?" I just gave him one of my sweet smiles.

After I watched the car sliding around as he went around the corner, I was afraid he might fall on the slick sidewalk at the store before he got back, and I would be the cause of it. When he returned I asked him, "Did you fall?"

He answered, "Oh, I just fell on my back," as if that were the best place to fall. He wasn't limping or anything.

Even before he took off his coat, I gave him a great big hug, which I had forgotten to do when he came home before. I said, "Speaking of birds, it looks like you're a tough old bird."

He opened his coat and gathered me into his arms, and whispered, "Mother, you're as spoiled as your cardinals."

I sat beneath my redbud tree.

The birds were singing songs to me.

I enjoyed their songs to the depth of my heart,

Thankful to them for sharing their part.

It was God's will that they to sing to me,

As I sat beneath my redbud tree.

Oh, to run with the wind with my spirits high.

If I could see higher, then higher I'd fly,

Until I reached heaven beyond the blue sky.

Kneeling at the portals, my Jesus and I.

I'd be with my loved ones who've gone before I,

There with my sweet Russell, the baby, and I.

Alas. How dreary would be the world if

There were no flowers,

No birds to sing,

No rippling streams to wade in,

No trees to give us shade,

No velvet green grass to play upon.

It would be as dreary as if

There was no sunshine to brighten our days,

No poetry,

No romance,

No promise of eternal life,

No home for our souls after physical death.

Nobody can conceive or imagine all the

Wonders that are unseen

And unseeable

In this big, beautiful world

And the glory beyond.

By the end of 1989, Mary had to take me to the doctor much more often because of the suspicion that I had cancer in my lungs or some other part of my body.

When Life on Earth Winds Down

1990 through 1993

I found that my memories kept running back to where I had lived when I was a child. In awe, my mind wandered through the woodlands where the flowers were blooming wild.

It is a place of refuge, so perfect and complete,
Where the saints of all the ages sit
around the Savior's feet.

It's a home place mansion, in heaven bright and fair,

Where families gather to visit and
be with our Christ up there.

I sensed that my God had a set schedule for the remaining
years of my life on earth. It just happened that a distant cousin
named Jack Pritchard came to visit me in May 1990. Jack was
a college professor at Oklahoma State University in Stillwater.
For the past eighteen years, he had done research about our
family, as far back in years as he could find census records to
knit them together.

One of the other ways he discovered family members was to
ask the students in his classes if any of them had family members with Logan or Pritchard as their last name. One day, as he
was calling out these last names, a student held up his hand and
said, "Sir, my name is Randall Buck. My mother's name is Nina
Logan Buck," and that's the way Jack found me.

After our visit, I wrote to him and sent him some very old
family photographs. He was putting together a family history
book titled *Grandmother's Old Trunk*. In a cousin's storage shed,
he had found an ancient trunk belonging to my grandmother
and grandfather, John and Sarah Logan. It contained many family documents and photographs. I wanted to supply some of my
own family photographs to include in his book. I also thought,
Well, here's an opportunity to get some of my poems published, so I
included some of them with the photos. He wrote back to me.

Dear Pearl,

Thank you for your letter and great pictures. I'm sorry
that you have had some illness. It's good that you are
feeling better.

Thank you for allowing me to leave a tape recorder on
during our visit to record the family stories you told me.
It's sad when you see a generation of family disappear. I

think about so many family members who have passed away since I started my research in 1972.

I'm hoping to start work composing a book sometime this year. I have enjoyed working with Randall Buck. He was one of my outstanding students. He is presently teaching at a school in Wagoner, Oklahoma.

I enjoyed your letter. You are a sharp lady. I'm glad you are family.

Sincerely, Jack

God works in mysterious ways to let us know he sees what's going on in our lives and to remind us there is a time to live and a time to die and that he has a mansion in heaven that looks just like we want it to look. I fully expect to see many ancestors in heaven, some whom Jack found that I wouldn't have known about if he hadn't done his research. I know I will see my Russ and our first baby. I asked myself, *Do you know why you're holding on to this present life so strongly?* I had to admit to myself, *God will know when the time is right.*

All this talk with Jack about family reminded me that I needed to write a letter to Daddy to tell him how much I was looking forward to seeing him again. It's really difficult to break the habit of hearing your lover tell you every day, "You are pretty. I really love you and wouldn't want to live on earth without you."

June 16, 1990

Dear sweet Daddy,

My heart is breaking today. It's now been eleven years this morning since we were called to the hospital to you. You passed away a day or so after we took you there.

I've been living that awful day over and over all day. I'm

so alone. I've cried all day. But it hasn't brought you back and hasn't relieved my sorrow. Eleven years is a really long time without seeing you except in my dreams.

I thank our blessed Father in heaven that he allows me to dream about you. My dreams are sometimes real sweet. I even laugh when I tell others about what we do in my dreams.

Daddy, I went through a dresser drawer recently looking for some hose and found the letters you had written to me when I was in California. You told me how much you still loved me and couldn't live without me. I'm thankful for those dear, sweet letters, Daddy. I always knew you loved me—maybe too much. Goodnight, Daddy. I hope I dream about you tonight.

November 30, 1990, I wrote one of my last poems. I had been in Tulsa for six weeks with Son and Jerry Ann while I took radiation treatment for my lung cancer. I went to the hospital at four thirty each afternoon, Monday through Friday. We scheduled the treatment with Dr. Brickner at St. Francis Hospital at that time of day so Jerry Ann could take me after teaching eighth-grade English all day at Edison Middle School in Tulsa.

I greatly improved my education during this six-week period of time. There was a large window in their dining room on the south side of the house. It allowed the winter sun to warm the floor where I sat to read. So they moved their set of encyclopedias into the dining room, the ones Jerry Ann used in high school, the 1944 *World Book Encyclopedia*. I started with the *A* book and read the parts that interested me, all the way to *Z*.

The radiation treatments really taxed my body. A time or two, I wondered about what I had gotten myself into. Also, I had time to meditate about how much I had written about longing to see heaven and wanting to be with Daddy again. I talked to God about it because it was he and his Holy Spirit who had given me this confident expectation of heaven.

As it turned out, he allowed me to be me. It wouldn't have been me if I hadn't fought for life in my physical abode to the very end, suffering death as my children and their mates cared for me in the middle of their very full and busy responsibility-filled lives.

That was when I was prompted by the Spirit to write a poem of acceptance about what he would require of me and my children and their mates, my other true children, over the next three years.

The breezy wind swept through the trees

And scattered all the autumn leaves.

I heard the wind whisper through each pine,

And it stirred this happy heart of mine.

Then cold, cold snow fell very fast

And buried all the leaves at last.

One weekend, Son took me back to Okmulgee so I could spend a weekend in my own house. As I was packing, apparently, he wrote a note to me and put it in with my clothing so I would find it when I was unpacking after I got home.

Dearest Mother,

Now it's my turn to write a note to you and tell you how much we are enjoying being with you almost every day. You are a wonderful houseguest. Jerry and I both love you and appreciate you and your great positive attitude. We thank God every day for parents who love Jesus and have given us an example of how to live and enjoy family. We hope you have a nice weekend, and we look forward to seeing you again Monday.

I love you.

Sonny

After the radiation treatments, I returned to my own house in Okmulgee, and Mary again took on the primary responsibility of taking me to the doctors and checking my medications. I probably didn't feel as well after the radiation as I did before. However, I had the satisfaction that we had made the only logical decision that had a chance of prolonging my life. In fact, the doctor told me and Mary that they had done all for me that they could do and that the length of my life was in God's hands. Well, that's where my life had been up to now, so why not trust him to finish the job?

By April 1991, it was time to write my Russ another poem about my remaining time on earth.

> As long as I can remember, I've loved you, Russ, my dear.
>
> And I want you to know I always want you near.
>
> Some days the days are long and I'm lonely as can be.
>
> So now I'm waiting and watching 'til God calls for me.
>
> And I know you are longing and waiting there for me
>
> As I am climbing up higher on the hill of Calvary.

By June 1991, my physical health kept deteriorating, and my spiritual health began to reach out like a little child for the healer of my homesickness.

> If you follow me, you won't be lost,
>
> For the river of Jordan must be crossed.
>
> The road is narrow that goes to the throne.

Just follow me, and you won't go alone.

For I am heading home—can't say when I'm going.

Just follow me, for the way he'll be showing.

God has a home for me and a robe as white as snow.

Just follow me. I know the way. I found him long ago.

✝

I was still in my own home in March 1992, when I had my last poem published in the church newsletter. I wasn't able to go to church very often, so I used my poems to stay connected with the ladies' Bible class. I sent this poem to them, and they asked the preacher to publish it.

Come walk with me.

Talk with me,

And happy we will be.

We'll walk the path, the narrow path,

That leads to Calvary.

We'll climb many mountains

Before we reach that home.

If we hold the Master's hand,

We'll never walk alone.

As we journey on this earth,

Jesus tells us of God's plan.

We must walk the narrow path

To reach his promised land.

Jesus will stand with arms outspread

To open the pearly gate.

Come walk with me, dear Christian friends.

I don't have long to wait.

I got a letter from my granddaughter Anne Russelle that gave me a good laugh.

March 23, 1992, Carrollton, Texas

Dear Grandmother,

Basketball season is over, and we miss it. Luke is lost without practice time to occupy him. Kirby tried to run away from home yesterday and is now grounded from friends. She's very dramatic. She asked Mark to put a full-length mirror in her bedroom so she can watch herself cry.

We are staying busy in our accounting business with tax season. I get really tense about work that needs to get done. Mark doesn't get bothered by it. That makes me even more tense. I am the world's greatest worrier. I am living proof that worry works. When I worry, nothing bad ever happens. So, that proves worry works. I hope you are enjoying being back in your own nest. I am glad you can be in your own house. Try to keep eating to keep your weight up.

Just before I moved from my house in Okmulgee to Mary and LaMoine's Lake Eufaula house to spend the winter of late 1992 and early 1993, I got a letter from my oldest sister, Blanche, who lived on Gold Run Mountain in California. By now, I was taking frequent doses of Percocet for my pain. I was hurting so bad I called sweetly to Mary, "Would you please give me just a little more painkiller?"

She screwed up her face with a combination of grin and wonder about what I was up to. "Is your pain a lot worse?"

"No. This might be the last letter I ever get from Blanche, and I really want to enjoy it.

Mary gave me instructions about the extra dosage I could take, and I scribbled it down on the back page of Blanche's letter.

Hi, dear sister.

I received your letter. It was very nice of your daughter to write it for you. I'm sorry you are feeling so bad. I haven't been feeling good myself.

I have eleven pine trees and four cedars in my yard. My kids and grandkids like to come here for visits. I'm an old, mean grandma. If the grandkids get out of line, I just bust their little butts. Their pop has a good vegetable garden, and he lets them help him in it.

I had a letter from Bertha last week, and she's doing okay. I'm making cookies, cakes, and pies because the kids and the grandkids are coming for a visit.

Well, my dear, I must say goodbye so I can walk to the post office to mail this letter to you. Goodbye, my darling. I love you.

Blanche

P.S. Thanks for the pictures.

Jerry Ann and Son came to the lake house to visit with me in February 1993. They used the visit as an excuse to stay at the Fountainhead Lodge on Lake Eufaula, an Oklahoma state lodge.

I was still staying at Mary's lake house in March 1993 when I received a birthday card from Jerry Ann and Son.

The printed card said, "We learned your secret for wearing a mother's smile in the most trying times. It wasn't a secret at all. The caring you bless your family with comes from your beautiful faith in God and your loving heart."

Jerry Ann added:

Dearest Pearl,

Happy eighty-seventh birthday! I know there have been days when you never thought you'd make it. But you did! And we're mighty glad.

Julie, Alec, and Jordan were with us this weekend. The kids are such goobers. They surprised us by making all the beds in the house today. Julie says Jordan is getting so she can be a pretty good helper. Julie pays her a nickel for this and that. Jordan loves to earn money, and she loves to go shopping with it. Wonder where she got that?

Well, darling, you know how special you are to us. We pray for your continued well-being during your "new year."

I thank you so much for sharing your precious son with me for these forty swift years. You did a mighty fine job raising him. He gets sweeter and more important to me every year. We were meant for each other, and you helped! Much love.

Jerry

Son added, on the small space remaining at the bottom of the card, "We love you, appreciate you, and admire you for the good example you've always been. We thank the Lord for you every day. Sonny."

✝

The remainder of my story wasn't about me. It was about my heroic children and their heroic mates, who became my constant caregivers. My children's mates became more than children to me because of the many personal and intimate things they had to do to help my body function the best it could.

It finally got so bad that it became a twenty-four-hour, seven-days-a-week job. Mary and LaMoine carried the bulk of the load over a long period of time, with some relief from the other two couples during the last four months I was alive. As one slept, the other nursed me as a parent would care for an only child.

I knew, although at times I didn't act like it, that I was being a terrible imposition on my children and their faithful mates, and there wasn't a thing we could do about it.

This is a good place for me to share some Hebrew poetry from Psalm 127. I practiced Hebrew poetry in some of my own poems. Hebrew poetry is made up of couplets. A line is written, and the next line says something very similar or expands upon the previous line.

> Unless the Lord builds the house,
> its builders labor in vain.
>
> Unless the Lord watches over the city,
> the watchmen stand guard in vain.
>
> In vain, you rise up early and stay up late,
>
> Toiling for food to eat—for he grants
> sleep to those he loves.
>
> Sons are a heritage from the Lord,
>
> children a reward from him.
>
> Like arrows in the hand of a warrior

are sons born in one's youth.

Blessed is the man whose quiver is full of them.

They will not be put to shame when they
contend with their enemies in the gate

Psalm 127:1–5 (NIV)

I didn't know that when I was a young mother that three other young mothers were raising up the perfect mates for my children, who also became arrows in my quiver.

Nor did anyone tell each of us that as life wound down for me, my worn-out body would become a test of the character of each of us when our staying power would be tested to the limits.

This may not seem like a happy chapter to end my story, but it's a realistic one. The happiness lies beneath the surface that shouts praises to God for his provisions for his own old and dying children. For me, it's a holy expression of the greatest love that can be shown to an aging and dying parent.

I wrote this to honor my children, especially Mary and LaMoine, and above all, Mary. She spoiled me with her constant presence, even as the stress and strain were draining her own life and energy away with mine.

I thanked God for these strong, straight arrows in my quiver in this three-year battle we all eight waged together with our "enemies."

I knew Son, Jerry Ann, Betty, and Buck wouldn't object to the lavish praise I heaped upon Mary and LaMoine for the many months of my care that was heaped on their shoulders.

LaMoine was mostly retired from the furniture stores he owned, although he did spend time, as required, to keep an eye on them and his other investments. LaMoine's mother and father had already gone to be with the Lord. She had required a considerable part of their time even before my health got so bad.

Buck was still working full-time as the president of a bank

in Richmond, Texas. Buck's parents, who had lived a few blocks from our house, had also passed over.

Son was working over fifty hours a week at his job in Broken Arrow. Jerry Ann was still teaching eighth-grade English at Edison Middle School in Tulsa. In addition, he and Jerry Ann had responsibilities at church on Sunday mornings. Fortunately for me and her mother in Bristow, Jerry Ann had her summer months to devote to the extra care both of us required.

In April 1993, Mary and LaMoine brought me back to my house in Okmulgee and essentially moved in with me because I was requiring more frequent visits to the doctor. I also required constant support of oxygen for my breathing. We obtained an oxygen generator with a long, plastic hose so I could roam around the house and even go out on the front porch.

Knowing I was growing worse each month and to give Mary and LaMoine some time off for themselves, Skylene decided to fly up from Texas to spend two weeks with me. Son and Jerry Ann met her at the Tulsa airport and brought her to Okmulgee.

I was glad that on that particular day I felt well enough to prepare chicken and dumplings. They really were tasty, and all four of us ate ourselves silly. It could've been because my normal taste buds were messed up and I was using more spices than usual to get the final taste I thought was right.

Betty drove up a week later to help Skylene. I was having frequent nausea, so Betty talked to the doctor about whether a feeding tube would be helpful. He told her it wouldn't ease the nausea at all.

Betty phoned Jerry Ann to inform her and Son about the doctor's decision. I asked to talk to Jerry Ann because she always cheered me up. She said Luke wanted to come up from Texas for the next few weeks to do his regular summer visit. She told him she might be very busy this summer. He said to her, "But Grandma! Don't you remember it's a tradition? Besides, I've also got Grandma Stokes in Tulsa for a backup."

At the end of the stay for Betty and Skylene, Jerry Ann and Son picked up Buck at the airport so he could drive them on the long trip back to Texas. When they arrived, we ate chili and then went out on the porch to visit.

Buck asked about the egg-crate foam cushions on my bed, on the chairs I used in the house, and even on my porch chair. He didn't know I had some bedsores we were trying to control.

As we sat on the porch, we heard Son and Mary having a conversation about how she and LaMoine would stay with me during the week and he and Jerry Ann would come down on Friday evening and stay until Sunday night. Son told Mary he had to teach a Bible lesson on Sunday mornings. Mary was in no mood to dwell on that sacred issue, so she gave him her standard answer. "Well, you'll just have to work it out."

It would take only one weekend of staying with me for Son and Jerry Ann to understand why Mary and LaMoine had to have some relief.

Son really didn't understand what Mary had been going through for so long, and Mary didn't yet understand that Son was his father's own reflection of the addiction to study and deliver each week's Bible lesson as their way of communing with God and his Holy Spirit.

Before dark, Buck, Betty, and Skylene were headed south for Texas. Son and Jerry Ann were headed east to Heber Springs, Arkansas, for few days at Red Apple Inn and then to St. Louis for a few days with Ryan and Carol. They spent a night at Tan Tara Resort in Missouri on their way back to Tulsa. I suppose Son had some intuition that he had better get some vacation time while the getting was good.

After their short vacation, Son checked in with Mary to let her know he was back in Tulsa. She told him they were taking me to the Eufaula lake house again, and Son said that would work out fine.

After that weekend, Son called Eufaula, and I overheard LaMoine say, "Pearlie is having the "hebbie-jeebies" again, waking up in the night and walking the floor, among other bizarre things. We will most likely bring her back to Okmulgee to be near the doctor."

Back in Okmulgee, where I had my own phone, I called Jerry Ann late one evening to have someone to tell my troubles to. I told her, "I feel like I'm neglecting my children by not feeling like talking to them." We talked about ten minutes, and I said, "I've got to sign off now because I want to talk to Betty before it gets much later." I could tell Jerry Ann was already in bed when I called.

Mary thought I was asleep, but I overheard her calling Son at his workplace on Friday morning the first week in July. She told him that she was worn out and needed him and Jerry Ann to come and stay with me that very weekend.

They arrived about nine o'clock Saturday morning in separate cars so Son could go back to Tulsa on Sunday morning because he hadn't had time to arrange for someone else to teach his Bible class. As soon as Mary gave them the pill instructions, she and LaMoine hurried off. I thought, *I can't blame them for leaving as soon as possible, and I sure feel sorry for these other two children who will learn a lesson this weekend they will never forget.*

Jerry Ann asked, "Were you expecting us to show up this weekend to give Mary a chance to go home?"

Jerry thought Mary hadn't prepared me for this surprise.

I answered with a bit of a gleeful grin on my face, "Mary didn't say you were coming because she thought it would upset me. But she didn't know I overheard her conversation with Son."

Mary had told Jerry Ann how I liked for her to sit beside my bed whether I was sleeping or not, so Jerry Ann pulled a chair up beside the bed. I noticed she had a three-ring binder in her lap and was writing in it. I asked, "What's that?"

"It's a journal I started writing this year about each day's events. I didn't have time to record Friday's events last night, so I decided to catch up if you go to sleep while I'm sitting with you."

I wanted to jump out of bed and dance a little jig. "That's just more proof that we're kindred spirits. What have you said about me?"

"I've written that Mary said you had fallen twice last week and that we need to hold onto you when you get out of bed to walk to your chair. I've written that your appetite isn't too bad and that you crave spicy foods like onions and peppers. And I can't believe this next thing on your menu. You eat pizza for breakfast, but you just eat the topping off of it. Are you sure you're not pregnant? Sonny's going to have to get after Mary for not keeping a close enough eye on you."

We laughed over those last remarks. I dreaded what would go into her journal. But I thought, as I put myself in her place, *I know she will record how pitiful I am now: skin and bones and white hair all slicked back, how all I care about is being clean. She'll say I can still move and walk, but I'm on so much Percocet and Xanax every three hours, day and night, that I mostly stay zonked out.*

I told Jerry Ann, "I never kept a journal. I like to wait awhile after each significant event, with my thoughts and words as seeds that must be given time to germinate and grow into a flowery bouquet of words or a poem."

The next time Jerry Ann came, she made potato soup for supper. She got two boxes of cornbread mix out of my pantry. They were both so old they wouldn't rise. She said, "It looks like I would be smart to put together a little grocery list for our next weekend with you."

I really had a pretty good night for this first night of their indoctrination as caregivers to an old mother. I only got up twice to go to the bathroom by myself even though they begged me to call them so they could keep me from falling. On the second trip, I quipped, "A person has to do some things for themselves.

Besides, I have to find out how much I can get away with from you two." I asked, "What kind of a night did you have?"

Jerry Ann said, "I hardly slept at all, but I heard Russ snoring from six to eight o'clock this morning."

That Sunday morning was the Fourth of July. Son was awake and dressed to get to church in Tulsa by the time Jerry Ann woke up. Things got really busy after he left. A nurse's aid came and gave me a *quick* bath. Fortunately for Jerry Ann, I slept most of the day. We went out on the front porch about four thirty in the afternoon until I got nervous. Jerry Ann gave me half of a Xanax, and I settled down.

I wanted to go to bed, but Jerry Ann wanted to keep me awake. We watched the Boston Pops Fourth of July concert, and then Betty called and we all talked. Jerry Ann managed to keep me out of bed until ten o'clock that night.

The next morning, I asked Jerry Ann, "What kind of a night do you think we had?" I was hoping to get good marks from this schoolteacher.

With her schoolteacher voice, she said, "Can you give me the definition for *hellish?*"

While she was cooking later in the day, I sneaked a peek at her journal.

Pearl was up and down every hour and a half. She had to move to the living room chair before midnight. She has a big, wooden bowl beside her chair full of self-medication. She does nose spray, throat spray, eye drops, and Bengay. She goes through the whole rattling ritual before each attempt to sleep. At 4:30, she needed an enema. I finally gave her an extra Percocet, and she slept 'til 6:00 a.m., ready to get up and start her rounds.

I thought, *This girl isn't cut out for this kind of work. How could one old lady be worse than 150 eighth graders passing through her classroom every day at school?*

I tried my best during the day for Jerry Ann to get some naps. In between, I tried to be a good host and visit with her. I asked, "What will Son be doing this afternoon?"

She brightened up a bit and told me, "This is the day Russ takes Luke to the firecracker stand on the east edge of Tulsa. Then they drive to a secluded, wooded area Russ found and shoot the loudest and biggest fireworks. Then, even though Luke isn't old enough to drive, Russ knows a secluded road about a quarter mile long where Luke can get under the wheel and practice his driving."

I laughed and said, "That sounds like something Son would do. When Sonny was about twelve years old and working with his daddy at the gas station, he drove cars around the driveway and up on the old-fashioned, inclined grease rack. One day when I came to the station, after shopping downtown, Sonny had to show off by backing a car up on the rack. I knew he was showing off for me."

The next morning, Monday, I heard Jerry Ann puttering around in the kitchen, and I could smell the coffee. I was sleeping now in the middle bedroom, the one Sonny slept and studied in when he was at home. It was closest to the small half bath we built into the closet some time after Son moved out. I rang my little hand bell to let Jerry Ann know I was awake. When she came to the room, I asked, "What are we having for breakfast?"

She informed me, "I'm having two pieces of toast and plenty of coffee to get my equilibrium. Then you're going to your chair to have pizza for breakfast while I strip the beds and do the laundry before Mary and LaMoine come."

LaMoine showed up around nine a.m., and Jerry Ann left a little after ten a.m. to return to Tulsa. She called later to let us know she had gotten home safely and said Son and Luke were already out shooting up the last of their fireworks.

On Tuesday, Mary called Jerry Ann to tell her that she and Son needed to be back in Okmulgee Thursday afternoon so they could go to Dallas to the Furniture Mart for four days. They needed to place orders for their stores in Okmulgee and Henryetta. By this time, Barbara and Butler owned a furniture store in Stroud, Gaines and Pat owned one in Shawnee, and Suzy ran one in Okmulgee while Johnny was buying and refurbishing old houses for rental property.

Mary took me to the Okmulgee hospital on Wednesday, July 7 for an IV. The next day, Son and Jerry Ann returned in the afternoon so Mary and LaMoine could get packed to go to Dallas. Son had taken off work early, and on their way to Okmulgee, they ate at an Italian restaurant so they could bring me some spicy spaghetti. I was so drugged and frazzled out by this time that I had to rely on Jerry Ann's journal to tell much of the remainder of my story.

Thursday, July 8

We have to crush Pearl's large pills now. She's having trouble saying everything just right but is pretty alert when she sits in her chair. She can't even concentrate well enough to clean her false teeth right. Russ insisted on doing the midnight, three o'clock, and six o'clock medications. I slept in the back bedroom.

Friday, July 9

I had to wake Pearl at nine o'clock in the morning for her pain medication. I sat her on the divan, and while I was getting her pills, she took off to the bathroom on her own. Fortunately, she didn't fall. She was able to swallow some small stuff today but didn't do much with her pizza and her Ensure nutritional supplement. She kept falling asleep. I believe she may be overmedicated. After waking me, Russ was off to Broken Arrow to work for a few hours. When the registered nurse came, she didn't see anything unusual about Pearl but suggested the disease was just progressing. Russ and I ate the remainder of the spaghetti and lasagna for dinner after he returned from work.

Saturday, July 10

Pearl was a little more with it today after Russ cooked her some bacon and an egg. After eating, she got up and started walking away. I asked her where she wanted to go. She answered, "Heaven." Then she stopped and thought about it and said, "No, I want to go to Disneyland first." She still can show a flash of humor. Bless her heart. She looks so pitiful. She now weighs less than ninety pounds. Russ got us Sonic burgers and onion rings for supper. We saved a little for tomorrow. Russ insists on doing the all-night getting up. He claims he sleeps in between.

Sunday, July 11

I got up at 6:15 a.m. to help with Pearl while Russ lay back down for a while. He left about eight o'clock to teach his Bible class in Tulsa. I hurried around and washed sheets and towels and changed beds. Pearl ate pretty well: mashed lasagna, mashed peas, and Ensure. A nurse's aid came and gave her a bath. At lunchtime, Aunt Lillian came from church for a visit. She is also a widow, the wife of Roscoe, big Russell's brother. For lunch, I fed Pearl tiny pieces of hamburger. She preferred straight mustard. Lillian left but returned with two cans of spicy V8 tomato juice. I could tell how shocked Lillian was to see Pearl so weakened. This became the longest afternoon in my life so far. Pearl and I were both exhausted. Mary and LaMoine arrived about seven o'clock. They also couldn't believe Pearl's worsening condition. When I returned to Tulsa, Russ met me at the Pancake House for a late supper. I'm absolutely zonked. Taking care of Pearl doesn't seem to bother Russ, but it eats me up.

Thursday, July 15

We had reserved a cabin in Colorado for a week before we started helping with Pearl's care. We decided to take the chance and go, even if we were called back early. To do this, we scheduled Thursday and Friday with Pearl. I got there by 8:00 a.m., and Russ went to work in Broken Arrow. Russ had an appointment with Buchanan Funeral Home at three o'clock in the afternoon to prearrange his mother's funeral. It seems so sad to me to pick out caskets when someone is still alive. Usually, Pearl is agitated when she finds me there instead of her Mary. Today, she didn't seem to mind that I was there instead. After her bath, she drank some V8 and some Ensure. Then we went out on the front porch. The Home Health folks had ordered her a hospital bed. Two of LaMoine's furniture store men came and moved her regular bed out to the garage. When Pearl saw the men bringing in the hospital bed, she wouldn't even look at it. Even so, she has been very sweet and loving with me today

Friday, July 16

The nurse came today to hook Pearl up to an IV. LaMoine arrived and had to make some alterations because the pole to which the IV was hung was too tall to be taken through doors. I left around 10:30 a.m., almost too tired to drive.

Saturday, July 26

Back from our Colorado trip. Back to Okmulgee. On Sunday morning, Russ was still up at 6:00 a.m. giving Pearl her meds when I got up. Russ went back to bed until nine o'clock. Then he went to the store for milk, eggs, and bacon. Pearl was able to eat a whole egg and two strips of bacon. She sat at the table with us and asked the blessing. She prowled around all afternoon groaning and feeling miserable. I made potato salad for supper, which she gobbled down. Russ has to feed her everything she eats. Russ got Kentucky Fried Chicken for our supper, and she ate some of it too. LaMoine arrived around 8:00 p.m., and I felt mercifully set free again. I'm understanding more and more why they want to escape so quickly each time we come to take our turn, and they've been doing this for months rather than weeks.

Sunday night, August 1 through
Wednesday afternoon, August 4

More of the same, except the nurse called and said she was on the way to hook up the IV again. This gave me an excuse to have the nurse ask the doctor if the IV was really necessary since Pearl was eating and drinking so much better. Doctor Alexander agreed it could be removed. Pearl said, "Thanks for getting me released. I don't think I could have laid still for a whole eight hours."

I thought since she was so lucid now it might be a good time to talk to her about the bell. I told her, "Pearl, that bell really aggravates me, and you use it every time I leave the room, and when I don't stay around close, you ring it even more and are real crotchety like you are this morning."

She just sweetly grinned at me and said, "Ah, you're just upset because your sweetie isn't here to help you."

Skylene and Bertha called on Tuesday.

When Russ got here for the Wednesday night shift, he messed with Pearl from eleven thirty on. I was sleeping in the back bedroom, which had a door that opened to the kitchen. Russ was trying to keep her quiet so I could sleep. At about four o'clock in the morning, she got up off the divan and insisted on going to the kitchen. Russ asked her, "Why do you want to go into the kitchen?"

Her answer was one of a mother who was tired of her kids running her life, so she gruffly answered, "Because it's mine!"

How do you argue with logic like that? Russ said he grumbled under his breath like a scolded boy, "Not at four o'clock in the morning."

Friday, August 13

I called LaMoine to let him know I was on my way. I arrived about two o'clock in the afternoon. Pearl was asleep when I got there. When she awoke, she was surprised to see me. They've quit telling her Mary is leaving because she gets so worked up when Mary isn't there. Mary is her security blanket.

Russ came from work and arrived at 5:30 p.m. Russ retired to bed at 8:45 p.m. to sleep until midnight. Pearl went to her room at 9:00 p.m., and we started the "nighttime routine." Before midnight, she was up to potty three times and rang her bell for me to come five or six other times. When Russ got up at midnight, as I went to bed, I felt ashamed as I thought, *Well, at least Friday the thirteenth is over.*

Saturday, August 14

I got out of bed at 5:30 a.m. and met Russ in the hall-way. He sent me back to bed to sleep until eight o'clock so I wouldn't be so cranky I guess. As he went to bed, I started the ministrations for the day. About the most helpful thing for Pearl is a Bengay rubdown. I've tried to avoid that mess on previous visits, but this weekend I'm slathering it on at the drop of a hat. The house reeks of it. Russ got up a little after 10:30 a.m. and, after eating something, went out into the yard to water the grass and Pearl's remaining flowers and probably to get away from the Bengay fumes.

Pearl's resurrection lilies are fantastic, four extravagant bouquets near the back door. When he came back in, he sat down to study his Sunday Bible lesson. Every few minutes, he would blow his nose. He said, "I'm either allergic to Daddy's Bible or Bengay. I think I'll go to the front porch to study."

Pearl went out on the front porch with him, and in a few minutes asked for a bite of food. I opened a can of chicken and noodle soup and gave it to her almost straight. I also tore up pieces of bread and put them in it. She ate about half of it dutifully and then wanted some of her meat and onion mess. I kept spooning in the soup and she looked at me and said, "You're not playing fair." But she finished it and went off to sleep, and I promised her the meat and onions for breakfast. Now that Russ and I are wide awake, she's sleeping just fine!

I baked brownies for us and for Betty and Buck because they are arriving tomorrow to take care of Pearl for a week. We ate brownies with peaches for supper, and Pearl enjoyed a few bites too. I used the brownies as a way to let Pearl know Betty and Buck were coming.

During the evening, Skylene called to see how Pearl was doing. We talked about ten minutes.

Sunday, August 15

The previous night, I gave Pearl two and one-half Percocet pills every three hours rather than the normal two. She slept like a baby. The next morning, she said, "I can't believe you had to wake me." For breakfast, I cooked some prunes for her. Her response was, "These prunes are too sticky for me to swallow." Then, with a mischievous look on her face that I loved to see again, she reminded me, "Besides, you promised me meat and onions for breakfast."

Morning went pretty well. I got the bed sheets washed and the beds changed. Buck and Betty arrived from

Texas at noon. We sat down at the kitchen table for chili and a short visit before Pearl awoke. This worked out well because I was able to coach Betty through the various procedures before returning to Tulsa.

Thursday, August 26

It was a blessing to have this two-week reprieve since school is back in session, and I needed to drive my mother from Bristow to Tulsa for doctors' appointments.

Friday, August 27 through Sunday, August 29

Russ and I drove to Okmulgee in rush-hour traffic.

Pearl seems much weaker and more pitiful. She's worrying about her mind being bad, and she complains that Mary and LaMoine aren't doing enough for her. She wants to be taken to the doctor frequently. She had to be in bed so much last week that now her bedsores are much worse.

While LaMoine was instructing us about the change in Pearl's medications, she was determined to go out on the front porch in the August heat. As sweetly as possible, he told her it was just too hot for her out there. She gave him an angry look and said, "LaMoine, you're going to be the death of me yet!"

That night, I mostly stayed in the room with Pearl as I graded papers. She wasn't too bad, just awake and only dozing.

The next day, Mary called. She was almost distraught with this ordeal and because Pearl had been such a big handful this week. We agreed the time had come to hire some nursing help full-time. I was less available because of my teaching, and Mary was just physically and emotionally wrung out after so many months. We considered Rebold Manor Nursing Home but decided to try to keep Pearl in her own house, if possible. Pearl's pain had become so great that the increased medication had made it much more practical for Mary to not be constantly there.

We had pizza for supper. We sat Pearl in her living room chair. Russ gave her a kiss and said, "Miss prissy, that's all the kissing you're going to get until we finish our supper."

After supper, Russ went to bed, and I got Pearl ready. She appeared to be doing much better with her new meds. She slept from ten o'clock to midnight. Of course, I was wide awake—my fault, not Pearl's. Then when I was almost asleep, I caught her trying to climb over the bed rails to get out of the bed. I really talked sternly to her about the dangers of falling. She went back to sleep, and in another hour, she rang her bell to apologize. Bless her heart. She wanted to get Russell up too, but I said no. Then, in a little while, she rang her bell again and said, "Well, I'm ready to eat. I promise to eat whatever you want to bring me."

I asked her if she wanted to ask the blessing for the food. She brightened a little and answered, "Thanks for suggesting that because I want to ask forgiveness for upsetting you, and I don't want to die unforgiven."

I thought, *There's nothing wrong with Pearl's mind. She covered herself with me and God in one sentence.* So I silently prayed, *Lord, I really hate it when I don't keep my opinions to myself.*

Sunday, August 29

Russ fixed eggs and bacon for our breakfast. He chopped his mother's into microscopic pieces and fed it to her. She ate it all and drank a 6-ounce can of V8 tomato juice.

Mary and LaMoine arrived at 6:00 p.m. We came home by way of Braum's ice cream store. I had a black walnut cone, and Russ had a chocolate milkshake. We watered the grass, unpacked, and were in bed by 9:30. I slept fitfully.

Thursday, September 2

Russ has to go take care of Pearl for twenty-four hours so Mary and LaMoine can get some rest. The nurse is to go to work next week. All of our kids are coming to spend the Labor Day weekend.

Friday, September 3

Russ called before I went to the school. He got two hours' sleep. He said, "Mother never sleeps more than an hour at a time now. No wonder Mary needs some relief."

I sympathized, "You'll be too pooped to enjoy the kids' visit." When he got home from Okmulgee, he wouldn't admit to being tired, but he showered and hit the sack around 9:00 p.m.

Monday, September 6

Jeb, Julie's husband, bought cinnamon rolls for breakfast. The donut shop he usually goes to when he visits us was closed on Labor Day. Ryan and Carol drove down to Okmulgee to see Grandma Jones even though we thought she might be too sick to visit. But she perked up because she knew Ryan had the making of being an author like she always wanted to be. She told them she enjoyed the visit greatly. We took Ryan and Carol to the airport to return to St. Louis at 6:00 p.m.

Friday, September 10

We ate at Mondo's Italian Restaurant and got to Okmulgee around 8:00 p.m. to give the nurse a twenty-four-hour break. Pearl looks much worse. She can no longer get up to go to the bathroom. I took the first shift. She wants someone in the room at all times. I put a wet rag on her face and used a small electric fan to blow air on her face. More cover. Less cover. I finally just sat beside her bed and graded students' test papers.

Saturday, September 11

We stayed with Pearl until 8:00 p.m. when the nurse returned, and we headed back home.

Friday, September 17

Russ and his boss went to the corporate office in Seattle, Washington, for a conference on Tuesday. I picked him up at the airport when he returned late Wednesday night. At noon on Thursday, the nurse called him at work because she couldn't rouse Pearl or feel a pulse. They agreed she should call an ambulance and take her to the Okmulgee hospital. They gave her an IV and were able to get her blood pressure back up. Mary and LaMoine got to the hospital and stayed with her until 7:30 p.m. when we got there. I stayed with her all night. She was in such misery and wanted me to be by her bed and pat her chest.

Saturday, September 18

Russ relieved me at five-thirty this morning. I went to Pearl's house and slept until 10:00 a.m. I made some vegetable soup from vegetables I had brought with me so I could make it for Pearl. I also baked some brownies.

I went back to the hospital so Russ could come home to eat and rest. Then he returned to the hospital so I could go the house to sleep and return at 9:30 p.m. to take the night shift again.

Realizing how bad she is, the hospital staff isn't quite so reluctant to give her medication more often.

She is still lucid at times and will even try to say something humorous.

Sunday, September 19

At 4:30 this morning, Pearl decided to get up. She was determined to bail out of bed. Trying to convince her she couldn't get out of bed, I suggested she just try to sit up. She sat up for a few seconds and fell back exhausted, saying, "I've got nothing. I've got nothing. I can't do anything."

Russ relieved me at six o'clock this morning. I fell into bed and slept well until 9:30 a.m. It was a good thing I took the phone off the hook because Aunt Lillian was trying to reach me for an update to give to the church that Sunday morning.

I was getting ready to go relieve Russ at eleven o'clock when he called and said, "Come on up to the hospital. I think mother is leaving us."

Standing in Pearlie's living room before I left the house, I remembered the first day I met my dear, sweet mother-in-law and future soul mate in this very room. This is the professional mother who gave me "my" Russ. It was our first date, April 28, 1951, and Russ had brought me home to show me off.

When I got to the hospital, she was gone, and her poor little body was at peace.

Russ had already called Mary and Betty. I returned to the house, and, using Pearl's address book, I made phone calls all evening to family members for the funeral, Wednesday, September 22, 1993.

Son sat beside my hospital bed, holding my hand as the last beat of my human heart was registered in the pulse of a vein in my left hand. The first thing I saw was the white throne and knew for a certainty about the hope that had been within me since I was a young girl. I had been judged as being righteous with God's own righteousness from the throne of grace where my Christ sat beside him.

Suddenly, I was back at the beginning of my story, in the prologue of my story, as my Russ and I and Baby Francis were under the fruit trees beside the river of life, listening to my funeral. As I listened to the laughter of our children, family, and friends, I bowed to my Lord and my God and said, "What a glorious day to be alive!"

Epilogue

When Life in Heaven Begins

My Russ, I, and Baby Francis continued our walk down the river of life with its fruit trees full of healing fruit. The trees began to change to oaks, cottonwoods, and pines like those I knew from my years at the old home place. I began to feel a healing that I never imagined I would experience. I hugged our baby to my breast with the knowledge that my life was being completed.

We walked around a bend in the river that looked more and more like Old Limbo Creek, except the water was much clearer than the old creek, and it flowed so gently I knew its waters held no danger in them.

My Russ said, "What do you see just up ahead, Pearlie?" When I looked, I saw an old bridge that crossed the creek, like the one back home, except it was made of gold rather than the black steel the old one was made of. We ascended the creek bank, and as we walked across the bridge, I could hear a violin playing.

I turned to my Russ. "That sounds like Mama's old violin!"

The look on his face told me his thoughts: *You're home, my Pearlie.*

Clutching the baby tighter, I ran up the hill. Sure enough, there was the old home place with house, barn, horse trough, water well, tater house, orchard, my flower garden, and Mama's Rose blooming beside the porch.

When Mama saw me, she stopped playing, and I called out, "Don't stop playing, Mama. That sounds heavenly."

Papa came toward me, and Baby Francis held his arms out and giggled as Papa took him and spun him around.

What a homecoming we had as friends and family welcomed me home!

After everyone had returned to their own home place, we sat on the front porch, listening to the heavenly sounds and looking at the glorious brightness that could only have been from my God and my Christ. Mama was rocking Baby Francis. My Russ got up and took me by the hand and pulled me toward the woods.

As we were leaving, I glanced over my shoulder and saw my Jesus standing beside Papa's well. He had a most tender and loving look on his face. He gave me a tiny nod of his head and in my heart, I heard him say, *Welcome home, Pearlie.*

"Where are you taking me?" I asked my Russ.

"We're going for a walk on your nature trail. You haven't seen it for a while. It's just like you left it as a girl but better. You'll need to revise your poem about it. I'll help you write it."

With the voice of a college professor, like the one he used when he talked in church, my Russ said, "Now, young lady, just tell me what you see. That's the best way to write a poem, if you remember what you taught me when we took our first walk here."

Holding hands and laughing like young lovers, we walked and took turns making up lines of poetry that came as easily as my spiritual breathing.

As we made our way back to the house, my Russ looked me in the eyes and, in his most tender voice, promised, "Pearlie, you'll never have to leave the old home place again."

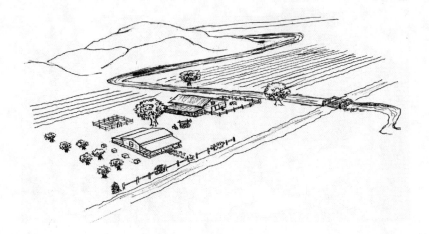